DOMINO
ENCOUNTER

Mr. Makuni

"The thrill of the intrigue in the plot is rhythmically woven into a captivating series of a flowing narrative that is pure suspense built around the escapades of the rich - romance, wealth and revenge keeps you turning page after page. Just irresistible"

SAMSON KIBII
STRATEGIC MANAGEMENT AND MARKETING CONSULTANT

"Betrayal, romance, and suspense all creatively spun into an amazing novel. This is a book you need to read...and read again!"

WILLIAM KHAYOKO
COMMUNICATION SPECIALIST

"For a first book, Waithaka is able to bring to life the characters and events in a way that makes you eager to turn to the next page. A courageous trail-blazer!"

PETER KAHORO
FINANCIAL MANAGEMENT SPECIALIST

DOMINO
ENCOUNTER

KINUTHIA
WAITHAKA

Empiris
Creative Communication Ltd.

Managing Editor: Lorna Seneiya Sempele

Design and Production: Blue 30 Designs

First published in 2015

Empiris Creative Communication Ltd
P.O. Box 37131 - 00200
Nairobi, Kenya
East Africa
Tel: +254 706 537 101
Email: empiris101@gmail.com

URL: http://www.empiriscreative.com

ISBN 978-9966-1793-0-2

Kenya National Library Services Cataloguing in Publication Data
A catalogue record for this book is available from the Kenya National Library Services

Jomo Kenyatta Memorial Library Cataloguing in Publication Data
A catalogue record for this book is available from the Jomo Kenyatta Memorial Library Services

Printed and manufactured in Kenya

Dedication

To my wife Winnie,
my son Lawrence,
and my two daughters, Silvia and Brenda.
You are my inspiration and
I love you all.

Chapter One

"I couldn't believe it when the doctor said it was my son," Lesley Angleton broke the news to her long time friend and sobbed uncontrollably after receiving a call from Dr. Rudolf.

"Calm down Lesley, what happened last night was accidental," Linda Ashcroft replied quietly after being told about the incident.

"No, no, no, Linda, it was planned; I heard he was physically attacked by a group of hooligans who had been watching him at the club, and who followed him for some time thereafter," Lesley replied swallowing hard.

The call came from the Radcliffe Referral Hospital in the early hours of Monday morning. Lesley Angleton was busy in the kitchen preparing breakfast for her husband who was in the bathroom. She looked out the open window, watching insignificant drops of rain drizzle down like flakes of snow falling from the soft mass of clouds above. The chilly breeze sliced through the air depositing its moisture on the dry, earth beneath. The call was from Dr. Rudolf, the personal physician who had known and worked for the family for years; he called to inform Lesley about their son.

———

Fletcher Angleton's face couldn't hide his anguish as he writhed helplessly on the drenched trench by the roadside; he gnashed his teeth from the pain. Bathed in blood from the deep cuts and bruises all over his tall frame, he could only emit faint wheezes and frantic whispers that were inaudible to the hustling passersby as they hurried past him in the eerie darkness. Seven hours of haemorrhaging and excruciating pain left him fighting for his life.

A group of school-going children gathered nearby looking bewildered as they stared down at his pathetic form in the filthy, muddy trench. The time was seven in the morning and the warmth of the rising sun could be felt filtering through the surrounding thickets.

Someone must have finally called an ambulance, for Fletcher could hear the unmistakable sound of its siren as it wailed from afar, drawing closer to his location at an incredible pace. The screeching sound of tyres against the hard tarmac road beside him made the youngsters shriek and scamper away into the morning mist to stare from a short distance away. A large, white ambulance, emblazoned with a red cross on each side, manoeuvred expertly close to the muddy trench, even as white-clad paramedics jumped out the back holding a metal stretcher and ran towards his contorted and drenched frame. They reached out for the almost dead Fletcher and gently lifted him out of the gutter.

"Thank God!" a young boy of about eleven exclaimed, "I thought the poor mite would die as we watched," he continued with a nervous giggle.

"I called for the ambulance," said a middle-aged woman nonchalantly as she stood nearby, with her pet dog yelping excitedly and circling around her chunky feet. They gave her a quick quizzical glance then continued staring at the drama before them.

The team of paramedics shuffled their way through the growing crowd and whisked the now unconscious man on a stretcher through the wide, open doors of the waiting ambulance. They left as fast as they had come.

———

Fletcher Angleton, an executive salesman of a pharmaceutical company, was a well-respected and executive man in Brighton, Sussex. That was where the rich and famous rubbed shoulders with politicians as they jostled for key elected positions within the locality. As an ambitious young man of twenty-six, Fletcher's life was spirited and high-level connections and the social expectations that went with them added to his daily bustle. This flurry of wheeling and dealing hoisted Fletcher's life to heights of fame among the moneyed, and kept him in a perpetual whirlwind of activity. He was used to hustling with all kinds of business people and found it difficult to pass unnoticed on some streets, where those who knew him would perpetually stop him to greet him or discuss some business transaction. He was used to this kind of attention and that is what made it impossible for him to detect that for some time now, he had been followed wherever he went by a ruthless web of hooligans who meant him harm. All this was because of his infatuation with Camila Ashcroft, a daughter of a real estate tycoon Michael Ashcroft; a self-made millionaire whose possessive streak over his only daughter led him to decree that there must be a perpetual human shield of protectors around her and those she interacted with, ensuring that her respectable frame and name were unsullied. The skulking group of hustlers had to also ensure therefore that they were around Fletcher as well since he was her fiancé, watching his every move. Camila's father was determined that even if it meant meting merciless bodily harm to anyone who might pose a threat to her innocence and life, he would not be deterred from calling for punitive measures on the culprit to protect his daughter's reputation. This brooding group of hustlers obeyed Camila's father's orders without the slightest hesitation and brooked no mercy for those who might inflict emotional or physical harm on her. It was obvious that Mr. Ashcroft was not amused by rumour-mill dribbling of Fletcher's rampant philandering with other women. What he had been hearing of Fletcher for some time now had irked him for it eroded his hard-won respectable standing in a touchy high-class community that thrived on such nonsense.

Dawn was breaking Monday morning after what had been a good night out on a Sunday evening for Fletcher. He left the Ogaden Night Club in the late hours of night behind a jovial group of revellers. He was holding hands with a young woman he had been entertaining throughout the night. His intoxication made him swagger pompously into the night, flattering his female companion jovially and without restraint. His faculties were flooded with alcohol, but what he didn't know was that his drinks had been steadily laced with a concoction of narcotics throughout the night as he cavorted with his giggly companion. He had been too drunk to notice what those louts around him were doing to ensure he was weak and helpless by the time he left the club.

After drinking all night, Fletcher finally left with his female companion. He staggered forward, his lanky frame weaving back and forth. To steady himself, he cradled her small waist with his arm and leaned heavily on her small shoulders. He was so focused on impressing his belle that his foggy mind failed to spot the hit boys hanging around and slowly trailing them as they watched every move he made. Suddenly, a familiar voice growled in his direction.

"You don't mess around with Camila and expect to get away with it Fletcher," Jose Cameron the gang leader warned him as he passed by.

"Get lost!" Fletcher shouted, the words hitting his inebriated mind like a hammer. He swung around towards the sound, but could not see clearly whom he had spoken to. He continued forward stubbornly despite being unsteady on his feet, holding his surprised companion possessively.

"I am warning you Fletcher, just go home and leave that prostitute alone," Jose continued.

"Hey look here, I am not a child to be looked after okay! So mind your own business and get the hell out of my face okay! Leave me alone, sucker!" Fletcher's voice, though loud, was slurred from intoxication and the frequency of his swearing was a sign of how drunk and drugged he was.

Fletcher Angleton staggered back and forth in the night, an effect of the laced shots of Jack Daniels he had downed. He wobbled down the terrain leaning heavily on the arm of his newly found lover. He couldn't know that he was being followed by Michael Ashcroft's dirty boys, and Camila's father, who drove slowly a short distance away watching the brood and Fletcher's reactions. After seeing his belle to her doorstep, Fletcher wearily continued towards familiar streets closer to his apartment. It did not take long for all hell to break loose. Fletcher did not see the first blow coming. He only found himself entrapped in a spate of pounding blows and kicks, coming from all directions. The hammering caused indescribable pain so he could hardly breathe, leave alone shout for help.

The beating was only meant to hurt and serve as a warning to Fletcher Angleton for his mischievous involvement while still claiming he had a serious love relationship with Camila. The instructions were very clear from Michael Ashcroft. Despite his wealth and influence Ashcroft was not brutish; he detested and hated Fletcher for his deviant and wayward behaviour with Camila in the past and that is all he wanted to make clear through this beating. The thought of his only daughter relating with a scoundrel like Fletcher had never sat well with him, but he had always tried to give Camila space to make her own choices in life, and for a long while, this had kept him from interfering with the relationship – up to today. He could no longer stand the shame Fletcher's trifling with anything in a skirt was bringing upon his head, as well as his daughter's. The fact that his prized daughter was hopelessly in love with this louse called Fletcher was a bitter pill he had to swallow. But today, Fletcher had to pay a price for the smelly garb of shame he had flung over the Ashcroft family. So Michael Ashcroft watched stoically as Jose indicated to his thugs to follow Fletcher and discipline him in the darker part of the street further on. He then turned his car around, and slowly drove back home. Jose also turned and walked back to the club to keep an eye and make sure no one had followed them. The hoodlums slunk after Fletcher and hungrily punched, kicked and dragged the bewildered man through the mud, before they seemed to tire and fling him into a miry ditch.

After slowly coming out of the fog of his induced coma on his hospital bed, Fletcher Angleton couldn't raise his left arm; the bruises inflicted and the pain were unbearable and one question swirled around his murky brain, 'what happened to me and where am I?'.

The curtains in the sanitized hospital ward, separating his bed from others around him, were pulled open suddenly and a voice ricocheted in his pounding brain.

"Fletcher Angleton," a voice said softly above his puffy and lacerated face.

"Fletcher Angleton!" The same voice called again this time with more vigour.

Fletcher's right eye was swollen and ripe with puss. He opened his left one to a blurred snap-shot of his ward surroundings. He slowly turned his blood-matted hair on the pillow to get a painful glimpse at who was speaking to him. Standing by his bedside was Dr. Rudolf the family physician together with Fletcher's mother Lesley. Upon seeing them, Fletcher strained to find his voice; the effort alone sent spasms of pain up and down his battered head.

"Where am I?" he rasped not recognizing the two people standing beside the bed.

"Don't worry Mr. Fletcher, you are in good hands," Dr. Rudolf told him quietly.

"What happened?" Fletcher went on, confused by the surroundings.

"You are in a hospital where an ambulance brought you after you were found unconscious in a trench by the road side in the early hours of the morning. Can you remember anything dear? Can you tell me what happened?" Lesley, his mother, was trying to sound calm despite the anguish she felt watching her only son helpless and beat-up on the hospital bed. Fletcher was tall and could barely fit into the small bed. The sanitized light-green sheets barely came up to his shoulders. As she tried to imagine what nightmare had descended on Fletcher, she cupped his forehead gently, pushing away sticky strands of his golden-brown hair from his bloodied, bluish face. A mixture of unparalleled anger and distress overcame her and her voice trembled when she tried to tell him how much she loved him. Tears blurred her vision and trickled down her soft, pale cheeks. She couldn't believe the helpless state to which her grown son had been reduced. It seemed like she was looking at someone else, not her energetic, bubbly, high-spirited and strong son. She quickly wiped the tear on her cheek away when she realized he was trying to peer at her from under a swollen eyelid. The fog in Fletcher's mind was clearing, and his memory rallied towards what was closest to his heart strings.

"Where is Camila?" he asked in a slurred, husky voice.

Before his mother could answer, Dr. Rudolf moved closer towards his patient. He bent down holding a syringe and carefully injected him with a strong dose of morphine that made Fletcher slump back on his pillow closing the only eye he could open. He quickly descended into a dark cloud of nothingness. This was the safest course to take the doctor said as Fletcher was in so much pain. Only sleep was the sure healer at this point, as too much movement and the effort it took for Fletcher to speak and move about could hurt him at this point.

"That will ease the pain," remarked Dr. Rudolf turning to Lesley for an instant and placing a gentle hand on her shoulder.

"Do you think he will come out of this muddle soon?" Lesley's question was the cry of a distraught mother. Her dove-like eyes were still tearful and they searched the doctor's face frenziedly for a flicker of hope.

"He will be okay, only today and tomorrow...or maybe three days and he will be good to go. He will definitely need a few days rest at home before he can be up and about though. He is responding very well to antibiotics. He's a lucky bloke after the battering he got and very lucky to be alive. Those bastards were bent on beating the hell out of him I tell you. I am yet to know what this fuss was all about," said Dr. Rudolf thoughtfully as he finished going through a few more checks on Fletcher. He removed his stethoscope from around his neck and held it loosely in his left hand after checking Fletcher's heartbeat.

"Wait till his father gets to the bottom of it all!" Lesley couldn't hide the anger from her face. She yanked off her gold rimmed glasses, with wrinkled strong hands and wiped her teary eyes.

"I think it would be good if you call Camila and tell her about it; you can come with her tomorrow as well if possible," Dr. Rudolf told her an understanding look on his face. He had known Lesley for decades and knew she loved her family dearly. She was obviously distraught at this heinous act that almost killed her only son. After giving her a few moments more to ensure she was alright, he looked at his watch and turned to lead her quietly past the curtains around Fletcher's bed. He needed to continue with his rounds and ensure the other patients were also alright. He drew the curtains firmly to shield Fletcher from view and walked purposefully towards the other ward beds.

Mrs. Angleton sobbed quietly and unashamedly. She turned and quickly went back past Fletcher's curtains before the doctor could stop her. She moved closer to him pulling the bed sheet up to cover his bruised and swollen chest and kissed him goodbye on the forehead before finally slowly walking away from the ward. She thought of Camila and decided to give her a call when she was safely out of the hospital.

Radcliffe Referral Hospital stood between Owen Street and Oak Tree Avenue. The hospital had a horizontal orientation and was spread over a fifteen-acre piece of land. Its modernistic architecture gave it a magnificent look. Most walls had rounded edges and there were many windows along each corridor to let in large amounts of light and allow hospital visitors to glimpse the carefully-tended and green landscape. Along the corridors, away from the wards were porthole windows so that one had the feeling they were walking along the belly of a large ship. The wall surfaces had a smooth plaster finish that made visitors feel like running their palms over them as they walked towards the wards and administration centres of the hospital. Above was a high, flat roof with other ceiling portholes to let in light. This was an attractive shift to greener architecture that maximized on natural light. Small horizontal grooves lined the walls, which were of subdued white to beige in colour. Only the up-market patients could afford this hospital.

As Lesley walked away from its imposing structure towards the parked cars, a sleek Mercedes Benz convertible flashed its parking lights at her. Fumbling inside her handbag, she pulled out a cell phone and held it against her left ear. She paused and leaned on the side of her car as she spoke on her phone in her usual commanding tone.

"Hello! It's Mrs. Angleton... Lesley Angleton. Is that Camila?"

"Hi Mrs. Angleton; it's been a long time, how are you?" Camila answered without excitement.

"I have something important to tell you," Lesley said in a guarded undertone, ignoring the polite greeting.

"You always have something new to tell me," Camila replied in a blasé tone.

"This is something different," Lesley said.

"Is there something wrong?" Camila asked her voice rising from sudden nervousness.

"I am at the Radcliffe Referral Hospital, Fletcher has been admitted with brutal head injuries he suffered last night after what the doctors said was an assault." She heard a sharp intake of breath from Camila on the other end, but continued while trying to compose herself. She graphically narrated every aspect of the ambush on Fletcher, her voice layered with obvious torment.

The conversation between Mrs. Angleton and Camila lasted for a while and it was obvious that Camila was now distraught as well. She kept gasping as she listened keenly to what Lesley was saying. The main reason Lesley had called was to try and glean as much information of her son's recent goings-on hoping that this would help her understand, even in a small way, why anyone would attack him. Lesley was prepared to fight to the bitter end for her ailing Fletcher until justice was done. Their conversation intensified as Mrs Angleton peppered Camila with questions about their relationship with little regard for the young girls' obvious distress and shock at what had happened to her lover. Despite Lesley's probing questions, Camila's responses did not help her connect the dots to shed light on why this heinous act had taken place. She was getting increasingly agitated at this fact, as was Camila with the insensitive prying from Fletcher's mother. Lesley drew a quick breath and sighed dejectedly; this conversation was not going as she had hoped. She finally said goodbye to an unhappy Camila and flipped her cell phone shut. Looking around as the intense wind swirled around her, Lesley felt her life was just as tumultuous. She finally opened her car door, got inside, and drove distractedly off towards her home.

———

The life of luxury and privileged circumstances didn't mean anything to Camila; the twenty-three-year-old daughter of a millionaire had an degree of discipline that belied her age and placed her squarely above her peers in terms of maturity and character. A holder of a Bachelor of Science degree in economics from Cambridge University and a Diploma in Business Administration equipped her well to manage her father's vast business as a trustee of the company, and a hopeful heir. With a towering height of five feet nine inches and with long, shiny, blonde hair falling seductively down the back of her size twelve body frame, Camila was the epitome of beauty and brains put together. She turned heads even without make-up. She was obviously intelligent and held her own in business meetings with no apologies. Despite this, she was not proud, and her agile stride and broad smile brought joy to those who worked with her in her father's expansive office.

But today, Camila was a different self. What she had just heard from her fiancé's mother had struck her with its full and unexpected force. She dropped her cell phone on the big mahogany office table in her living room and slumped back onto her swivel leather chair. She realized she was trembling with shock and realized how traumatized she had become after hearing the sad news of her boyfriend. She adored Fletcher and imagining him in such a helpless state caused searing tears to streak down her high cheek bones, over her soft skin. Her breathing became heavy and uncontrollable. She felt overwhelmed and slightly woozy. She closed her eyes and tried hard to think clearly. 'How could this be? Why would anyone in their right mind try to harm Fletcher? Granted he was a daredevil who irked some around him with his sense of self-importance, but he was also undeniably captivating when he smiled and spoke with those he loved. When he was happy, he had a boyish twinkle in his deep blue eyes that drew women to him like a magnet. His salesmanship was superior to most because he knew how to hone in on the kill when he sensed that a client was interested in what he was selling. He had that effect on Camila all the time; the ability to draw her in even when she tried to resist him, and get her to give in to all his whims even when she was trying to play hard to get. He was warm and affectionate, but could be calculating and hard to business associates. But, she could think of nothing that would get anyone to harm him in this way.

As she thought of all Fletcher meant to her, she cried as she sat at her office desk.

Startled by the news of his son, Michael Angleton a senior accountant with a chartered group of companies left his office in haste and torpedoed across the spacious office with long strides, mumbling to himself as he yanked the door of the impressive office building open. The time was eleven fifteen in the morning and the cool breeze blowing against his face once he left the office was welcome, as he had broken into a sweat just thinking of what he had just heard regarding his son. Janet Cooper, his personal secretary, followed hurriedly behind him, mystified by his strange and obvious agitation, as well as hurried departure. She called in a loud voice.

"Mr. Angleton, Mr. Angleton! What is it? Please tell me what's going on; is there something I should know?"

"What!" Michael shouted absentmindedly whirling to face her. "Oh Janet, I am sorry for shouting, didn't mean to, just one of those bad days." His mind was occupied with frightening images of his ailing and battered son, based on what Dr. Rudolf had briefly told him on the phone.

He leaned heavily on the rails that served as a perimeter to the pavement leading to the car park outside, contemplating what he should do next.

Mr. Angleton removed a handkerchief from his trouser pocket and wiped his now sweaty face. Composing himself, he looked at Janet Cooper again and shook his head.

"Can you just tell me what's going on? You look different, what is it sir?" Janet asked in exasperation, yearning for the truth. It was rare to see her normally composed boss so frazzled.

"It's about Fletcher," Mr. Angleton said still wiping his face, struggling to maintain his usual air of professionalism before his personal assistant of many years.

"Is it something serious? Maybe I can help," Janet went on urgently. She had no idea how weighty the matter was.

"How I wish you could!" Mr. Angleton answered in a laboured whisper.

The love and pride he held for his son was something he never hid or denied, and this bestial act of ambush that had left his son incapacitated on a lonely hospital bed, a far cry from his usual charisma and jovial self, was more than Fletcher's father could bear. Mr. Angleton was known to rise above myriad life challenges that threatened to get between his profession and family life, but the thought of a band of hooligans descending on his son was nightmarish to say the least! "I will get those hooligans," he said to himself under his breath and through clenched teeth. Of course he didn't have the slightest idea where he would start as he said this. His son was still heavily sedated and had yet to name any of his attackers.

Mr. Angleton felt like a caged and angry bull.

Shaking his head in frustration, he strode heavily across the road towards the roadside parking where his new Toyota Celica was stationed, leaving Janet Cooper staring agape as she had not yet gotten a response from him. She stood and watched her boss in consternation, unsure of what to do. But her perplexity lasted only a moment, and in a bold move and with long strides she followed Mr. Angleton quickly to the car and sat on the front passenger seat before he could drive off. Without a word, Mr. Angleton started the car and sped towards the Radcliffe Referral Hospital.

Chapter Two

The stream running through the golf course was the only barrier between the two groups of golfers – each from a different side of the social canvas. To the west of the ridge were local folk who gathered around occasionally and played golf for leisure, with no great meaning attached to the sport, or care for who might win. On the eastern side of the ridge, was a gathering of the elite, semi-professionals who cherished every moment of the game, their peculiar life's challenges whirling through their minds as they swung at the balls on the green.

Jose Cameron, the caddy of Mr. Ashcroft, was trotting by his side pulling the caddy bag as Michael and his associates tested their swing power from slope to mound to dip; each master golfer determined to outwit the other; high class friends in an unspoken but palpable fight to a classic finish.

Mr. Ashcroft, with a grey polo neck T-shirt, and donning a white cap with a *Nike* trademark on its visor, walked a few steps ahead of Cameron. He shielded his eyes with a gloved hand as he keenly followed the golf ball he had driven with a smooth and powerful swing from the tee. He was a professional golfer as well as an astute businessman, and with astonishing accuracy and agility, he would swing his golf club hard and with precision to win most of his rounds. He was by far the best among his associates.

Dr. Carter, a practicing neurosurgeon with a keen interest in real estate and a personal friend to Mr. Ashcroft, caught up with him as they approached the fourth hole. Although not as good as his buddy, he displayed a fine swing, his shoulder muscles bulging and taut, and his tall agile frame turning to his left smoothly. His eyes became slits as he keenly watched and prayed that the blowing gust of wind would buoy his ball to the desired position. It narrowly missed a sand bank and fell two meters short of the target. It rolled down a final slope to rest by the bank of a flowing stream.

"Did you see that?" Dr. Carter asked excitedly, not directing his question to anyone in particular.

"Golf is not a game of strength mate; it's all in the mind with this game you know. Had you controlled your strength and focused on accuracy, I am sure you would be smiling more broadly now. I am familiar with the smile I am talking about; often comes when I strike a mega deal," said Mr. Ashcroft slyly.

"When will you ever commend my game? You know too well that I have trounced you before and if I continue like this, I surely will defeat you. You just watch buddy, this is my day," said the flamboyant Dr. Carter in high spirits as he strode forward lugging his expensive, water and fade-resistant caddy bag behind him. Sometimes he preferred to shirk the help of a personal caddy, opting instead to carry his own bags. It gave him the satisfied feeling of having done some much needed workout.

The two middle-aged men enjoyed a light banter as they strode under the shadow of the Willow trees that majestically lined the foot path. The soft, soothing sound from the stream that cascaded from artificial waterways and meandered on to the wild bush in the horizon brought on a sense of relaxation, but it could not deter Dr. Carter and Michael Ashcroft from the ever titillating subjects of world trends such as global warming and ecological contamination that always seemed to dominate the minds of the elite. By the eighth hole Dr. Carter was enthusiastically jabbing his golf club at the distant horizon and gushing on about Mother Nature and how the extreme floods and hurricanes resulting from climate change had stripped away the fertile top soil of diverse lands in countries worldwide, and how unfortunate it was that no solutions to this ecological mess had yet been found. His homily progressed to the whole idea of devolution of power, world domination by certain nations at the expense of others, and how greed led to a perpetual destruction of the innocent in the world. 'What a world we are leaving behind for our children! When will sanity ever reign?' It did not bother Dr Carter that no one in particular seemed enthralled by his soliloquy. He carried on unperturbed between enthusiastic swings at the golf ball.

It was getting cloudy at an alarming rate, with winds blowing with increasing pressure at the surrounding perimeter bush. The cold weather wrapped itself around each player like a cold flannel coat, but Jose, as he walked behind Michael with the caddy bag, felt the cold seep into his body more than those around him as he wrestled with disturbing thoughts of Camila's father and the imminent revenge attack he could sense hurtling towards him for the ambush he had ordered on Fletcher that night outside the Ogaden Night Club. He knew too well that, if Fletcher died on that hospital bed, from the brutal lashing he had received that night, the wrath from Camila's father against him, if he found out that he was involved in the attack, would be like a thunderbolt blasting mercilessly at him from the skies. The brutal ways and methods his hired sycophants used had been bloody and injurious and it was too late to undo any of that. The damage had already been done and there was no way out. He could only play the nail-biting waiting game and hope that Fletcher Angleton would pull through the coma, for all their sakes

Michael Ashcroft had no idea what his daughter's lover had gone through as his instructions had been quite clear and he had driven off before it all began. Haunting physical discipline was what he had directed, as a clear warning to Fletcher that his shenanigans with déclassé females were not going unnoticed and were demeaning Camila and her celebrated family members. He had not intended any lasting physical harm or injury. It was simply a way of bringing Fletcher in line with his wishes as Camila's father. No more! But the worst had happened due to Jose's unbridled and destructive zeal; him and his troop of brigands! To make the matter worse, Jose had exposed himself by turning up at the Ogaden Night Club himself on that fateful night despite the fact that he would be recognized by Fletcher. It mattered little that he hadn't actually laid a hand on Fletcher during the final assault. Jose's mind was in tumult even as the golf players around him strode along, focusing on their swings and the undulating green before them, oblivious to the tortuous thoughts that were whirling madly in Jose's mind as he hauled Ashcroft's cabby bag along.

As they approached the eighteenth hole, Dr. Carter reached into his pocket, drawing out his cell phone that had been ringing intermittently and distracting him. The call was from Dr. Rudolf at the Radcliffe Referral Hospital. He raised his golf club as a sheriff would raise his gun to halt bandits; a signal to the golfers who trailed him to stop and give him a minute. He then raised his small handset to his large ear. His face turned pensive as he listened to Dr. Rudolf's conversation. It became increasingly severe as the doctor's voice intensified in pitch.

"Just a second Dr. Rudolf, are you talking about Mr. Angleton's son? Michael Angleton!" Dr Carter interjected in obvious disbelief as he knew Mr. Angleton and his family very well.

"Yes! I am talking about Fletcher and we need you here right away!" Dr. Rudolf's voice on the other end was quivering slightly as he explained in detail what had led to Fletcher's hospitalization. He did not leave out even the tiniest detail as he recounted all that had transpired and culminated in Fletcher being wheeled into the large hospital, comatose after a thorough thrashing outside the Ogaden Night Club.

"What the heck! I will be there within the hour," Dr. Carter said murmuring obscene words under his breath before putting the phone back to his ear.

The phone call lasted a number of minutes as both men dissolved into a medial discourse on Fletcher's clinical condition.

The expression on Dr. Carter's face reflected how distraught he was increasingly becoming. When he finished talking to Dr. Rudolf, he sullenly walked to his curious companions who had moved slightly on ahead to give him some privacy, albeit listening keenly to Dr. Carter's side of the story. They could sense that something disastrous had happened and they became sure of this when Dr. Carter strode past them like an army general without uttering a word. It was clear he expected them to follow even though he had not taken the time to explain his sudden aggravation. Those who knew Dr. Carter would swear that he abhorred violence especially when meted on innocent people. He seemed to hold lofty ideals of a world rid of barbaric acts. His thoughts on Fletcher were captured in a sudden angry swing of his golf club. He hit the ball with such force that it flew away in no particular direction and was swallowed up by the wind.

The golf game degenerated in an instant. All players followed Dr. Carter off the course, eager to know what had led to his abrupt change of heart, as Jose ran into the rough to look for the lost ball.

It was getting late; four thirty on a Monday afternoon and the warm rays from the sun were fading away fast as the clouds gathered. The nifty wind was now laced with a chill that caused the players to pull light scarves out of their bags and tie them firmly around their necks. Michael Ashcroft was the first to question the doctor's weird change of attitude. Fidgeting, clenching of fists, and swearing, were unusual characteristics of the good doctor. The other golf partners could now barely contain their curiosity; they wondered what had caused the eminent doctor to suddenly lapse into gloom after such an energizing game. Dr. Carter finally turned to face them and relayed the disturbing news of the ambush to the curious group. At first, he didn't mention who the man was.

Although the events of the day had been well planned, and the imminent investors' meeting at the Grand Regency Hotel had not been cancelled.

Dr. Carter found himself in a dilemma, caught between the will of his friends and peers, and the call of duty that had abruptly arisen at the hospital. As a doctor, hospital emergencies were always his priority. Dr Carter naively thought of himself as the only person within the vicinity who was privy to the harrowing incident Fletcher had gone through, but the truth of the matter was that Jose had been briefed by his bad boys about the near-fatal ambush through a telephone conversation with them earlier.

"Those crazy people," Dr. Carter hissed to himself, "How could they do that for crying out loud?" he continued this time in a loud voice.

"Come on doc. what is it? Mumbling under your breath won't solve anything," Michael asked in obvious frustration, throwing his large hands up in the air in exasperation.

"I am urgently needed at the Radcliffe Referral Hospital," Dr. Carter said with a distracted, cross face, as he glanced hurriedly at the increasingly cloudy skies above. The foreboding weather aptly captured his sullen mood.

"Urgently?" Michael's face was etched with concern.

"Yep, very urgently, in fact I should be on my way by now," Dr. Carter answered still gazing at the skies.

"So what is it then? Is it somebody I know, or is it a family member?" Michael prodded. This is quite unusual coming from you, but you don't have to tell us if you don't want to," Michael knew how to draw information from reluctant client's easily, and he used this tactic on Carter now.

"Family friend, Fletcher Angleton, is in a coma and needs a neurosurgical examination," Dr. Carter stated absentmindedly.

Without uttering a word, and with his head bent slightly to one side, Michael Ashcroft moved closer towards Dr. Carter careful not to allow any uneasy or overly curious expression to show on his face. Further ahead, leaning on the fence, was Jose looking gloomy and wiping his sweaty face with his palms. He avoided any direct eye contact with the two talking gentlemen. As their conversation intensified in low tones, Jose could tell something was wrong and with trembling hands, he lit a cigarette inhaling the smoke deeply while straining to follow the heated but almost whispered conversation. He drew closer to Dr. Carter and Michael, but acted disinterested like a lone lunatic aimlessly wandering about the neighbourhood.

Abruptly, the heated tête-à-tête came to an end and Dr. Carter turned quickly to stride off the green towards his car that was parked at the distant clubhouse. He brusquely waved goodbye to Jose as he passed by, walking determinedly towards the car park. Moments later, he was gone.

Pretending nothing has happened, Jose pulled the caddy bag towards the parking, forcing a grin on his face and fumbling in his pockets for Michael's car keys. Unwelcome beads of sweat dripped down his moist forehead.

Mr. Ashcroft with his cell phone clung to his left ear followed suit and stood a few meters from the idling car where Jose was cocooned in the driver's seat revving the engine nervously as he waited for his boss to join him in the car. Both of them had succeeded in pretending they knew nothing of Fletcher's damning incident, although underneath their controlled countenances, they both wrestled with alarming thoughts.

Mr. Ashcroft finally opened the back door with his free hand and sat back-left in his sleek Lexus before being driven off slowly from the periphery of the golf course and out the club's exit by Jose. They drove by St. Paul's Cathedral and towards the ring-road connecting the Marine Park to the Parade Highway.

"Turn left at the next turning and drive straight to my office," said Michael Ashcroft in a deep, hoarse voice as he scribbled furiously in his pocket diary.

"Yes sir," Jose replied obediently as he manoeuvred the black Lexus smoothly on the busy highway. There was absolute silence as the two men drove towards the city centre. It didn't take them long to get to the office building as there was not much traffic on the road. The time was six twenty-five and other than the security guard standing at attention at the office building entrance, there was nobody else in sight.

"There is something I need to know from you," continued Michael once they were safely behind his private office doors. "Do you know why we came directly to my office from the golf course?" he asked Jose as he quietly tapped the key-ring in his hand on the large Mahogany desk in his expansive and expensively furnished office.

"No sir," Jose answered staring at the floor as he stood submissively before his boss.

"I need you to tell me everything," Michael said; the last word clipped off and stated in a higher pitch to emphasize it. "Do not leave out any detail of what you brutes finally did to Fletcher that night." It was clear Michael was disengaging himself somewhat from the unrestrained and incorrigible onslaught that Fletcher was dealt that night.

Like the professional of long-standing that he was, Michael Ashcroft slowly crossed his legs, leaned back and stroked back his well-kept hair with his long, strong fingers as he levelled his stern and unflinching gaze at his employee. He launched into a detailed cross-examination of an increasingly timid Jose, insisting on a graphic and detailed description of the humiliating assault meted on Fletcher Angleton. Michael's stern demeanour and the clipped manner in which he fired questions at Jose made the man's bulky shoulders become progressively heavier until he dissolved into an embarrassing sniffling giant. Jose could tell that dire consequences lay before him for the Fletcher blunder. He struggled to respond to the peppering all the while wishing he was miles away in an inconspicuous bar, drowning the fear that was building up in his chest with a few bottles of Jack Daniels.

The verbal onslaught finally came to an end and Mr. Ashcroft commanded Jose to get out of his office and to return the following day with hard facts detailing who the individual culprits in his mob of bad boys had been on that fateful night outside the Ogaden Night Club. Michael was determined that there would be no wiggle-free room for any of them to get away unpunished if any police investigation was initiated by the Angelton's.

Jose Cameron snuck away from his employer's thunderous visage knowing that any erstwhile chivalry from Michael to protect his devoted employee had waned to the lowest point and there was nothing Jose could do to bring it back. Mr. Ashcroft's harshness in this matter stemmed from his intense loathing of scandal, given his respectable standing in society.

It didn't take Jose long to locate one of his goons via a quick phone call, a local guy working in the construction industry in Brighton; one who was always broke enough to jump at the slightest promise of a quick buck or free drink. That is why Jose had picked on him in the first place, to carry out the ambush on Fletcher, because of the money Michael had promised each of them. A snap meeting was called to seek a way of disentanglement from the mess that had inadvertently ensued from the attack.

"Ten o'clock sharp tonight! Yes! We all meet at the Ogaden Night Club; make sure you get the other guys and bring them over. Without fail, okay?" were Jose's quick words to the man as he beckoned to an oncoming Taxi. His tone was commanding and angry, an attempt to salvage whatever shred of self-esteem he had remaining after the debasing dressing-down he had endured from Ashcroft, his boss.

The person who mattered most to Jose Cameron was his girlfriend Amanda Walters, a postgraduate student at Oxford University. The last time he saw her was a month ago and sometimes a pang of loneliness would overcome him especially when the going was rough. He needed some tender loving care and not having her around at this irksome time made him feel crabby. Despite the fact that she was more educated than he was, she always had time for him, and made him feel like he was the only man in her life.

He grabbed his cell phone and broodingly dialed her number. The strain in his voice told her everything and so she agreed to see him that weekend. She was never one to ask him too many questions. A spare key to his flat meant she popped into it off and on whenever it pleased her. Jose couldn't wait to see her, and just the thought made him feel slight relief and forget what he sensed lay ahead regarding Fletcher.

Chapter Three

It was eight thirty in the morning. Camila stood contemplatively by the balcony of her spacious three-bedroomed bungalow. Her shapely, long legs, attached to a well-formed and lithe frame, were barely concealed by the light-pink gown wrapped loosely around her body. It was clear she wore nothing underneath. She was a woman who was comfortable in her skin.

Camila Ashcroft's mind was far away. She pondered the heinous crime that had put her soul-mate and lover into a coma. She couldn't shake off the image of a swollen, weak body from her mind. As an old friend of the Angleton's, she knew Fletcher as a noble and quiet person who hated violence. He was known for his tolerance and respect as well as the fact that his charming, handsome face was so disarming. He had a way with the women who flocked after him, and he was outstanding in marketing whatever product or service he sold so that he could wheedle commitment from the most resistant prospects. It was difficult to resist his alluring nature. Camila continued to mull over their love relationship, recalling the romantic and heady moments they had shared. She wondered how everything could go so wrong.

A soft morning breeze swirled around her silken face. It brought with it an indulgent and sweet aroma that wafted from the flowers blossoming in her back garden into the room she was in. Camila did not hear that her door bell had been buzzing for some time. A flickering shadow of movement outside her front door caught the corner of her eye as she stood in her spacious kitchen. She startled and swung around to face the door when she realized that someone had been standing outside her front door.

It took a moment before she could regain her normally calm demeanour; the events over the past few days had frazzled her quite a bit. She moved towards the door to check on who had come to see her.

It was her mother Linda Ashcroft.

"I am sorry mum, didn't hear the bell ringing," she said in a matter-of-fact tone as she opened the large oak door and let her mother stride quickly into the hallway.

"It's alright my girl, I know what you are going through after the horror that's been visited on Fletcher," Linda told her daughter without donning her usual smile.

"I know. I still can't believe it. Thanks so much for coming over," Camila replied.

"I tell you what," her mother continued soothingly "at least Fletcher is out of danger, that's for sure."

"Is he? How do you know that?" Camila asked looking at her mother curiously.

"Your father called Dr. Carter at the hospital this morning and learned that Fletcher was now out of danger," she answered.

"So how is he faring now, is he talking?" Camila asked with both of her hands holding the sides of her mouth as she waited for her mother to reply.

"Oh yes, he is responding very well to the treatment and I understand Mr. Angleton will be meeting with your father to discuss the events," she told her daughter, "can I have some coffee please?" Linda walked purposefully towards the kitchen as she continued; she rubbed her hands together to warm them up.

"Oh my God, I feel so lost I am not even being a good hostess! This has been such a stressful time for me; of course, let me make some coffee for you," Camila said walking closer to the kitchen table where the kettle was connected to the lone socket on the wall.

The relation between mother and daughter was protected by a shield of immense affection. Linda made her daughter's needs a priority without being idolizing. She never failed in her maternal duties and found ways of carving time out of her demanding work schedule for her daughter's important needs. Mother and daughter had an enviable and comfortable friendship, and liked spending time together.

Linda Ashcroft has been married to her husband for the last twenty-six years. They were obviously affluent and she revelled in the full support of her husband. Linda was an enthusiastic and gallant woman, a graphic designer by profession and a radiant housewife who basked in enjoying her family's company. She was gifted with leadership qualities as demonstrated by her zeal as leader of the region's Mothers Guild, a post she protected and to which she gave her all. At forty-seven, she defied her age, maintaining a youthful appearance and an enviable level of energy. Despite her innovative designer skills, Linda preferred to support her husband's business ambitions, and chose to work as his personal assistant in his auspicious office. Once in a while she also took on some design work, but her husband's business was now priority number one. She had endured many difficult moments in her marriage and professionally as his personal assistant, to see him build his venerable business empire successfully.

Spending time with her mother helped soothe Camila's mind and she was relieved that Fletcher was now officially out of danger. They chit-chatted about nothing in particular, enjoying each other's company as they sipped coffee and nibbled on pretzels and small mince pies. A more relaxed Camila finally excused herself to go to the bathroom, leaving her mother watching the early morning news on the TV in the living room.

Camila walked towards her bedroom, her long legs causing her hips to sway seductively with her gait. She entered her bathroom a few meters away from her bedroom and let her loose gown fall freely to the floor, exposing her shapely, naked body to the massive mirror hanging from the wall in front of her. She bent over the king-size bath tub in the huge bathroom and absentmindedly turned the silver faucets, to let the steaming hot water run into the tub. She dribbled a blend of herbal essence into the running water to create a foamy lather that released a relaxing and fruity aroma into the air around her. Slowly, she stepped into the large tub and using a silky-soft sponge she slowly but firmly massaged her soft skin in circular motions. Doing this always helped any tension seep out of her body. She ran her hands over herself dreamily as her mind wandered to Fletcher. She missed him all the more as she remembered his firm loving arms cradling her against his broad chest when she felt lonely or needed a shoulder to cry on. She inhaled the aromatic scent that rose up from the steaming water and allowed her tired body to succumb to its relaxing warmth. She wished the moment would not end, but the absurdity of what had happened to Fletcher drew an uninvited chill into the room, and abruptly thrust the warmth away.

The soft music filtered in from the sitting room through the thick, glass panels separating the bathroom and the veranda. It brought a soothing therapeutic melody to Camila's now slightly troubled soul. Thoughts of Fletcher Angleton still in the hospital flooded back however, bringing a sharp awareness and slight pain to her mind. Camila finally stood up and carefully stepped out of the bath tub, water and foamy bubbles dripping down from her blushed, warm skin. She grabbed a soft, thick towel that was hanging loosely on a side rail and gently wiped her body dry. She wrapped herself with the towel and strode to her bedroom, its warm yellow, brown and tanned hues drawing her.

Linda waited quietly for her daughter to finish washing. She sipped her second cup of coffee and listened in silence to the broadcast from the television set hanging on the wall of the well-furnished room.

Camila indulged in soothing herself with a slow massage using her favourite lotion and forgot all about the time. This inevitably invited an outburst from her now ruffled mother when she finally joined her in the sitting room.

"This is what I really don't like," said Linda indignantly.

"What's that you don't like mum?" Camila asked naively.

"You know very well we are supposed to be going to the hospital and you take all the time in the world to take a bath. I know you needed to relax away the stress you've been through, but surely…., for nearly a whole hour?" Linda's voice trailed off on a high note, despite her efforts to mask the frustration she was now suddenly feeling.

"I am sorry mum; I honestly didn't notice," Camila said defensively.

"You know there are other matters waiting to be attended to and of course your father will be waiting for us in the office," Linda continued.

"Ok mum, I am now ready," Camila continued trying to placate her flustered mother.

"Next time, try to be time-conscious and nobody will complain!" Mrs. Ashcroft was troubled by her daughter's lack of concern when it came to time-keeping. All the happenings at the hospital had apparently snuck under her skin and she was finding it difficult to dispel a lining of frustration in her mind.

"Okay, okay. I didn't take that long mum, so don't be so mad with me, I said I am sorry," Camila said with a knowing smile. "Let's not turn this into something more than it is. Honestly, you know how all women get carried away in front of the mirror sometimes. I am sorry but next time I will try to be faster," Camila was trying to deflate the angry bubble her mother was struggling with.

"Okay, let's get on with it then shall we? Let's not dwell on that too much," Linda said as she finally felt the irritation lift. She gave her gold wrist watch a cursory glance as she bent to quickly pick her large designer handbag.

The pair headed towards the door and Camila couldn't resist a last but quick side-glance at the long mirror hanging in the hallway. Linda just shook her well-coiffed but slightly gray head in dismay.

The two ladies were immaculately dressed as they strode confidently and side-by-side towards the parked cars in front of the apartment complex. Their body language displayed that they were at home in the elite class to which they belonged. With fashionable attire and a perfect finish to their make-up, you could hardly tell mother and daughter apart. Not surprisingly, glances were cast in their direction as they confidently strode past passersby. They spoke to each other in low-tones unaware of the admiring glances and stir they caused in the homes of their equally affluent neighbours' homes.

Camila got into Linda's car and they slowly drove away from the spike-studded main gate that led to their apartments, towards the narrow drive leading to the main road. Mrs. Ashcroft navigated the big Range Rover with ease as her daughter fumbled with the car radio looking for the frequency of the music station she liked. It was getting brighter as the day progressed, with sunny spells bringing freshness to the day. Above them; the sky was blue with an occasional white cloud lazily floating away. Sparrows flew about freely in the sky and watching them lifted one's spirits. It was promising to be a good day.

It didn't take them long to get to the Radcliffe Referral Hospital as the roads were clear of traffic; it was ten forty-five. Linda Ashcroft parked the car and she and Camila quickly got out and strode across the front parking section of the hospital. Neither of them noticed the sleek Mercedes parked a few feet away. It belonged to Lesley Angleton who had come earlier and was now standing by the oval-shaped reception desk just inside the front entrance of the hospital. She was casually talking with a young man in a white overcoat; one of the orderlies in charge of non-medical needs and maintaining cleanliness in the hospital. She turned her head slightly to the right and noticed the two approaching women. Lesley greeted them with a frosty smile and led them down the wide corridors of the hospital leading to the wards until they reached ward fifteen where Fletcher Angleton was sitting up on his hospital bed. He grinned widely when he looked up and saw his visitors. He had been enjoying a huge bowl of oats porridge, which he now promptly kept aside to quickly embrace his fiancé and greet the other visitors.

Camila's immense relief was obvious to all as she held Fletcher's curly locks close to her chest and kissed his forehead tenderly. The others politely waited their turn to say hallo. Fletcher delved with graphic detail into his harrowing ambush by the thugs that night at the Ogaden Night Club. He touched the now healed lacerations on his face; the stitch marks could clearly be seen despite the fact that the swelling had reduced markedly. He was enjoying the intensity of distressed emotions on Camila's face as he embellished his detailing of the ambush. She was obviously pained and concerned for him and a part of the man in him basked in her reaction. He covered every minute detail of the incident outside the Ogaden Night Club the night he had gone there to meet with friends for a drink. He was careful however to omit the details of the pretty damsel by his side with whom he was philandering while there that night. Fletcher was a sly enough man to know where his bread was buttered.

"The first person to approach me at the night club was Jose Cameron, if I can remember correctly. And on a table not too far away from me were four rough-looking guys, I didn't feel uneasy because they didn't seem too concerned with me, and I don't think I had ever seen them before. In fact, when I finally left the club I was not aware that I was being followed by anyone. You know how it is when you are just having a fun night with you guy friends; you don't really pay attention to who's on the other tables around you. You're just having a good time, and I had been really tired that week, so I was out to let off some steam, you know." Fletcher was narrating the incident to the three women who were keenly following his story; they were nodding and shaking their heads at intervals depending on how his narration ebbed and flowed. He was in his element; the centre of attention is where he loved to be.

"Then what happened?" his mother asked him when he hesitated for a moment; he was making his ordeal sound like a thriller.

"They followed me the minute I stepped out of the club…at about midnight," Fletcher lied before he continued animated. "A sixth sense made me turn around and that is when I felt a heavy blow on my head. One of the brutes must have knocked me with something, you know, like a huge rock. It felt huge! I fell down and that's when the other three jumped on me, punching and kicking and with heavy blows to my face and body until I lost consciousness. Next thing I knew, I was in this hospital bed," he stated waving his palm from the back of his head to his feet as he came to the end of his narration before his spellbound audience.

"Did you recognize any of the culprits?" Camila interjected with great concern.

"To be honest with you, I didn't recognize anybody but if Jose was involved because I saw him hanging about and he was shouting nonsense out to me but I can't remember what exactly. I swear he will never know what hit him if it is confirmed he was part of this crazy mess," said Fletcher heatedly as he recalled the pain he had been in the past few days in hospital. Fletcher believed in living his life to the full and the thought of someone trying to steal that from him made him feel outraged.

The idea of Jose's possible involvement in this heinous act came as a big surprise to Camila and Lesley, but they remained mum knowing that if this were true, it could spark a family feud with catastrophic consequences. Mr. Angleton had confided in Lesley his wife the night before that he would leave no stone unturned to find out who was involved, and ensure they were nailed and that they paid dearly for what they had done to his son. He swore to seek retribution without caring who would get hurt. It would be almost impossible to diffuse the situation.

Michael Ashcroft on the other hand was working to deflate the tension that was building between the two wealthy families. He clearly understood that any bad blood between the two power brokers would inevitably tarnish his name in society and could very well bring down his vast business empire. Although Fletcher was out of danger, the bone of contention was now firmly in place between the two families, threatening to blast all that they had built over the years in all directions.

Two families that commanded great respect and wielded immense power in business and political circles in their society, had no idea what deceit and unbridled grudges had unleashed on their erstwhile closeness. The looming darkness and hostility hurtled towards their peaceable elite world and it was too late to undo the avalanche that Jose and his hooligans had wrought. Their brutish greed and criminal conduct had caused damage that was irreversible.

The looks on the faces of both Lesley Angleton and Linda Ashcroft belied the turmoil in the hearts. Instead they depicted an inner serenity and control as they watched the young lovers greet and catch up with each other. Stakes were high for both families yet the looming feud was inevitable.

As the time passed, Fletcher Angleton's medication started to draw him into a deep sleep that he could not resist, though he desired much to continue with his enthralling account. His eager retelling of that fateful night dissolved into slurred and tired phrases. He leaned on his pillow, still clutching Camila's long, soft fingers and fell asleep before their observant eyes. He looked like a small boy trying to keep clutching a lollipop despite a weakening cloud of slumber descending on him.

"Let's go," Mrs. Angleton said to the rest in a whisper as she turned slowly away from Fletcher's hospital bed.

Without uttering a word, Lesley Angleton bent towards Fletcher and smoothed out the bed sheets on his narrow bed, a habit she had honed over the years as she watched over him from infancy, and then she walked slowly past the curtains separating the beds in the ward. She was followed by Camila who now seemed to be lost in a world of her own.

As they walked down the corridors, none of the three women spoke. Each tried to come to grips with the happenings that had violently assaulted their formerly amenable lives. These were the sorts of stories one heard about from the inner-city, ghetto-like communities of the lower classes. But, in more sophisticated circles to which they belonged, one hardly heard of such hooliganism. Each woman wondered silently what was happening to their secure world and felt a slight and unwelcome fear curl around their hearts.

A few yards into the car park, Mrs. Ashcroft cell phone started to ring persistently and jolted them out of their reverie.

"Hello my dear," she answered quickly after dipping into her designer handbag for the handset. It was her husband.

"Hi, I couldn't make it to the hospital; I got tied up," Mr. Ashcroft said. "The meeting took longer than anticipated and you know these meetings for directors, one of us had to be there. Anyway, how is the young man responding now?" asked Mr. Ashcroft. His wife gave him an update on Fletcher's situation and he responded in the low and distraught tones she expected. He keenly followed the detailed description of the attack and additional points from the doctor's medical report at the hospital. The greatest worry he had was how he would clear his name with the Angleton's family because it was now clear to all that Jose Cameron was working for him and was involved in the atrocious attack. The rumour mill always worked overtime and at lightning speed. He needed to act quickly if he was going to sort this mess out. "Anyway, see you at home soon. I am through with work here so I am going to head there as well now," he said then hung up.

By the car park, the three ladies bid each other farewell with promises to meet sometime soon as their cars pulled out of the parking area. They headed in two different directions. Camila, though struggling with what she had heard from Fletcher that evening, found the courage to ask her mother to tell her honestly what she knew about the whole thing. Fletcher was her boyfriend but he was also the victim, and it was her father's associate who was the prime suspect from the little she had heard. She had every right to know as much about it as she possibly could although her mother was a bit reluctant at first to tell her anything. Seeing that Camila was not going to stop pestering her for the truth, her mum finally opened up and carefully described what she had heard about Fletcher's waylay that night. She was however careful to quickly point out that nothing concrete had yet been found out about the attack.

"The only thing your father has told me is that, he will make sure that everybody involved in this will be caught and severely punished," her determined tone helped soothe Camila's distraught spirit.

"Mum, even if that's the case, why would Jose of all the people try to harm Fletcher? Is there any reason that I don't know about. I don't understand, they have been friends for a very long time, why would he try and hurt Fletcher?" Camila's voice trembled as she peppered her stressed mother with these questions and she finally broke down and sobbed uncontrollably, wiping her tears off her soft cheeks with the back of her palms, careful all the same not to smudge her makeup. Her mother drove on listening keenly to Camila's queries and clutching the steering wheel hard until her knuckles stood out white and taut. She was trying hard to maintain some control over her own emotions which were also threatening to overcome her.

"I know how you feel my love, but this will surely come to an end," she said to Camila as she parked the big Range Rover outside the Italian restaurant, the Riverside Hotel. They sat for a while as Camila cooled down and wiped her nose with a pink, flowered handkerchief. She breathed in deeply a number of times and looked up at her mother. Her eyes were red and she had messed her usually perfectly done mascara despite her efforts not to but she was calmer.

"Any plans for the day?" she asked her mother.

"Let's get in here for a meal, and then I will drop you at your apartment," Lesley said looking at her watch. "I don't have anything more important planned today, other than making sure you are okay." She smiled at her daughter and waited as she quickly sorted out her make-up, before they both stepped out of the car and headed to the hotel, which was not too far off the side of the road.

It didn't bother Camila that she had cried in front of her mother. They had always had an open and honest relationship and did not hide even their deepest emotions from each other. It was just that all the mix-up of emotions in her heart after the attack on Fletcher was difficult to deal with. Learning the truth of what had happened to Fletcher and seeing him today in the hospital alive and healing, knowing that someone in her father's office had something to do with bashing him unconscious was all too hard for her to deal with. What made things worse was the uncanny sense she had that her father had been involved in this whole mess; that he could actually have had a part in making it happen was like a nightmare beginning to claw at her mind. Camila had always looked up to her father and couldn't believe that he could ever be involved in any fishy business, and definitely not of this ugly nature. Her mother had been careful, even as she tried to explain what she had learnt of the incident that night, to mask what she truly felt. Her face showed no hint of what really took place or what she feared was really confronting their family. She took pains to calm her daughter and give her the impression all was as it had always been. The saintly look on her face would have fooled anyone. In her heart however, what she really felt was like a big boulder was hurtling in their direction, about to smash all that was sane and important into smithereens.

Chapter Four

The time was ten fifteen at night, but instead of cool air and stillness, the air was humid and muggy. Ogaden Night Club was teaming with revellers of all ages and music filtered through its lofts to the heady patrons below. The queue outside was getting longer and longer as people jostled to get through the doors into the popular joint. The inside was shadowy with tinted lights hanging overhead, casting different patterns around the corners where patrons lustily drained their bottles of beer and tantalizing cocktails. Sweaty bodies intermingled as people moved about from bar to table, and the air was smoky.

Sitting in a secluded corner was Jose Cameron animatedly conversing with Henry Forbes, a well-built character of Caribbean origin whose taut muscles displayed the formidable frame of a hardened athlete. Henry's shaven head proudly displayed a dragon tattoo and his bulging bloodshot eyes were fearful enough to make anyone avoid his gaze and melt from his presence. Holding a bottle of Budweiser in his left hand and a cigarette in his right, it was obvious that Henry brooked no nonsense; a man with no conscience who was capable of the worst atrocities. His position as the leader of an infamous hit squad made even those who considered themselves his collaborators wary of him. Although Jose Cameron had verbally warned his other die-hard lieutenants not to fail to attend this meeting Henry was the only person who came to this meeting that was to determine the fate of Jose in relation to the disastrous events that almost led to Fletcher Angleton's demise from this side of heaven.

"I told you I don't want any excuses from anyone. You told me you've communicated with the other guys and that they would all be here by ten. What do you think this is, a kindergarten outing or what?" Jose growled at Henry.

"Let's give them a few more minutes; it could be that they are just late," Henry answered his head bent away from Jose's angry glare. Despite his large body, he didn't like to ire Jose. He knew that though Jose was smaller, angering him would be unwise as he had links to powerful people who could do him some harm.

"Listen! You guys have really put me in real trouble. I am supposed to report back to my boss tomorrow morning with a detailed explanation of what transpired that night and I don't give a hoot about any excuses from any of you! If, and only if, in fifteen minutes they don't turn up I will expect you to give me a very detailed description of what happened after I walked back to keep an eye on the club that night, otherwise you'll all be in real trouble," Jose retorted with a raised voice, banging the table with a clenched fist. A few of the revellers from the tables around them looked up at them for a moment with questioning glances, then got back to discussing their own scrapes in life just as quickly.

Never before had Jose Cameron been so agitated. He was desperate to sort the impasse he was in as quickly as possible. He shook his head in frustration before he stood up suddenly and staggered towards the bar where he ordered a double shot of neat, dry gin. He angrily tossed his head back and gulped it down in one move before ordering another one. Wiping his face with a white handkerchief he drew from his back, trouser pocket, he wobbled back to his seat. The look on his face said it all when he found that Henry Forbes had long disappeared!

"What the heck!" Jose shouted in consternation, looking around the dark lounge frantically. It only took a few seconds for him to accept he had been duped. He angrily walked back to the bar and pulled out a stool. He sat down frustrated and decided to order another drink.

Alone in the night club and the effects of alcohol taking control of his already distraught mind, Jose was wondering what alibi he could come up with to get himself out of the mess that they unleashed on Fletcher that night at the Ogaden Night Club. He ruefully mingled with the crowd of revellers with hope of finding Henry hiding in some corner, or even finding any of the others but no one else from the hit squad appeared. The alcohol was taking its toll and before long his socializing with the frenzied drunks dissolved into a mad gyration of every limb to the loud club music, all cares of before thrown out the window as he wiggled and weaved to the wild rhythms and melodies.

It was finally at three thirty in the morning that Jose disentangled himself from the crowd in the club and staggered along the well-lit walkway. The crescent moon and the stars in the sky were partially hidden by dark clouds. A slight drizzle fell slowly down and soaked into the soft grass beneath his feet. His mind was troubled as he staggered back and forth inebriated. Other than an occasional wild fox crisscrossing the path before him, there was not a single soul in sight to appease the tumultuous thoughts in his tired mind. 'What an egocentric loser!' he swore under his breath, referring to Henry Forbes. I am gonna get that louse!

The long walk to his residence sobered him up somewhat and the cold, wet wind caused chills to run down his spine. He pulled his large coat closer about him. Walking alone caused a sudden fear of the unknown to creep up his being. He looked furtively around him at some point and despite his large frame, Jose felt vulnerable. His mind was playing frightful games on him, and his thoughts strayed to his boss and what plot had been hatched against Fletcher. He knew only too well what Michael Ashcroft and those in his league were capable of. He quickened his step in the lonely night.

A drenched and shivering Jose finally covered the thirty-minute walk to his flat, although it had taken him almost one hour in his inebriated state. He fumbled in his pockets for his keys, and it seemed like eternity before he found the right one to his front door. Inside his one-bedroom flat, nothing seemed in order as clusters of magazines and newspapers filled every space on the oval-shaped coffee table in the centre of his living-room floor. In one corner of the room, and placed on a glass-topped stool, sat an ashtray that was full of stale and smelly cigarette butts. They emitted a repulsive stench so he quickly walked to the window facing his back yard and flung it open for fresh air. He grabbed the ash tray and dumped the butts into the garbage bin in his small kitchen to the left and walked on to his one bedroom. Oddly enough, the bedroom was usually neat and immaculately arranged compared to the rest of his flat. The bed was with a white silky bedspread smoothly covering every corner of the massive Victorian bed with double pillows matching the spread. A gargantuan wardrobe with double doors stood by the wall and long drapes on the slightly opened window swung lazily from side-to-side allowing a cool breeze into the room.

Jose Cameron felt so exhausted after the long and fearful walk, not to mention the uncontrolled gyrating and drinking he had succumbed to at the club, that he just slumped onto his bed and lay there face up, with his clothes still on. When he fell asleep, it was a fitful experience. He tossed and turned most of the night, having angst-ridden hallucinations of his boss chasing him down a muddy embankment. In the dream, Jose was slipping and sliding, grasping at wet bushes as he fled. No matter how fast he ran, Michael seemed to be a whisker away, shouting obscenities and waving what seemed to be a shot-gun over his head. Even as Jose ran screaming, he would look back and find Michael's eyes were bulbous and bloodshot, and a black liquid trickled from their corners. The nightmares weakened Jose's sweaty body and wound up his already strained mind. It was almost morning before he finally drifted into a deep sleep.

—————

The tap on the front door was soft but the voice that followed it unsympathetically loud the morning after Jose left the Ogaden Night Club. Ten o'clock in the morning and he was still cocooned in his bed, the hangover of the previous night causing a searing pain inside his head. It was only the continuous loud banging on his door that finally woke Jose up. He rubbed his puffy eyes and jumped out his bed as a cold-sweat broke out on his forehead. He was familiar with such thumping on doors; it could only be the police.

"This is Sergeant Morgan," the voice from outside thundered, "open the door...police," the same voice ordered.

"Okay, okay!" Jose shouted gruffly as he swung his tired legs over the edge of the bed and reluctantly walked towards the front entrance of his flat.

Standing right in front of the door was the towering figure of Sergeant Morgan Clifton, a criminal investigation officer from the Metropolitan Police Department. He was in plain clothes and smartly dressed in a grey, striped suit, a light blue shirt and a crimson coloured tie falling over his fat belly but not quite reaching his belt. Sergeant Morgan looked like a typical salesman from Brighton waiting to unleash a marketing pitch as he waited patiently for Jose to open the door.

"I am Sergeant Morgan Clifton from the Met Police Department," he introduced himself calmly displaying his identity badge close to Jose's sleepy eyes.

"What is it Sergeant?" Jose asked still trying to shake off the fear and the hangover that was mixed together in his head.

"Sergeant Morgan Clifton," was all the Sergeant replied as he strode purposefully into the house without waiting to be invited in.

"Okay Sergeant Morgan Clifton, what can I do for you?" Jose was getting increasingly frustrated as he couldn't understand what this sudden visit from the police was all about, although in the recesses of his web-filled mind, he sensed it had something to do with Fletcher.

"I am here to ask you a few questions regarding an assault that took place in the early hours of Monday morning close to the Ogaden Night Club. Are you aware of anything like that?" Sergeant Morgan's voice was controlled but his eyes were piercing as he whirled around to face Jose, who had closed the door behind him and was now standing sandwiched between the front door and the imposing sergeant.

"What are you talking about?" asked Jose visibly shaken and sensing that the die had now been cast.

"I am talking about Fletcher Angleton, do you know him?" Morgan's reply sounded more like a statement than a question.

"Of cause I know him," Jose answered rubbing his eyes with the back of his hand to avoid a direct stare into the sergeant's searching eyes.

The Sergeant drew a note book out of his coat pocket and held a small ball-point pen over it, poised to jot down anything he thought was important to his investigations. He liked the officious look he cast when clutching a pen and notebook.

"When was the last time you saw him?" asked the Serge, looking up briefly into Jose's face after each question.

"Couple of weeks ago, can't remember the exact day," answered Jose and continued, "what's all this about Serge?"

"Sergeant Morgan Clifton, how many times do I have to keep reminding you?"

It was clear the man expected to be addressed with respect, and it was not going to be any different with Jose.

"Okay Sergeant Morgan Clifton, I just want to know what the hell is going on," Jose replied defensively.

"All I want to know from you is whether you were involved or collaborated with the people who attacked him and whether you know anything that would assist us with the investigations, simple," Sergeant Morgan explained without hesitation. "Do you have a problem with that?"

"No, no, no…I don't even know what you are talking about. Listen, I am really tired so if you don't have any reason to arrest me…I think you should leave me alone," Jose ventured, hoping this would dissuade the Sergeant from going on with his questioning. "I mean, I don't have anything to do with what you are asking and if I hear of anything I will no doubt let you know. Why would you imagine I know anything about this anyway? I mean, I know Fletcher of course, but why would you suspect that I had anything to do with…what even happened out there, you haven't told me exactly what happened?" Jose was speaking hurriedly, but he tried to force himself to become calmer, and speak slowly. He could sense that the sergeant did not have anything concrete linking him to Fletcher. He had to be careful with what he said. He didn't want to put himself in more of a mess. But, he had a niggling thought, 'why had the sergeant come to him?'

"If I hear of anything, I will let you know," he said sidling past the sergeant's large frame and settling on the sofa in his medium-sized sitting room. He crossed his legs to feign relaxation.

"I am in charge of the investigations into what happened to Fletcher at the Ogaden Night Club when a group of hooligans ambushed him on his way home, and beat him up so badly that he ended up almost dead, and in hospital. So far, information I have received seems to touch on you as well, so it is up to you now to co-operate with the police and that way, everything will be alright in the end…if you had nothing to do with it," Sergeant Morgan said in measured tones as he keenly looked Jose over from head to toe. He paused for a moment waiting to see if Jose would say anything else. When this was not forthcoming, he briefly touched on what he had heard from other sources about that fateful night and turned to head towards the front door. He threw a quiet but ominous warning over his shoulder to Jose, that he would get to the bottom of this case no matter what, and that this would not be his last visit. "You might have more to tell me then," he said before he slammed the front door behind his broad back, leaving a shaken Jose staring after him. The sergeant's presence seemed to linger in the flat even after his angry exit.

Jose finally got up and locked the front door then moved to his bedroom, as if that would dispel the fear that he now felt. He sat on his bed and thought of what had just transpired. He felt isolated as he tried to comprehend the events unfolding. He wondered what to expect from this sudden development. Standing up, he checked his jacket pockets and took out his cell phone intending to call his boss to hear his take on things, but just imagining his boss's face on the other end of the line made him think better otherwise. He wasn't sure of the reception he would receive and he wondered what difference it would make anyway. His hands shook nervously and drops of sweat glistened on his face. He shuddered as he slumped back onto his bed. All efforts at going back to sleep failed miserably.

He clicked his tongue in annoyance as his phone battery gave out and he heard an annoying beep. Normally he would charge his phone battery before sleeping but the state he was in the previous night had caused him to forget to do so. He had only himself to blame. 'Damn!' Jose sat up finally and lit a cigarette. He dragged at it urgently in an effort to calm his frayed nerves. He got off the bed, holding the lit butt in his left hand, and paced the room slowly in deep thought. 'What was to become of him and his boss? He did not even want to imagine losing his job. Whose fault was it anyway that Fletcher was done in that night? His boss was behind all of it, yet it seemed he was quickly being tagged as some sacrificial lamb! Damn these aristocrats! And why did Henry disappear into thin air suddenly after the ambush on Fletcher?' Jose's spinning thoughts were driving him crazy. 'What's going on for goodness sake?' Jose hissed to himself as he walked towards the bathroom. The time on the digital clock hanging on the wall read 12:45 in the afternoon. 'Maybe I should have gone with them instead of staying back to keep an eye on the club,' he thought to himself angrily.

Henry Forbes was nowhere to be seen. The door to his house was locked but the windows were partly open. A lone cat sat lazily on the window sill facing his small verandah, its long black and white tail swished slowly back and forth as it dozed in the warm sun. The slight breeze was refreshingly welcome as it brushed on the faces of passersby. Jose knocked on the door several times getting increasingly frustrated at the haunting silence from within. He finally turned and went to sit in his van, which was parked a few metres around the corner from the entrance to Henry's house. He waited for about an hour, growing increasingly agitated as he wondered where Henry was. He was just about to give up and leave when a shadowy figure emerged from behind a thicket a short distance along the road. Jose could tell from the stealthy amble that Forbes was finally coming back home. It was obvious he was being watchful for he kept turning his head to see if anyone was following him.

If Henry spotted Jose, he would find a way of disappearing again without the slightest concern for the consequences on Jose's life. This feud between the Angletons and the Ashcrofts needed sorting the soonest possible otherwise Jose would lose his long-standing friendship with them, as well as lose his only means of livelihood. He also always lauded it on his friends that he daily brushed shoulders with the high and mighty; it would be too embarrassing to lose all that. Speed was of essence if he were to clear his name of this Fletcher debacle. The notion of losing his position within the Ashcroft's family was unimaginable as he would ultimately lose the benefits and luxuries of working with the rich and famous, and he had become accustomed to the perks that came with the job. He had to get a water-tight plan of claiming his innocence and preserving his relationship with the two families and Henry Forbes was an important element of this solution.

Jose was well-concealed a few metres from Henry's door. He was partly hidden by a large tree not too far from Henry's front entrance. He watched keenly as Henry guilelessly ambled towards his front door as a deer would blindly stumble towards a pride of hungry lions. Henry Forbes jiggled his keys in his pockets as he got nearer to his door. He pulled out the bunch of keys once he was at his door and inserted one key into the door's lock. He turned it. It was then that he felt the heavy clamp of a man's hand on his back. He swung around in shock and came face-to-face with Jose's livid countenance. Without a word, Jose shoved the sheepish Henry into his flat and as soon as they were both inside, he promptly locked the door from the inside.

"So, you think you're just gonna leave me hanging like that huh? I am not going down alone I tell you. What the heck did you think you were doing disappearing like that, first at Ogaden then the other night when we should have talked about this crazy thing? Huh? Huh?" Jose was inching up against Henry's chest, his dark eyes boring into Henry's skull as he yelled his head off into Henry's shocked face. He was obviously incensed and released a string of obscenities while threatening in the same breath to expose Henry to Sergeant Morgan Clifton. The anger on Jose's face was palpable and Henry knew that these were not just empty threats. He could tell that Jose was capable of doing anything to exonerate himself if that meant he would salvage his prized relationship with the two most powerful and rich families in Brighton. Physically too, Henry knew he was no match for an angry Jose Cameron. Everyone in Brighton's underworld knew of Jose's Black Belt in Tae-kwon-do and other Martial Arts, but what was most terrifying were the connections Jose boasted of that could enable him to make one disappear or be incapacitated for life. The thunder in Jose's face revealed how angry he was with Henry and that he would stop at nothing if Henry did not give him the information he required of what really happened that night, so that Jose could consider what he should do to get himself out of the mess. Henry fearfully staggered backwards and plonked himself into a small chair in his living room. He fumbled in his pocket and removed a half-smoked cigarette, which he lit with shaky fingers and sucked hard at as he listened to Jose's tirade. He nervously narrated all that had taken place after Jose had indicated to them to follow Fletcher and do what Jose's boss had wanted. Every harrowing detail slipped past his quivering lips as he stared into Jose's thunderous face. When he was through, Jose ran his fingers through his hair as he glared at Henry as if he was wondering whether to punch him in the face. He couldn't believe what he was hearing! 'How could they have let everything get so out of control?' He then spat on the wooden floor in anger, and stormed out of Henry's house making it clear that the only option would be for Henry to own up as the culprit of the Ogaden Night Club misadventure otherwise Jose would have his neck. Henry watched him leave and sank into his chair in relief. He held his breath for a moment, with his mouth and eyes open. He wondered what to do as he took a few breaths to calm himself down. He was not sure of his next move given the options Jose had spelt out to him. Just the thought of encountering Michael Ashcroft and owning up to what they had done at the Ogaden Night Club incident was unimaginable. Henry was tired and he shivered slightly from the effect of Jose's visit. He walked slowly to his bedroom, lit up the only cigarette he had left, and went straight to bed. He puffed on the cigarette and directed the smoke up at the ceiling as he mulled over what had taken place over the past few minutes. He wondered if there was another option other than facing Mr. Ashcroft and confessing to what they had done to Fletcher in their deliriously drunk state that night away from the Ogaden Night Club. He wondered over and over what he should do until he fell into a fitful slumber.

Chapter Five

Both Michael Angleton and Michael Ashcroft were talking in low tones within the safety of Mr. Ashcroft's big and tastefully furnished office in town. The talks ranged from politics and business to sports and leisure, a safe chit-chat that helped them avoid the crisis they faced as two families, at least for some time. Mr. Angleton finally broached the issue of Fletcher and his hospitalization and the heinous act that had transpired at Ogaden Night Club. This private tête-à-tête between two societal giants was a desperate bid to avoid an all-out feud after Jose's muck-up. It was five forty-five.

"I think we can do with a tot of vodka," Ashcroft said flexing his arms.

"That sounds good to me," was the answer from Mr. Angleton. Both men were eager to release some tension.

Standing up, Mr. Ashcroft strode across the office floor towards a drinks cabinet that stood against the back wall of the office, just behind his mahogany desk, and came back holding a bottle of vodka that was halfway full. He also carried two small glasses in the other hand. He studiously placed them on the office desk, pouring the contents in equal portions into the two small glasses.

"Here you go," Ashcroft said handing one glass to Mr. Angleton.

"Thank you…to our mutual understanding," said Mr. Angleton grimacing after raising his glass and swallowing the neat stuff.

"You are most welcome and although I am still waiting to hear from Jose, I think it would be okay if we just went on with our discussions as the matter rests squarely in our hands," explained Mr. Ashcroft in a low tone.

"I think this matter is in *your* hands and not mine Mr. Ashcroft," said Michael Angleton emphasized.

"I know why you are saying that Mr. Angleton but I think it's very wrong to speculate," Ashcroft replied trying to hide his unease at the direction the formerly amicable conversation was going.

"The only thing that I want to know is…why and how did Jose get involved in harming Fletcher in the first place, since that is the information that is clearly coming through to me from my sources…and I never doubt them. And because he is your employee, did you ask him about it?" Mr. Angleton's voice was raspy though he tried to contain his anger.

"I know how you feel and I am in a dilemma myself. I told him to investigate what exactly went on with Fletcher and to bring his findings to me first thing in the morning. I am still waiting for him! Can you imagine the louse hasn't even bothered to call me? And his cell phone has been switched off the whole day! I don't understand," said Mr. Ashcroft his facial expression betraying his mounting anger with Jose. He wasn't sure how to proceed with Angelton without having heard from Jose, and it was immensely frustrating. It made him feel blind sided by Angleton's questions about the Fletcher incident. He had hoped that Jose would have been back with some word by now from his hooligans, and that is why he had set the appointment with Angleton at this time. But, without some confirmation of the details from Jose, he wasn't sure what was safe to say.

"Well, you called me and arranged for this meeting. Look at the time now, is it not six fifteen?" asked Mr. Angleton trying to compose himself.

"I don't think I should rely on Jose and even if he does show up, I will definitely chastise him myself for failing to report back to me in good time. I had given him specific instruction about this meeting and how important it was for him to be here. I don't know what has happened," Ashcroft interjected.

"All said and done, this is not my business. If nothing is forthcoming, I will be left with no choice but to take the matter in my own hands regardless of the consequences. And by the way, do you know Sergeant Morgan Clifton?" Angleton queried suddenly.

"I think I know him," answered Mr. Ashcroft carefully.

"Already, he is in on the case and I am quite sure he will be visiting you soon. You and your family have been our friends for a long while and I don't want this matter to get out of control." Michael Angleton's remarks were couched in underlying sarcasm. It was clear he blamed Ashcroft for this debacle even though he didn't have any evidence to prove what he sensed deep inside. He had however, always trusted his instincts.

"So has the Sergeant asked you anything yet?" asked Mr. Ashcroft gulping down his shot of vodka.

"He came to my office during the day but I was not there. My secretary Janet Cooper told me," answered Mr. Angleton.

"That means you don't know how far he's gone with the case?" countered Mr. Ashcroft.

"I told you I was out of the office, why the concern? It doesn't bother me at all...in fact I am happy because at least somebody from law enforcement is working on the case," retorted Mr. Angleton.

"Just asking," parried Mr. Ashcroft.

"Can I have some more please," said Michael Angleton pushing his empty glass towards his friend.

"I like vodka at times like these you know," Ashcroft said topping both glasses.

"What do we do now?" asked Mr. Angleton.

"I don't know at the moment because, either way, I still have to get Jose," answered Mr. Ashcroft.

The two gentlemen continued downing a few more tots as they discussed Fletcher and how he was doing. Sipping the vodka to calm their nerves helped dissipate the feelings of frustration they both struggled with. Light banter as between old friends was peppered with statements of concern over Fletcher's health, Camila's grief and confusion, the love relationship between the two children of the two most powerful families and the tension that this incident put between the two families. True enough, both Michaels were great friends and their business acumen was above reproach. They had worked together on many projects over the years and each man nursed a keen drive to succeed in whatever project they invested in. If they had a strategy on how to deal with this muck, they were both adept at hiding it from each other; each held his trump card to his chest. Michael Ashcroft was undoubtedly wealthier than Angleton but he had learned to mask this reality under a veneer of modesty. He was not boastful and often times preferred to keep his views on issues a secret until he was completely sure of what was going on.

It was getting late and there was no sign of Jose Cameron anywhere. It was not worth waiting any longer. Michael Angleton stood up, his hand extended to his friend. He was tired and eager to leave.

Mr. Angleton felt that he had spent enough time in Mr. Ashcroft's office and that they were not making any headway on Fletcher's case. He was eager to leave for home. Suddenly, his cell phone rang and he paused. Standing partly turned away from Mr. Ashcroft, he picked his phone, his left palm raised in the air.

"Hallo dear," he said softly on realizing his wife Lesley was calling. He stood in the doorway to Michael Ashcroft's office as he spoke into his cell phone.

Michael Ashcroft tried to glean from watching Mr. Angleton's face what the conversation was about; he could tell the caller was Lesley Angleton and he worked hard to feign disinterest but he hoped desperately this was not a call to herald even more disastrous news on Fletcher from the hospital. He already had enough muck to deal with in his hands regarding Fletcher.

He followed every inflection in Mr. Angleton's voice and was relieved to note an exultant twist to it.

"What?" said Mr. Angleton with a delighted look on his face, "Great!" he continued as Mr. Ashcroft wondered what was going on. He breathed deeply as he waited for Mr. Angleton to finish his conversation with his wife. He had not noticed that tension had made him hold his breath for some time.

"When did this happen?" asked Mr. Angleton who had now turned and walked back to Mr. Ashcroft's desk with the phone to his ear.

"Okay, great I will see you shortly," he said before putting the phone in his pocket and recounting to Mr. Ashcroft that he had just heard from his wife Lesley that Fletcher had finally been released from hospital. He was obviously thrilled that his son was finally coming home and for a moment it seemed he had put aside his suspicions on Mr. Ashcroft's involvement in the whole macabre incident and excitedly shook hands with him over the large mahogany desk.

"That's great!" said Mr. Ashcroft standing to shake Mr. Angleton's outstretched hand.

"Yes, I am rushing home now to see him, so let's catch up on these issues later then when you hear from Jose, shall we?" said Mr. Angleton as he headed back out the door. "We need to have some clarity on this whole issue quickly."

"Yes, let's do that," said Mr. Ashcroft to Mr. Angelton's retreating figure.

He then walked slowly to close his office door and stood for a moment pondering what had just happened. It was clear that Mr. Angleton suspected some underhandedness in this whole Fletcher thing, and the news he had just received on his son's release from hospital, was but a small breather. Until he was able to hear from Jose he could not be clear on what strategy to use on the Angleton family regarding the Fletcher case.

'Argh! What exactly had happened to Jose? Why had he not turned up for this meeting?' Mr. Ashcroft thought angrily to himself.

He knew that in due course, the two families would need to openly discuss what had taken place no matter how uncomfortable it was, and hopefully in the presence of Fletcher. He wasn't looking forward to such a meeting at all. However, he was glad Fletcher was out of danger. This had been a harrowing experience and he knew that though Fletcher had made it alive, the matter would not end that simply.

―――――――――

Fletcher's mood was mixed; he struggled with immense loathe and relief at the same time. The former feelings stemmed from the harrowing pain his body and mind had been subjected to and the resultant hospitalization he had gone through, and the latter from the fact that he was out of danger and able to see and touch Camila again. He paced up and down swearing under his breath as his father watched quietly from his favourite armchair. They needed to talk about all of that as a family first though, so Fletcher had to take his focus off Camila even though her presence a few paces away overshadowed all else in the room.

"Do you mind making a cup of coffee for us?" Michael Angleton asked facing his wife.

"Oh why not," answered Lesley waking up and taking short quick steps towards the beautifully arranged kitchen. It had fitted cabinets with most of everything in a calming spectrum of pastel colours.

"Count me out mum, I am okay at the moment," said Fletcher gently scratching a scar on his face. His scars had started to heal and this came with an infuriating itch that only led to more pain when he scratched.

"Why? I thought you need it more than everyone else," his father said knowing that a cup of tea would calm him down.

"Coffee doesn't go well with the concoction of medication that I am taking," Fletcher said lamely.

Camila who had been quiet most of the time stood up and walked to the kitchen where Lesley was busy preparing coffee for the family.

"Need a hand? I just don't want to be glued to the sofa doing nothing," said Camila.

"That's very kind of you my dear, on the left drawer there, you'll find some snacks and biscuits that I think we can all do with," answered Lesley.

Meanwhile, the discussions between father and son were still going on in the sitting room away from the hearing of the two women. Michael Angleton calmly interrogated his son trying to gather as much informa-tion as possible about the ambush. He wanted to be careful not to omit any important details. He knew the way forward was to know everything before blaming anyone for what had happened to his son. All needed to be graphically explained because not even Camila had an idea what had actu-ally happened to Fletcher. She only knew that Jose Cameron was involved.

"Coffee is ready everyone," said Lesley placing a tray with steaming cups of coffee onto the side table in the living room while Camila followed behind her.

"Can I have some orange juice?" requested Fletcher not referring to anybody in particular.

"Oh sure, I will get you some," Lesley answered happy that her son was at least taking something.

The family sat quietly for a while enjoying their coffee and biscuits as Fletcher sipped on some cool cocktail of fruit juices. He also thoughtfully nibbled on some biscuits. Cool music was playing in the background and competed with the TV programmes one could also hear and see from the wide-screen hanging on the wall. The family seemed at peace, each member in his own thoughts; an occasional cough from Fletcher who was still healing from his chest injuries punctuated the air. It was good to be home together.

Michael Angleton finally stood up and tapped his son lightly on the back.

"Can we go for a little walk? I feel like I need to stretch my legs. You know how sitting down the whole day in the office can be quite agonizing for my joints," Michael said giving his son a knowing look.

"Come on dad, I am not in the mood and again I think it's a bit cold outside," grunted Fletcher.

"I know, I know," said Michael leaning towards his son.

Neither Lesley nor Camila understood the whispering that went on between father and son but Fletcher Angleton finally stood up and donned his leather jacket as he followed his father to the door.

"We won't be long," Michael Angleton said as they walked past the sliding doors that led to the back yard.

"Okay but don't keep us waiting too long," said Lesley as she stood up to clear the small coffee table.

The walk presented an opportunity for the two gentlemen to talk in detail about what had taken place that fateful night at the Ogaden Night Club. Without omitting any detail, Fletcher Angleton narrated his ordeal, sometimes pausing and wondering aloud why it had happened. His father listened keenly without interrupting his son who sometimes seemed overwhelmed by emotion. Fletcher knew what his father was capable of doing to whoever was behind all this, and the notion that Camila's father knew about it or was indirectly involved made the situation even more delicate and frustrating to both of them. His mind was tired and fragmented thoughts whirled around inside his tired head. He desperately needed an answer to this sudden and frightening turn of events. He struggled with anger as he continued recounting his suffering to his father, concerning what had happened after he left the club that night. "Dad, do you think this happened because I am having a relationship with Camila, because that's what's coming from the rumour mill, you know?"

"I won't say yes or no because it would be very wrong for us to jump to any conclusions before Mr. Ashcroft has sat down with his guys to find out the truth," Michael replied as he was still at sea about what had really happened to his son that night. He also didn't want to tell his son that he suspected that Michael Ashcroft had anything to do with the incident.

"And have you spoken to him?" Fletcher asked in reference to Jose Cameron.

"Of course not, if I hear anything from their quarters you will definitely be the first to know. I don't know how this mess is going to end, and I sense it won't go down very well," Michael said signalling with his finger that they should go back into the house.

Their talk had been intense but not conclusive. They both secretly feared the worst - an all-out war between the two families–but none was verbalizing this fear. They knew without a doubt that this calamity would inevitably tear the two families apart. Fletcher wished ardently that he could protect Camila from being affected by it all. This was what was weighing most heavily on his shoulders. He felt that it was his duty to prevent the impending fiasco, and especially the ramifications that could result and affect his relationship with Camila.

"Camila," Fletcher called his girlfriend gesticulating with his hand as soon as they got back into the house.

"What is it sweetheart?" Camila asked walking towards him from the kitchen.

"I don't want you to go home tonight, the thought of being alone is already giving me a nightmare," said Fletcher in beseeching tone.

"No my love; I've got to go because I have a lot of work pending that must be done early in the morning. I will try my best to see you tomorrow afternoon," said Camila.

"I really hoped that you would stay," Fletcher said lovingly.

"Not today my love," Camila said walking towards the door.

She brushed past Lesley after giving her a quick hug, turned her head back and waved goodbye to Fletcher's father before blowing a kiss to her lover. She strode outside towards the car park before driving off into the twilight. It had been a tiring day and it was true that she needed to get to the office early the next day. But, she knew deep inside that she was avoiding spending time with Fletcher because she wondered to herself repeatedly who he had been with at the Ogaden Night Club that night. It bothered her too much and made it impossible for her to imagine being close to him tonight. She drove to her apartment with her car radio on; her favourite jazz tunes nudging the disturbing thoughts out of her weary mind. The soft music helped her relax and feel more positive. It was good to have Fletcher out of the hospital all the same. She smiled to herself as she thought of him away from the cheerless hospital ambiance. It was nine at night and only the distant sound of vehicles driving on the highway not too far ahead could be heard. She was going to call it an early night.

Chapter Six

James Wilcox was walking alone through the streets of Brighton in the early hours of the morning. He normally used this route after his night-shift as a security guard in one of the large and prestigious malls in town. He wore a black tweed jacket and black trouser; his white shirt couldn't be seen in the dim light of the early hours. As usual, he had removed his guard's uniform and donned his every day clothes when he was leaving work.

James was a towering figure of six feet and well-built with muscles rippling under his shirt when he walked. He cut an image of a confident man who could hold his own against anyone. Women easily took a liking to him, though he was married.

The street was lined with trees on each side. There seemed to be no one else in sight, although as James kept walking, he caught a glimpse of a person walking unsteadily on the road ahead of him. He increased his pace so as to overtake him and create some distance between them. He was eager to get home and it was getting rather nippy.

A few more steps and he came alongside the wobbly stranger who at this juncture was leaning against a post by the curb. He seemed to be wondering which direction to take. In fact, he seemed totally confused and lost. Knowing his whereabouts well, James decided to help the poor bloke and at the same time was curious to know where the miserable looking man was headed. He was in for a big surprise.

"Henry, is this really you? What the hell are you doing at this time alone on the streets?" James asked bewildered when he recognized his friend.

Henry Forbes was just as shocked to see James and completely lost for words. He stammered in a disorientated fashion and gazed absentmindedly in all directions as if haunted by an evil spirit. He turned and looked at James.

James Wilcox, a punter of illicit deals knew Henry Forbes very well through their regular meetings in hidden corners in the suburbs, to seal one deal or another. Their activities in the black market were hidden from authorities, and the dangers and challenges they had overcome together over the years had created a strong bond of friendship between them. They had become street-wise together, in order to survive.

"You mean it's you?" Henry looked just as shocked to see James, but he also looked relieved. He was obviously inebriated and seemed frustrated about something. He was thankful he had someone he trusted to walk down the road with him, especially after his encounter with Jose earlier in the day.

The two brigands walked side-by-side as Henry narrated the details of Fletcher's ambush near the Ogaden Night Club and how this had caused a rift between him and Jose. They both had habits and associations that were questionable but despite their shady addictions, neither of them had a history of being violent. The Fletcher situation was therefore unfolding in a fearful and unbelievable way. They feared the two powerful families and knowing what each could unleash sent shivers down the spines of the two friends. James listened keenly as Henry talked and they hurried their steps to James' house as they realized this was something they needed to discuss behind closed doors. Henry began the tale with a slight slur for he had been drinking, but the cool air and walk made him increasingly sober so that he was able to graphically capture the Fletcher calamity that he and his hooligan buddies had agreed to unleash that night. It took them around forty minutes to get to the house where James lived with his expectant wife. It was a two-bed roomed semi-detached house that was tastefully furnished and neat. They were glad to finally get into its welcoming warmth.

James did not really understand what had transpired between his friend Henry and Jose that day but the fact that the two most powerful families in Brighton were in the mix made him shiver slightly. He was glad when they finally got to his house. Jose Cameron was not new to him and Fletcher

Angleton still considered him a friend so James felt rather confused about how he was going to deal with all that was tumbling out of Henry's mouth that evening.

Their whispered conversation filtered through the open door leading to the kitchen where Pamela Wilcox was busy preparing breakfast; she knew what James liked after his night shift. She couldn't help eavesdropping and the little she heard scared her stiff. Everyone knew who the top families in Brighton were and how much power they wielded over the goings-on in the life of the common man. They were elite, therefore they were feared. She edged closer to the door and leaned against the wall listening keenly to what Henry was whispering urgently to her husband about the Ogaden affair.

"Tell me and be very honest, were you personally involved in this fight?" Mr. Wilcox asked holding his chin in disbelief.

"I was drunk," answered Henry looking down sheepishly.

"No, I am asking of your involvement in the whole arrangement, right from planning it," retorted James thumping his chest as he often did when he was feeling vexed. He wanted Henry to be honest and to the point; he did not like ambiguity.

Realizing his avoiding tactics were not going well with his friend, Henry Forbes finally opened up and told James what had transpired and how Fletcher had ended up in hospital in a coma. He also recounted how, because everything had gone worse than had been planned, the two families, the Ashcrofts and the Angletons, were grappling with possible major fallout with each other. He also told James how Jose Cameron had met with him earlier and threatened him with dire consequences if he did not sort everything out without Jose losing his rapport with his boss. James kept shaking his head in disbelief as he listened. It seemed like a major nightmare was unfolding before his very eyes. He interjected several times in an effort to clarify issues.

"I had to leave early because I knew the police would be coming for me at my house and with no ready answers I was not prepared to gamble with my future," Henry said in a sulky voice.

"I know how you feel but still I can't understand why commonsense did not prevail. Surely even Jose should have sensed how terribly this might turn out," commented James squinting in frustration.

"I also regret it myself, but nobody seemed to have sanity at that time, we had all taken a few drinks so…you know how it is," Henry mumbled shamefacedly.

"Where was Cameron at that time anyway?" Wilcox asked curiously.

"He had stayed behind after Fletcher came out of the club to watch in case someone who knew any of us, or even knew Fletcher, would come by the place. We are the ones who followed Fletcher and…" Henry voice faded off since he had already told James the details. He continued when James didn't say anything "we finally fled leaving the poor mite in a dirty trench." Henry looked up at James, and without realizing it, he started to bite his finger nails nervously.

"Okay you see now, Jose planned it and left you to do the dirty work! That's crazy man! Don't you guys see how you were set up? Jose and his boss will get away with it and you'll take the fall man! You guys are in real trouble unless you think of something fast…like getting out of the country. Man! They'll definitely get you. Think!" James insisted feeling sorry for his friend. He could see that Henry felt like a trapped hare.

"I know man and that's why I am glad I have come to you for help, it's not easy to deal with this alone," Henry said with shaky voice.

"Exactly what do you want me to do?" James asked.

Without a word Henry looked beseechingly at his friend.

At that moment, Pamela opened the kitchen door pretending that she had heard nothing. She placed three cups of steaming coffee and some snacks on the dining table. The atmosphere was tense but she didn't say a word. Pamela was normally quiet but James could tell she was somewhat edgy but she didn't have the courage to ask about the goings-on. The quiet was unnerving as they munched on the snacks and sipped the hot coffee. It was obvious that the two boys did not want to let her in on what had gone on and this irritated Pamela. She finally got up after a few minutes and reluctantly cleared the table and walked to the kitchen with the empty cups on a tray. She gently closed the kitchen door behind her sensing that they wanted to keep this to themselves, and left the two friends to continue with their secret conversation.

The glare of the morning sunlight was filtering through the drawn curtains sending in warmth and a semblance of sanity. The sky was clear and the sounds of chirping birds flying above were a sight to behold. All this serenity was shattered however when they all suddenly heard the loud siren of a police car as it cruised around the corner close to their apartment. The car careened to the curb opposite their main door and Henry Forbes rushed to the window to see what was going on, a petrified look on his face. He peeped through the window cautiously, settling down only when the sound of the siren faded away as the car raced on to corner ahead and disappeared in the direction of the main highway a few miles ahead. They must have used the road next to James' house as a short-cut to some other place. Henry could literally hear his heart beat against his chest from the fear that had gripped him. He already had sweat on his large forehead. He looked pleadingly at James who had stood up from his seat in the living room. James wondered how to help his friend as he could tell that he was in a tight corner and had run out of ideas. The police car had scared the hell out of all of them. He needed to protect Pamela from any negative consequences from all that Henry had shared with him, and the only way to do this was to tell her the truth and see if they could help his friend together. He got up and called out to her in the kitchen. He wanted to help Henry, but she needed to be in on the plan.

"Pamela!" He called out to her.

"Yes…coming," answered Pamela from the kitchen.

"Can I see you for a minute," James said as he gently led her towards their back garden.

Pamela followed her husband looking up inquiringly into his face.

"You may have heard a little bit of what I was talking about with Henry," James started "you remember Henry, he's been here before…?" Pamela nodded quietly wiping her wet hands on the back of her black trousers. She had been washing the coffee cups when he called her out. James continued, "Well, it's about an assault that happened on Sunday night and unfortunately my friend Henry was involved and someone got badly hurt. In fact, they had to rush the person to hospital and he was in a coma for a few days. Now, I don't know what to do because he needs my assistance and before I make any move I thought it would be better to let you know," said James almost in a whisper so that Henry, who was still in their sitting room, wouldn't hear what he was telling his wife.

"Don't tell me that you want to involve yourself with this mess! Look at me, I am very pregnant with your baby and I am not ready to lose you through some mix-up with people I know are hooligans. You are better than that James!" Pamela sounded desperate and frustrated at the same time. She feared for her husband and her words were forceful as she sensed there would be a bad ending to all of this.

"I know how you feel but I am not trying to put us into any trouble and you know that...you know I love you and I would not do anything to hurt you. This fellow needs my help and that's why I called you aside because I don't want to do anything stupid behind your back! Please don't feel offended. Remember last time when your brother was in trouble, didn't he come to me for help and didn't I help him? So why are you against me helping my friend this time around?" James could tell that she was struggling especially because he was playing the guilty card on her at this point since he had helped her brother when he was in a tough situation.

"Don't use my brother as an excuse, that was that time and this is now," said Pamela belligerently. "I can't believe you are using that with me!"

"Okay, I am not going to do anything stupid alright, but remember when we moved into this house, Henry was the only person who agreed to loan me some money when I was in need, he wants me to help him now and maybe it's payback time, remember every dog has its day," James was more authoritative now so as to pressure her to agree with helping Henry. Pamela sighed dejectedly and James could sense that she was thawing somewhat.

"Ok, ok. But please, don't get yourself tangled up with friends and their feuds whose beginnings you cannot really know. These families they are dealing with are not your regular small boys. Your friends should have known better than that!" Pamela retorted feeling she had been cornered into something she didn't want.

After a few more minutes of trying to console her, James walked back slowly to the sitting room where his friend was seated absentmindedly toying with a picture frame. Henry's face still looked distraught despite his gallant effort to overcome the palpable fear he felt. He only had James to turn to now and he needed their support if he was going to find a solution to this problem he was in. James was his only trusted companion. James nodded knowingly towards Henry, an indication that they had come to some kind of agreement with Pamela. Henry breathed a sigh of relief. Shortly thereafter, the two men walked out of the house towards the main street talking in low tones. James continued asking Henry questions as they walked along the road just so he could be sure he had fully understood all that Henry had shared earlier. He knew very well what the consequences of hosting Henry in his house might be, especially if the police came knocking. Pamela was also getting crankier the bigger her belly became so it was not going to be an easy ride.

"Do you want a cigarette," asked Henry as he jiggled his pockets around looking for a lighter.

"I quit," answered James.

"Oooooh, good for you! But I thought I saw you smoking not too long ago," retorted Henry.

"Once in a while when I am having a drink…by the way did you know that smoking is the worst habit one can have?"

"Yea, I know but sometimes the stresses of life and loneliness drive us to do things we don't' really want to do," said Henry Forbes sadly.

"Well, let's try and learn from the mistakes of the past shall we!" said James slightly irritated by Henry's defeatist attitude.

"I suppose," answered Henry with his head still bent.

"By the way, as Jose left your house yesterday did he tell you where he was going?" James asked suddenly turning to face Henry.

"He never told me and even if I had asked him he wouldn't have," Henry answered puffing out a long trail of thick cigarette smoke.

"I am asking because I think I need to have a word with him as well," continued James.

"You know that guy, he is a crazy man who only pretends to care for someone when his boss is around coz that's when he's sure to gain something," retorted James with obvious hatred.

Their conversation continued for a while as they walked through the streets leading to a public park. They sat down on a lone bench overlooking a large pond teaming with fish of different colours and species. Located in the middle of the pond was a beautiful fountain with a statue of a naked woman whose bosom was covered with a big fig leaf. Other than a couple of pigeons cooing unhindered on top of the statue, the place was ideal for a private discussion. They needed to decide how to overcome the impasse before them that hung like a menacing dark cloud of rain.

It was getting brighter as the day progressed and though James had not slept the whole night because of his night shift, he decided to stay by his friend. Strong sun rays warmed the air and absorbed the early morning dew that had settled overnight on the well trimmed lawn in the park. Tall eucalyptus trees lined the perimeter and their refreshing scent wafted over them carried by a soft breeze. Despite everything, it was promising to be a cheerfully sunny day.

James tried to be empathetic as he listened to Henry's long and mournful recap of their scandalous attack on Fletcher. It was clear that Henry only had James as a confidant in this matter. Henry was shaking his head with shame and embarrassment as he graphically dwelt on the events again and again, including his encounter with Jose Cameron the previous night. James finally stood up to stretch his legs; He patted his colleague on the back. It was clear he had heard enough for one day. He needed to get his head around all the details.

"Let's meet here again at two o'clock this afternoon because I also need to have my moment to think on the best way I can help. Remember my wife is repulsed by what you guys did and I can't blame her for that. I need to convince her that you were not directly involved and that there was a slight misunderstanding, okay?" James spoke in a calm tone but with a touch of finality to it. Without looking back, he told Henry that after talking some more with Pamela, he was sure they would come up with a suitable way of helping him, and then he said goodbye and left. There was nothing Henry could do except sit quietly in the sun and watch his friend James walk away. He however felt better now that he wasn't alone thinking of a way out.

Chapter Seven

Traffic on the main highway was congested and a slight drizzle trickled from the grey skies as heavy-goods vehicles competed with smaller cars on the slippery tarmac. Some miles ahead, road engineers and maintenance workers were busy building a bridge connecting the east side of the city to a new housing estate. It was getting late and motorists were grouchy as they snaked their way home on the crammed highway. The time was six thirty and it was starting to get dark.

Fletcher Angleton had taken this route hoping it would be the quickest and shortest way to Camila's home. His cruising dissolved into a slow crawl behind the other disgruntled drivers when he got to this highway. He cursed under his breath and looked at his watch in frustration. Since the attack Fletcher found that his fuse was shorter and shorter, and he didn't want to get to Camila's feeling all grumpy. Next to him on the passenger seat was a bouquet of flowers; a tag hang loosely from its shiny wrapper. Driving slowly through the traffic, Fletcher manoeuvred his car up the hill leading to a diversion. He was sweating as he drove through the narrow, one-way-traffic side roads. It took him more than one and a half hours to reach his destination, a journey that normally took him only fifty minutes.

Pensively listening to her favourite music and sitting on a sofa in her living room, Camila Ashcroft swayed her head to the musical beats filtering through the speakers in the corner of the room. It was eight o'clock when the buzz of the door bell startled her. She smoothed down her hair in front of the big mirror on the corridor wall as she walked to the main door. It buzzed again. She didn't know who was at the door but was pleasantly surprised when she pushed it open to find Fletcher standing there with a sheepish grin, holding a bouquet of flowers and whistling his favourite tune.

"Oh my...you'll never cease to amaze me. Come in, come in," Camila gushed smiling excitedly as she reached for the flowers. "How are you darling?"

"I am okay, how about you my love?" Fletcher answered offering his fiancée the beautiful bouquet and giving her a peck on her soft cheek.

"Why at this time of the night? We agreed that you'll be calling before you come over," Camila was all smiles as she talked.

"I know, but don't forget that I don't need customs clearance to see my fiancée any time of the day or night," said Fletcher "I drove for almost two hours owing to a freaking jam on the main highway just to see you. In fact, that's why I am late. You know I also don't like knocking on your door too late at night."

"Oh come on, no problem at all. This is great!" Camila said embracing her lover with both arms tightly around his chest, "come on in," she continued holding his left hand and leading him into the house. She held the beautiful orchids to her nose and breathed deeply with a wide smile on her face. It was obvious she was delighted to see him.

"Thanks for the flowers darling, they are so lovely and they have a gorgeous scent."

"You are most welcome," said Fletcher as he walked through the sitting room to the kitchen. It was obvious he was familiar with his surroundings, "any soft drink in the fridge?" he asked.

"I think there are some cans of coke in there, just have a look," said Camila placing the orchids into a silver vase that her mother had given her. She then went to the kitchen and got a small pitcher with water to pour into the vase so that the flowers remained fresh for a few days.

"Got it," he said closing the fridge and carrying the chilled can in his left hand. He flipped the small silver ring at the top open and tilted his head to enjoy the cool drink for a minute. He breathed deeply and wiped his lips with the back of his left hand before he looked at her again.

"I thought you would ask for a Lager instead," said Camila cheekily.

"Doctor's instructions, no messing around this time, you know I am still on antibiotics," he explained.

"Well, let's follow the doctor's orders then shall we?" Camila said giggling,

"Even after the medication, I will still give myself a couple more weeks before touching any alcohol," continued Fletcher as he tilted his square jaw and drained the can of coke. The drive here had left him parched.

"Shall we bet?" Camila parried. "I know by next week you'll be back to your guzzling habits. Don't you know that saying 'old habits die hard'? I dare you." Camila was all smiles as she teased her fiancé, and her face radiated with joy.

Standing side-by-side in the kitchen, the two lovers swapped stories and punctuated them with kisses as lovers do, each completely comfortable in the other's company. Minutes turned to hours. The window in the kitchen was open and the fresh cool air wafted into the room. A glimpse of the crescent moon was visible from the open window, and the stars above twinkled in the night sky as they embraced more passionately as time went on.

Camila held her lover's hand and pulled him slowly down onto the sofa where they sat down listening quietly to the news on the television before them. Fletcher stroked her hair tenderly. They were both lost in dreamy thought as he wondered to himself whether to talk about the unpleasant incident of the Ogaden Night Club again. He knew it was an unpleasant topic for her but she was the only person he could confide in regarding the details. He looked at her from time to time hoping to gather enough courage to venture on the issue. Not being a nocturnal person Camila was already dozing off, her head leaning on his left shoulder. It was getting late.

It was past ten o'clock when Fletcher Angleton stood up from the sofa set and walked towards the kitchen. He opened the tap of the cold water allowing the water to flow freely for a while before putting some into a glass. He was still feeling thirsty. He tipped the glass and drank thirstily. He put it gently on the work top in the kitchen and stretched his hand out to close the window as it was now getting a bit nifty. Drawing his hand back he accidentally tipped over a container of cutlery. Everything fell out and crashed onto the floor with a loud rattle. He whirled around concerned for his sleepy lover and found her startled and staring at him in wide-eyed confusion.

"What's going on?" she mumbled sleepily.

"Nothing much sweetheart everything is okay, my butterfingered mistake," he answered smiling.

"Come over here," Camila said looking at the clock hanging on the wall. Fletcher gulped down what remained of the glass of water.

He sat quickly by Camila's side and intently looked into her face. She immediately realized that something serious was up and knew instinctively that it was about that night at the club with Jose. All sleep left behind her eyelids went out the window.

"Tell me what you know and please do not lie?" Camila urged him.

"I wanted to discuss things with you and in fact that's why I had to see you today, but you looked so tired, I thought you preferred to sleep early tonight," Fletcher said gently as he wondered where to start.

"I want to know everything. Please tell me," Camila probed.

"I don't know whether your dad knows about it or not but I have come to understand that, Jose Cameron has been arrested and is already being held by the police for questioning at the police station," said Fletcher trying to maintain his cool.

"What! I haven't heard anything about that and I think my dad is not aware as well because we talked during the day over the phone and he didn't tell me that bit of information," she said innocently.

"Sometimes things happen faster than we get to hear," Fletcher answered scratching his chin.

"All I know is that Jose has not reported to work since that day, and my dad is considering giving him the sack," Camila said stroking her long hair, a look of confusion on her face.

Fletcher narrated the story scene-by-scene without leaving anything out. He explained to Camila how Sergeant Morgan Clifton visited his father in the office during the day to break the news and that Jose had been cooperating with the interrogators. Although his father didn't talk in depth about how far they've gone with the investigations, one thing he told Fletcher was that no one had been charged so far as they were still looking for concrete evidence and for the other collaborators in the ambush.

After a lengthy explanation, Fletcher confessed to Camila that whatever happened, he would not let the culprits go free and was determined to get his revenge. "There is no way I am going to let those hooligans continue to roam the streets freely after what they did to me," Fletcher hissed clenching his fists against his now moist forehead. "I would always live in fear of them attacking me again," he continued. "I will kill them if I have to," he swore. "I was bullied at school when I was a small boy and those times are over now. There is no way I can stand back like a coward and live with it, no way!" said Fletcher "If they don't get put in jail, I will do them in myself!".

"So what do you plan to do babe, because I don't want you to get into trouble," Camila said touching Fletcher gently on the cheek.

They discussed the issue at length, going back and forth on the details, from the Ogaden Night Club to this issue with Jose and what this horrible incident could unleash on their lives and on the relationships between the two prominent families. It was clear that the police were trying to cover all bases through the interrogations, but Fletcher still felt he needed to do something.

"I will go to the police station personally tomorrow and seek an audience with Jose if they agree…I hope they will," said Fletcher shaking his head.

"You said that you'll take action personally if these guys are let free by the police. What exactly do you intend to do…I don't understand?" Camila asked again in worried tone.

"There are many things I could resort to in order to sort this mess out once and for all, you know," said Fletcher avoiding Camila's eyes. With some extra cash anything is possible and those blokes could be done in, then nobody else ever needs to go through the harrowing experience I went through," said Fletcher heatedly. "I promise you that somebody will definitely get hurt; I am not going to let them get away with it. You know that."

"I am scared," Camila said desperation tinged her voice. "I don't want you to do something stupid. Something could go horribly wrong. You need to be careful. I don't want to lose you," Camila insisted clutching his shirt sleeve. "I came close enough to losing you when you were in a coma in hospital after the attack. If anything additional happened to you Fletcher, you know that it would kill me," she said cupping his angular and handsome face with her long, manicured fingers, so that she could look him in the eyes. She felt that this way she would be able to read his every thought and somehow keep in touch with his true feelings. Every time he started to talk about Jose and what he had gone through, Fletcher seemed to grow distant from her, as if he was fading into a world of his own; a place where she couldn't reach him or truly understand the hurt he was going through.

"I know that, and I am not stupid, Don't you think I care how you feel babe?" Fletcher asked. "I know what it must have been like for you too, not knowing whether I would come through the coma, or whether I would die," he said as he moved a long, blond strand of hair off her beautiful face. "It kills me though as a man when I think that there are some blokes out there somewhere who actually think they got away with their heinous plot to harm me in that way…and that nothing's been done about it so far."

"That's the problem with you men…you can only think about your own egos! What about me, doesn't what I fear or think matter?" Camila said frustrated that he could even imagine putting himself in harm's way to pay his detractors back, even if it meant both of them could be irreparably damaged from his choices. She turned away from him broodingly and took the remote from the chair next to her. She turned the TV on and stared at the flat screen on the wall ahead, without really focusing on what was showing on it; she was simply looking for a distraction to the pain she felt inside. She felt at a loss of what more to say to him.

None of them could eat that night. Camila kept throwing hurt-filled glances at Fletcher. She was afraid and angry at the same time at what this could lead to. He couldn't bear to make eye contact with her either as he struggled with his own thoughts as a man. He understood her fear but nothing could dampen his consuming need for revenge for what he had gone through. They struggled to hide their emotional pain and haltingly kept up some civility and chit-chat. The sound of cars passing by the apartment could be heard from time to time coming through an open window in the kitchen. Despite their efforts to dwell on simpler, less painful things: their childhood memories and experiences, the weather, and their love relationship, the prior discussion on Jose and his band of rebels had soured the atmosphere. It was clear this was going to be a problem that would take some time and even more heartache to solve.

The week flew by and though much had taken place, the lingering suspicion Michael Angleton had that his friend Michael Ashcroft had something to do with Fletcher's attack nagged at him and this made him even more agitated and difficult to work with at home and at the office. He was now keeping close tabs with Sergeant Morgan Clifton on how the investigations were progressing and was determined that he would keenly follow the case to make sure that no stone was left unturned, and that he would pinpoint the culprits and bring them to book. The sergeant seemed well-informed and skilled at his work. In fact, Michael had carried out his own investigations on the sergeant and found that he had many years experience dealing with such cases. He therefore felt confident that, in no time, what had taken place at the Ogaden Night Club would become very clear, and payback time was not far away. Whatever the case, he was determined not to let the guilty go unpunished.

Lesley Angleton felt the same and just as poignantly. Though on the face of it, she looked quiet and humble, she was over the moon with bitterness over what had happened to her son, and she held a strong desire in her heart for justice to prevail in the end. How to pay the culprits back for what happened to Fletcher was constantly on her mind. She would wake and it would be the first thing she thought of. It was one thing to deal Jose Cameron and his cahoots, but they feared that if it came out clearly that their family was involved in the attack, especially because Jose was Michael's employee, and it was common knowledge that Jose had worked for him for many years and was very devoted to him to the extent of carrying out his bidding without question, then this would be a big mess indeed. The tabloids would be full of speculative sleaze; it would bring unbridled shame, vengeful anger and misery on all involved, and definitely trigger an all-out war between the two prominent and powerful families, as her husband was not one to take it all lying down.

The arrest of Jose Cameron was just a beginning of this misfortune. If the sergeant were to confirm from him that Mr. Ashcroft was involved with the foul play in any way, only God knew what avalanche would ensue. Alarm bells were gonging in everyone's mind and pressure was building as both families awaited the outcome of the investigations. This could be the beginning of the end.

———————

It was shortly before midnight. Camila, who had finally dozed off next to Fletcher, roused slowly and stretched her arms up in the air above her, before standing up. She headed straight to the bathroom. The past few hours had been draining emotionally and physically; she needed a quick shower to freshen up. After ten minutes she came back wearing a pink nightdress; her pretty toe-nails were coloured shell-pink as well. She was barefooted and in a better mood after the shower. All the anger brought on by Fletcher's venting about Jose and what he intended to do about the case dissipated when she had dozed off earlier. She stood by him and looked down at him with fresh feelings of affection. He had watched her sleeping there beside him the whole time but sleep seemed to have eluded him. He was silently trawling the television channels, remote control in hand. With a dreamy smile Camila walked slowly to where Fletcher was seated and ran her palm seductively down his spine. He turned slowly and looked up at her radiant face, dropping the remote on the seat immediately. Fletcher was streetwise enough to know desire when he saw it, and he wasn't one to pass up such an invitation. He stood up slowly, looking straight into her alluring eyes and followed her leading hand to the bedroom. He flicked off the lights to the sitting room with a backward swipe before he entered the bedroom.

The fragrance emitted by the scented candle placed on the side table next to the bed was warm and inviting. It filled the room with a heady amorous ambiance. The long window drapes allowed a slight breeze to filter into the room. Their shadows played on the four walls, taking on the soft hues of the different coloured bulbs hidden in the large lampshades above them. The bed was not strange to Fletcher Angleton but he took his time, playing gently with the folds of the silk bedcover, taking in the scent of her lovely hair as he touched her hair and face gently. They continued to sit for a while on top of the bedcover fondling each other lovingly.

"It had been a mind-numbing day and thank God it's all over now," said Camila softly.

"Yeah, I feel good it's all over," Fletcher said sighing.

Camila turned to the small stool next to the ornate, four-poster bed and turned off the lights before turning back to her lover.

"You know my dear, I don't know what I would do without you," said Fletcher smiling tenderly at her.

"Things will work out in the end," Camila said pulling back the bedcover to reveal an immaculately clean, white bed sheet.

With the candle light still glowing, their conversation waned slowly and they allowed the stress of the day drift out the open window, passed the silky white curtain sheers, as the night sky folded over the neighbourhood.

In the early hours of the morning, Fletcher awoke still holding her tight against him. He lay there mulling over recent events.

In the quiet bedroom, Fletcher started reconstructing the events of the past few days from the time he was ambushed to the moment of his hospitalization. An underlying anger would always flare up inside him when he went over the events. He swore to himself that he would not let the culprits get away with it. He felt a slight movement from Camila and turned to face her. She was still in deep sleep and he just lay there watching her beautiful oval-shaped face. It was five in the morning when he finally drifted into a world of unsettling dreams.

Chapter Eight

Janet cooper was sitting quietly on her desk when the telephone rang. It was a Friday morning. The open-plan office was busy with people moving about tending to different clients as the month of April was quickly coming to an end. Businesses dashed to balance their audited accounts for submission to the Tax Office before the end of the year – every businessman's annual nightmare. Maria Kosgei, young lass of African origin, was walking self-importantly between the lined office desks dropping letters into each in-tray. A few metres ahead from where Janet was sitting was Michael Angleton's empty seat. He was conspicuously absent. It was nine fifteen in the morning when Janet picked up the phone.

"Michael Angleton's office, Janet speaking, how can I help?" Janet picked the phone and listened keenly to the speaker on the other end.

"This is Sergeant Morgan Clifton; may I please speak to Mr. Angleton?"

"I am sorry Mr. Angleton is not in the office at the moment. Can I take a message?" Janet asked picking up a pen. She quickly snatched a writing pad from a desk close to her and took some notes.

"Yeah…tell him to get in touch with me as soon as possible," said the Sergeant from the other end.

"Is it anything serious?" Janet asked, curious and concerned at the same time.

"It's something he knows about, but just make sure he gets the message," replied the Sergeant hanging up the phone.

As a senior partner in the company, Michael Angleton's absence was easily noticeable as junior staff relied on him on a daily basis for direction on the running of the company. Although he hardly dealt with clients directly, his fatherly figure commanded respect and discipline within the organization and also made staff feel that everything was in control. Janet Cooper was his personal secretary. She stood up from her desk and walked across to Mr. Angleton's table where she placed the hand-written note where it would be clearly visible in front of his big swivel, leather chair.

"Good morning Mrs. Cooper," a young man passing by greeted.

"Good morning," she answered looking up for only one second.

Walking briskly along the long office corridor with photos of business tycoons in ornate frames hanged up along the side walls, Janet Cooper took the left turning leading to the small staff canteen where she made herself a strong cup of black coffee before returning to her desk. A lot was going through her mind. She knew what had befallen her boss's son. She also knew he was now out of mortal danger after struggling through a coma. What she didn't know was that Michael Angleton had vowed to do whatever it took to pay back the culprits. She also had no idea before the Sergeant called that the case was now under intensive investigation by the local metropolitan police department. She sensed that this was the reason why Angelton had not come to the office. She mulled over the issue a little longer and wondered what was really going on, but she came up with no ready answers to the questions whirling through her mind. She went back to her office and sat down with the hot drink in her hands. Then she leaned back on her chair pensively stroking her hair with the tip of her pen, while slowly sipping her coffee. She needed the warmth that seeped through her tense body. Closing her tired eyes, she breathed deeply of the coffee's sweet aroma. She sensed that things could only become clear when her boss came back to the office.

At exactly half past eleven, Michael Angleton walked into the office followed by three smartly dressed fellows who were private investigators. They were however not familiar to Janet. He did not bother to introduce them to her. He strode past his staff, nodding politely without a word and ushered his visitors to his desk. He pulled three chairs from the side and the three gentlemen got comfortable. Noticing the small paper on his table before sitting down, he quickly read through it before nodding towards

Janet and flipping it over on his table. He sat down and faced the private investigators as Janet slowly made her way back to her desk

Before any issues were put on the table for discussion, Michael reached for his telephone and dialed the number on the note. He flipped it over to make sure the number he had dialed was correct before he threw it in the bin at his feet. After a minute and a half, shaking his head and mumbling to himself, he replaced the receiver. He tried the number again but there was still no response from the other end.

"Life is strange. Someone calls you, and you're not there, and when you are available, you try to call that person, he is not there. Strange eh?" said Angleton without referring to any particular private investigator.

"Yeah, I know, try again in fifteen minutes, maybe your friend's having a hard time in the John you never know," commented one of the guys with spectacles over his hooded eyes. Michael chuckled slightly.

"Anyway, let's get down to serious business! We have a lot of issues ahead of us and the sooner it's all done away with the better for all of us," said Michael Angleton his facial expression now more serious.

"Yes, let's do that. This is a complex issue. We are dealing with people we don't know," commented the same guy with glasses.

As he took the three guys through his plans, Michael Angleton kept warning them to keep it top secret and especially to make sure that the Metropolitan Police who were investigating the case did not speak of the plan to anyone. The task for the private investigators was to locate and monitor the residences, and if possible also follow the daily movements of Jose Cameron and Henry Forbes because they were the main suspects in this case. They were the leaders in their cluster of fools. The idea was to listen in on all their conversations with their friends, especially in any pubs they visited. It was possible that in an inebriated state they would spill the beans of exactly who was behind the Fletcher attack at the Ogaden Night Club, who had sent them, and how the whole plan had been hatched. Tongues wagged more freely when men were under the influence of alcohol. There was a lot that Michael could learn if the investigators kept close tabs on the hoodlums. He felt that he would get to the bottom of all this, one way or another.

After lengthy discussions, Michael Angleton stood up and firmly shook hands with each of the three men. "Not a word!" he warned making eye contact with each as he held their hands in a firm grip. He directed them to keep him informed of any development as the days progressed.

———————

Linda Ashcroft walked purposefully across the street from Boots within the town centre and heard her cell phone ringing inside her handbag. By the time she took it out to speak it had gone off. She quickly scrolled through the call log to see who was trying to reach her. The phone rang again and she flipped it open. Her husband's voice came through the other end.

"Hello there," she answered.

"I wondered if you are busy today sweetheart," said her husband.

"Well, I am in the town centre but I wanted to check my suppliers; It's been three days and we haven't received any deliveries yet," she said, the despair clear in her voice.

"Yes, I know. Sometimes they can be quite frustrating," her husband said distractedly. He continued, "I am in the office. If you can just pass by, there are a few things I would like to discuss with you."

"Is it something you can tell me over the phone?" Linda asked shielding her face from the wind.

"No, I can't tell you over the phone, once you are through with your stuff, come over to my office I will be waiting for you," although he was sounding calm, Michael's mind was troubled.

"Okay, give me about one hour and I will be there," Linda Ashcroft answered an instant before the phone went dead.

It was sixteen thirty in the afternoon when Linda Ashcroft pressed the door bell to her husband's office. An elderly man, who was well known to her, opened the door leading to the big office. Ernest had worked with them for many years as an office assistant and he knew Linda well. He ushered her into Mr. Ashcroft's office.

As usual Mr. Ashcroft was busy with his computer, feeding in data from a voluminous journal that was open on his right side. He turned briefly, stood up and drew her near to peck her cheek; their traditional greeting. Linda proceeded to the adjacent lounge where she made herself a cup of coffee in surroundings that were familiar and welcoming to her. As if nothing was troubling his mind, Michael Ashcroft continued with his work. He knew his wife well to know she wouldn't be offended if he finished off what he had been working on for the next few minutes before speaking to her. He didn't want to lose his train of thought although he was the one who had called her in to his office in the first place. Likewise, Linda knew her husband did not like to be interrupted especially when he was engrossed in his work so she focused on her coffee and looked out his large windows that enabled her to pan her eyes over most of the attractive landmarks in the city.

Ernest, who had opened the door earlier, disappeared into the corridors leading to other staff offices. After a few minutes, Linda approached her husband's desk and sat next to him pushing a tray full of correspondence slightly to the side. Without fuss, Mr. Ashcroft logged off his computer and faced his wife; he could tell she was now eager to be filled in with the latest developments. It didn't take them long for their conversation to change from domestic matters to serious issues afflicting the family.

"I think you know what has happened so far regarding Jose Cameron," started Mr. Ashcroft speaking in a low tone.

"Camila told me about it this morning before I left the house. But you seem rather bothered, I thought you had already fired him for his being absent from the office for so long without bothering to let you know of his whereabouts?" Linda answered innocently. "Well, that's not the issue I wanted to discuss with you here. I feel he knows too much about us as family and my fear is that, he might disclose a lot about my private life if he feels embittered by his sacking."

"You don't have to worry about anything," said Linda sensing he was quite disconcerted about Jose. "If he wants to tell the whole world your history, let him go ahead. In fact, it is good they nabbed him because even the Angletons are relieved. Remember, Jose and his collaborators assaulted Fletcher their son," retorted Linda totally oblivious of Michael's role in the whole mishap.

"You don't understand my sweetheart, it's not like that, there's more to this issue than you think," answered Mr. Ashcroft wiping his spectacles with a serviette he picked from the small coffee table to the side of his desk. Ernest always kept a few there for his use during the day.

"Is there something you know that I don't?" asked Linda peering into Michael's eyes curiously.

"Yes, there is something I didn't tell you," said Michael Ashcroft.

"Don't tell me you were involved!" Linda exclaimed visibly uptight.

"The truth of the matter is that, Fletcher Angleton had been seen several times in bars and night clubs cavorting with shady women, behind Camila's back -- with prostitutes," said Michael emphasizing the last word in thinly veiled anger. "As a father I have every right to protect my daughter from such rubbish," Michael Ashcroft was fidgeting nervously now. "So all I did was to tell Jose to warn Fletcher if he was still interested in a serious relationship with Camila. I wanted him to behave himself as his shenanigans were shaming her," Michael quickly added defensively, removing his exquisite designer handkerchief from his coat pocket and quickly wiping his moist brow. He continued "but instead of Jose using diplomacy he instructed his friends to physically assault Fletcher. Now my worry is that if Jose tells the police about it, I am sure the Angleton's will come to know about it and it will not go well with us as family friends. We are also respected in this community so the media would have a field day with this whole story if it is found out what really happened or that I had anything to do with it. I don't know how to resolve this whole mess! You have no idea how this incident can spiral out of control." By the time he was through with his confession, Michael Ashcroft was unable to look his wife in the eye. They had always tried not to keep things from each other, especially if a decision's ramifications could affect the family. He was embarrassed and her shock at what he had just narrated to her was palpable.

"What!" Linda Ashcroft was aghast. This was the first time she was hearing of this. "How could you do that for goodness sake? Do you know what it means? Why didn't you just talk to Fletcher and warn him..." Linda had stood up, unable to even sit near her husband with the disturbing feelings rising up in her chest. "Why couldn't you talk to him yourself?

Didn't you have the guts to do so personally?" Linda was obviously upset. Michael sensed her mix of anger, shock and fear at what she had just heard him confess to her. She paced around his massive desk. She was slightly bent from tension, with her one arm wrapping her cashmere jacket tightly around her mid-section as if she was suddenly feeling cold or feeling some back pain.

"I felt I was too old to deal with him myself. He is like a son to me, that Fletcher. That's why I sent Jose to warn him but unfortunately it didn't end like I expected. I imagined those hooligans wouldn't do more than rough him up a little bit, or even just threaten him verbally," Michael lied. "To be honest", Michael paused and looked at his wife intently, as if trying to draw her with his eyes to trust him again, "I am afraid and I just needed your support and understanding. Who else would I share this with?" He looked down at his feet like a doleful child.

"So what will you do? You know the Angleton's will vow to seek revenge once it is clear that you had anything to do with what happened to Fletcher," Linda said in a strained voice. If your name is mentioned it will definitely trigger an all-out war and bring shame to our family," she continued clenching her fists to her chest as if to hold her small frame in place. Her knuckles looked white.

"I don't know what to do...before it's too late," said Michael trying to compose himself and focus more on looking for a solution.

"How about Camila, do you think it's wise to tell her?" Linda asked. "You know how much she looks up to you as her father. She would be shocked to learn you had anything to do with hurting her fiancé."

"No! I don't want us to tell her anything...and never at any one time. She would never forgive me because there is no way I can make her understand!" Michael was trying to be assertive.

"Okay, do you have an alibi to cover your bloody mess?" Linda asked shaking her head.

"I am thinking and this time I need your help, do you know this fellow, the investigator, I can't remember his name?" Michael asked.

"Which investigator?" Linda asked, "What about him?"

"Well, I am told he is the one in charge of the interrogation and I think he is the right person to talk to," answered Ashcroft carefully.

Linda sighed audibly, getting the drift of what he was saying. She looked at him quietly then said after a minute, "Fair enough, use your contacts, and use them wisely, remember we just can't afford anything stupid happening… in addition to all that's already taken place." She shook her head like she was trying to shake off a bad dream.

"Try to contact Camila and see if there is anything she knows because I know Fletcher would not keep quiet about it, and we need to know exactly what he knows or suspects," instructed Michael quietly, relieved that he had told her but struggling with guilt from the obvious pain it had caused her. He knew he could always count on her support but he had not expected that it would all come to this.

Their talk lasted almost two hours. In all the years Michael had known Linda, even if something shocked or frightened her, she still tried to maintain a level head at the end of it all. It was clear she always had his back. However, the slight throb in her temples revealed how disconcerting the whole discussion had been for her. Their many years together also meant he knew how to assuage her fears when he needed to. He couldn't keep anything from her, but he knew she was hurt and afraid of what this would mean for their family. But, he hadn't wanted her to learn the truth about his role in this whole muddle from anyone else. He owed her that much. He watched her drawn face and knew that the way forward was to get in touch with Jose Cameron sooner than later and sort it all out. He was determined to use even fake promises or other means to twist his arm and get Jose to swear that under no circumstances would he reveal that Ashcroft had anything to do with what had happened to Fletcher. A storm was brewing fast and bearing down hard on him and his family, and he had to do all in his power to steer them clear of its angry path.

The moon was shining bright above them by the time they stepped out of his office building. The discussion had been delicate and painful for Linda but she was a strong woman. She took everything by stride and no one in the office would have guessed there was anything troubling her by the time she strode confidently past the few staff still working late at their desks. They stepped out into a cool night breeze that brushed against their cheeks lightly. Ashcroft looked up at the star-studded skies as they ambled slowly towards the office car park, their hands interlinked; both were lost in thought. They reached the parking bay behind the tall building and walked farther down to where Linda had parked her big Range Rover. He kissed her lightly on the lips as they parted ways.

"I might be a bit late tonight," he said quietly as he looked into her eyes meaningfully. "I need to see someone before I come," he told her before she nodded understandingly. She turned and got into her car and slowly drove off into the fast-descending darkness.

After his wife had driven off, Mr. Ashcroft turned and walked to his car and sat there for five minutes thinking of what to do next. His mind was filled with questions of how to get the right person to contact Sergeant Morgan Clifton without the Angleton's family knowing about it. Suddenly, he remembered his good friend Dr. Carter of Radcliffe Referral Hospital. He flipped open his phone and dialed the doctor's number.

The telephone at the hospital's reception desk rang and a tired female voice answered.

"Radcliffe Referral Hospital, Rachael speaking, can I help?" said the receptionist.

"Give me extension 612 please," replied Mr. Ashcroft feeling slightly irritated by her obvious emotional labour tactic. HR training needed to undo the belief that sounding excited when you were actually very bored and tired just didn't fool any client.

"Who is calling?" asked the receptionist.

"It's Michael Ashcroft and I would like to speak to Dr. Carter on extension 612," he answered.

"K…Hang on a sec", she said quickly.

After being entertained by a monotonous musical tune from the other end, the unmistakable voice of Dr. Carter finally sounded clearly on the phone.

"What is it this time?" Dr. Carter asked feigning irritation though it was obvious he was happy to hear from his long-time friend.

"Something has been going on for a while and I feel like I am getting ulcers," stated Mr. Ashcroft. He was too tired and tense to beat around the bush.

"I told you to refrain from drinking too much vodka," Dr. Carter said jokingly.

"It's not what you think buddy, it's more than that…I desperately need your help."

"What's the problem then big boy, especially at this time of the evening? You are supposed to be heading off to your lovely wife to rest." The doctor knew the Ashcroft's well and had always been their family doctor, and a personal friend to Michael.

"Well it's personal and I need to see you soonest. Can you spare a few hours tonight? It's only eight-thirty," requested Mr. Ashcroft.

"You remember the research I was doing about genetic mutation?" asked Dr. Carter. Tonight I will be confined in the medical laboratory most of the time but if it suits you, we can always meet tomorrow morning at eight at the Grand Regency Hotel." Dr. Carter explained.

"Okay, that will be fine with me," Ashcroft replied. He chit-chatted on other non-important issues for a few minutes, then he said goodbye and slipped the phone back into his coat pocket and started his car.

Feeling lonely and dejected, Michael drove his Lexus through the busy high street towards his home. His mind wandered over the Fletcher mess and he cursed under his breath. The main gate to the front entrance of his house was locked as usual and he had to get out of the car to open it. After parking his car and locking the gate behind him, he proceeded to the main door opening it with his set of keys without bothering to ring the door bell.

Linda Ashcroft was already home and she was sitting on the sofa in the living room with a glass of wine in her slim hand. She was listening to the news on the television against the wall. Tom, the pet cat, purred softly as he dozed on her laps. She was intrigued by what her husband had shared with her earlier in the day but wasn't clear what the import of it all would be for their family. When she got home she wished desperately that her daughter Camila had been home to keep her company and to ward off the disturbing thoughts she was grappling with since the discussion with her father. She startled when her husband walked dejectedly into the living room.

"How's everything my love, you got home okay?" Michael asked his wife.

"Yeah, just trying to relax, do you want a cup of coffee or maybe tea?" she asked.

"A cup of tea after a quick shower will do me good, but before that I need a shot of vodka to warm me up," he said walking to the cabinet next to the window "by the way did you talk to Camila?"

"No, I decided to keep quiet and think about it first, and she isn't in yet," Linda answered.

"That's okay," he said placing his glass of vodka on the table and removing his coat at the same time with a free hand.

"Did you manage to do what you had planned? You mentioned that you needed to meet with someone first before coming home tonight," she asked curiously.

"It was Dr. Carter I needed to speak to him but he was busy. I will have to see him tomorrow," Michael replied.

After a quick swig of his drink, Michael walked upstairs to his master bedroom where he had a quick shower, donning himself with a warm light gown before he walked back downstairs in warm flannel slippers. He felt a lot more relaxed. He sat on his favourite armchair and sipped at the steaming cup of tea that had been prepared by Linda when he was in the bathroom.

"You know what Linda, I just love you," he said starting to feel the relaxing warmth of brew course through him. "I know what I told you today, was so shocking, but I am so glad you were around."

"Hmmmh? Yes, it was, but we will have to find a way out of the whole mess," she sat close to him and nestled against his chest.

"Well, you are just the person I need when I feel low," he said soothingly stroking her hair.

"I feel the same way," she said looking up at him lovingly.

He put his arms around her and kissed her softly on her pink lips. They got up and walked side-by-side towards the bedroom, holding hands. Many years, and many challenges faced together, had only served to deepen their love for each other. Deep inside they both knew they would fight to the utmost to make sure no wedge came between them.

They talked for some time before they fell asleep, about his business and other social things they faced daily in life, but Fletcher Angleton dominated their talk as they weighed the pro's and con's of the options before them. They needed to see how to end the matter without raising too much dust. It was important to maintain their friendship with the Angleton's family.

"Darling …what do you think is the best way forward?" Linda asked her husband, leaning towards him.

"I will get an answer tomorrow after my meeting with Dr. Carter," he said.

"But does he know why you called him?" she asked again.

"No, some of these things you don't talk about on the phone because you never know who is listening," he answered yawning.

"I know." She knew how investigative journalists sometimes paid to tap the phones of the high-and-mighty so that they could glean what their lives were like, or inadvertently get a scoop on a story. "But remember to tell me everything darling," she said. "Incase anything goes wrong, I feel I should be in the know. That is the only way we can avoid embarrassment," said Linda Ashcroft earnestly looking up at his face.

"Okay. Don't worry about that. But if Jose refuses to keep his mouth shut about my involvement, I will make him pay, even with his life if I have to," said Michael gruffly. "I will stop at nothing. I will make sure he gets a clear message dissuading him from divulging anything about the whole debacle, and a strong message at that. Remember our relationship with the Angleton's must be protected and what Camila as our daughter goes through is also of paramount importance to us, now and in the future," said Mr. Ashcroft pulling the bed sheet close to his chin.

"I know you care very much for your daughter but you must consider what this issue can trigger if not properly handled," Linda said.

"Don't worry my love; just leave it to me and remember to keep quiet about the whole thing," Michael said pulling her closer to him.

"Good night sweetheart," she said.

"Good night my love," he replied as he closed his eyes and sighed deeply.

The day's events had taken a toll on them. With fingers interlinked, they drifted off into a deep sleep and floated away into the nether world where all the angst of each day always floats into nothingness.

Chapter Nine

The air inside the small cubicle at the police station was tense enough to cut through. On one side of the table was Jose Cameron and sitting right opposite was Sergeant Morgan Clifton flipping through a file and poring through the details on each page without saying a word. It was a Saturday, two days after Jose was arrested. A young lady in police uniform entered the room without knocking and walked straight to where Sergeant Morgan was seated. She whispered urgently into his right ear as he leaned his head to her side slightly, listening keenly to what she was saying. She looked hatefully towards Jose after she had finished telling Clifton what she had come to tell him and walked out of the room. It was obvious what she thought of him based on what investigations had already been carried out on the Fletcher case. She closed the door behind her after throwing Jose one last mean look. Two minutes later, a slight tap on the door and Sergeant Morgan stood up and opened it.

"My name is Michael Ashcroft, we've never met before but I am sure you've been expecting me Sergeant," said Michael as they shook hands.

"I've been told about you by a friend and I am sorry we couldn't meet yesterday because of work pressure here. It's been really hectic. Sit down," said Sergeant Morgan pulling the only vacant chair in the room for Michael.

"I am here because this young man works for me and I've been very concerned about his welfare, it's quite unusual for him not to report to work and I was surprised when I came to know about what happened. Has he been charged with anything?" Mr. Ashcroft asked pretending that he knew nothing about why Jose was at the police station, or what the situation was concerning Jose and his work at the office.

"It's good to know that he's been working for you, but if you don't mind, tell me the last time he worked for you?" Sergeant Morgan enquired watching Michael closely for any reaction.

"Before I answer your question, can I have a moment with him alone please? It will only take us a few minutes and then he will be all yours," requested Mr. Ashcroft.

Sergeant Morgan Clifton hesitated for a moment. He wasn't sure of the wisdom of granting such a request, but he had been taken by surprise, so he said before leaving the room, "I have a lot to do so please don't take too long with him".

It started as a normal conversation between Michael Ashcroft and Jose Cameron, but Jose knew his boss well enough to know from the steely glint in his eyes that this was no joking matter. Mr. Ashcroft's eyes were dark and piercing as he slowly approached his former worker who was now so uneasy that he felt he was close to wetting his pants. The small room had nothing except two small cabinets against the wall that was away from them. Jose had nothing to lean on to hide his fear. His trembling frame stood lamely in front of Michael Ashcroft.

Mr. Ashcroft used every tactic he knew, short of physical harm, to get Jose to promise that no matter what happened he would keep his mouth shut and not mention the Ashcroft family anywhere while under interrogation by Sergeant Clifton.

Jose knew very well what crossing the Ashcroft line meant. Pinned against a wall on one side by Ashcroft's wild look, he nodded nervously at intervals as he listened to dire warnings come out of Ashcroft's snarled lips and gritted teeth. Michael spoke softly so that the sergeant could not hear them, but his warning was loud and clear. Jose dared not ask any questions and knew that not toeing the line meant instant death sooner than later. Michael made it clear that if Jose did exactly as he was being told, he would live and even have safe passage to any location of his choice, including a new job, organized quickly by one of Michael's many and powerful connections worldwide. All Jose had to do was make sure that Sergeant Clifton was no wiser about Ashcroft's involvement in Fletcher's attack. Not a word would be said of any instructions from Michael that Fletcher should be taught a lesson so that he would stop his faux pas with hookers and flirts in town. In less than ten minutes, Michael had made his point extremely clear and though Jose wondered how he could trust his boss concerning the promise of keeping him safe and getting him a new job if he kept his mouth shut, he knew better than to argue. Jose was not stupid to pre-empt his freedom just yet, and there was no telling what was true at the moment as all seemed so blurred and unpredictable when one was petrified as he was. So, Jose just watched wide-eyed as Michael retreated swiftly after the stern warning. Adrenaline was still pumping through Jose's trembling frame.

Michael turned for one instant at the door and said, "Remember, the society holds our families in high esteem and I don't want any trouble between us -- you understand?" Mr. Ashcroft said in a whispery voice.

"Yes I do understand but surely this was not my fault," said Jose in a trembling voice.

"Not your fault indeed! Do you know what this means to me?" retorted Michael again his anger brimming.

"It was a mistake and I thought you of all people would understand sir," said Jose Cameron defensively.

"I hope this will end up well for all of us but do not underestimate the family of Michael Angleton, they are capable of doing anything within their power and influence," the veins on Mr. Ashcroft's face were bulging from a mixture of anger and apprehension.

The door swung open unexpectedly and with his usual majestic walk, Sergeant Morgan Clifton walked in. Although Mr. Ashcroft tried hard to control his anger, the distortion on his face and the clenching of fists betrayed the palpable tension between him and Jose, whose sweaty face also disclosed his fear, and gave Clifton a hint that all was not going well between the two men.

"I am sure you've had enough time now and if you need more time to talk to your employee Mr. Ashcroft you'll have to come back tomorrow. I have a lot on my hands and we want this case done away with as soon as possible," said the Sergeant displaying a cold smile.

"Protect this young fellow because I don't want to lose him. He is one of my best workers," Ashcroft said deceitfully while walking out the door without turning his head to say goodbye to Jose or the Sergeant.

Michael Ashcroft strode across the High Street with his agitated mind swimming with many ideas of what could happen if Jose did not stick to what they had agreed. He narrowly missed knocking down a very pregnant Chinese woman who was approaching from the opposite direction. Michael absentmindedly apologized to the mortified woman and headed to the only café within the vicinity.

Built during Victorian times, the cafeteria's interior displayed artefacts from that era on its cream-coloured walls. A dim spectre of light shone through the small stained-glass windows towards the entrance. It was generally dark inside and few patrons mingled and sipped at their drinks as low music filtered from the hidden wall speakers.

With slow strides, Mr. Ashcroft walked to a seat at the farthest dark corner and sat down.

"What can I serve you sir?" a waitress promptly asked picking up a menu from the table next to Michael's and placing it in front of him.

"Coffee," Ashcroft said curtly, taking his cell phone out of his pocket.

"Anything else sir?" she asked displaying the menu for him to see.

"Nothing else, thank you," said Michael Ashcroft scrolling through the numbers listed on his cell phone as she picked the menu and went off to get him what he ordered.

The coffee on the table was getting cold as Michael tried repeatedly to get through to his doctor friend. He was tired and the fine lines on his forehead showed the strain he had been through because of this Fletcher incident, but he was becoming increasingly confident that his business associate would come up with a good plan that would deal with the events ahead.

Dr. Carter was sitting in his office at the Neurosurgeon Wing of the Radcliffe Referral Hospital reading a medical journal when the telephone on the table rang. Raising his eyebrows after recognizing the voice from the other end, he realised that it was getting late in the morning and that they had promised to meet together. He knew that Michael Ashcroft could not be calling him for another round of golf because the sky looked like it would burst with rain anytime. He said hallo and Michael took the plunge, albeit with trepidation, and began to narrate his dilemma.

"Dr. Carter, how are you getting on?" he asked looking at his wrist watch. "I don't know how tight your schedule is but as a matter of urgency, I need to see you as soon as possible, I am sure you are the only person I can confide in about this matter at the moment," Mr. Ashcroft started in a tight voice.

"Yes, I got carried away and just remembered that we were supposed to meet up this morning.

"What is it this time Michael. I thought you told me you'll be dealing with serious business issues. I imagined you were trying to ensure you avoid the mistakes of the past. Don't forget how you lost a fortune last year by irking the very people who were sitting on the tendering board! I hope you are awake this time man!" Dr. Carter had no idea what the trouble was and supposed Michael's call had to do with some business deal going awry.

"This is a totally different issue and I am not ready to talk about it over the phone. I don't like to discuss private matters on the phone. I seriously need to meet with you on this…urgently," emphasized Michael, his voice tight tinged with frustration.

"Well, I am in my office and you can come in at any time," replied Dr. Carter sensing his friend's desperation.

"I am on my way," said Michael throwing his phone into his pocket.

With his cup of coffee untouched and without another word, he paid his bill, and gave a generous tip to the waitress before leaving the café.

The drive to the Radcliffe Referral Hospital took Michael Ashcroft twenty-five minutes less this time. It was eleven-thirty in the morning and traffic was light. He cruised through Queen's Drive to the town centre and quickly slipped into the hospital's parking bay.

Saturday as always was Dr Carter's preferred day of the week. Except for emergency calls, nothing else of great import would be scheduled for the day. He was therefore sitting at his desk leisurely flipping through the pages of an in-house magazine when the door to his office swung open letting in a harried Michael Ashcroft.

"Don't tell me your business is in trouble?" Dr. Carter enquired with a teasing look at his best friend as he extended his hand to greet him.

"Come off it man; this is more serious than anything else you've thought of before," blurted Mr. Ashcroft earnestly, grabbing a seat nearby and quickly swivelling it around to face the doctor's. He slumped into it like someone who had just come to the end of his tether. A veneer of desperation was obvious on his face.

"So what is it then? Come on guy, you know I hate guess work," countered Dr. Carter drawing his leather seat closer to Ashcroft's. It was obvious his friend was thoroughly flustered and this had piqued the doctor's interest.

"It's all about this fellow," replied Michael Ashcroft in hushed tone as he looked around the room to make sure there was no one else in the office.

"Which fellow?" the doctor asked.

"Fletcher Angleton," answered Mr. Ashcroft.

"What about him -- as far as I know this matter was resolved because you told me you'd had a one-on-one with Mr. Angleton --. Why do you guys keep going backwards reviving bygones! This is all rubbish and you know me very well. I don't like this. We should be thinking about how to persuade the Tendering Board to allot the tender to us for the supply of building materials to the Ministry. Why are you forgetting things Michael," Dr. Carter was obviously angry with his long-time friend as he assumed this was all about a business deal they had been trying to turn in their favour with the Tendering Board.

"Shut-up and listen!" Michael was quickly and equally frustrated by his friend's scathing accusations, and more so because he was totally off the mark as this was not the issue that was bothering him.

"Look here my good friend," he continued, "When things get out of hand we try to resolve them the best way we can, whatever the consequences. Don't forget what you did five years ago when your brother Tony was hijacked. You came to me because you knew I had connections and nothing was too tough for us to sort out together at that time. Remember? We managed didn't we? I am not talking about any business deal...this is something touching on my personal life, and the lives of those in my family so don't just jump to conclusions and assume I am talking about one thing, when I am referring to something totally different." Michael waved his hand up in exasperation, like someone trying to shut a wearisome sound off.

"I need to resolve this matter before it gets out of hand. Now my question to you is, are you ready to help me?" Michael's narration was way too emotional for the doctor to ignore.

"Okay," said the doctor realizing that Michael was truly distraught and that this had nothing to do with his business wheeling and dealings. "But please I don't want to involve myself in anything where somebody might get hurt. What happened last time is still fresh in my mind okay!" Dr. Carter said spreading his arms wide in exasperation.

"Don't worry, it won't happen again," blurted Michael confidently.

"What's the problem then?" asked the doctor.

It was clear that Michael had a weight on his shoulders and needed someone to help him make some difficult decisions. This was not the place for such talk. They needed a more private place, where no one could eavesdrop on their discussion. Michael made it clear that this was a sensitive issue so they left in a hurry to seek a more quiet location.

According to Michael Ashcroft, the plan was to silence the only witness who knew what had really happened to Fletcher, or what part he had played in the assault. The repercussions could be dire if the truth were exposed. They needed to silence Jose Cameron. But there was one major problem because this guy was still in police custody and nobody had the faintest idea what he had already disclosed to the authorities. Even though Michael had warned Jose earlier at the police station, he felt he could not trust him to keep his word; there needed to be a Plan B. The earlier this problem was sorted out, the better.

Behind the gigantic tree in the church backyard not too far from the Radcliffe Referral Hospital, where they had driven and parked their cars, were clusters of lonely, marked and unmarked graves, running all the way down the slope to the very edge of the compound. An elderly couple holding hands was slowly walking down the well-tended walkways occasionally stopping to chat quietly to each other, as though discussing a long lost friend. The flowers were so beautiful and the unadulterated greenery was refreshing. The lady clutched a bunch of flowers in her scrawny hands and linked her other one into her old partner's hand. It was clear they were headed to one of the marked graves. The old couple finally stopped and laid the bunch of flowers on a fresh, soft mound before them. After a respectful silence to a loved one they had lost, they walked away from the grave hand-in-hand. They absentmindedly passed by the seats along the path where Dr. Carter and Michael Ashcroft were now seated engrossed in the scheme at hand animatedly whispering to each other with their greying but well coiffed heads slightly bent and close to each other to prevent passers-by from hearing their frenzied exchange.

Time was running out and they were getting no closer to a solution. To make it worse, the elderly couple walked back to where the duo was seated and innocently sat on a bench opposite them. Michael looked up at them, with slight irritation marking his eyebrow and quickly changed the topic. He had briefed the doctor on all that had transpired since the night at the Ogaden Night Club, and was just about to launch into his encounter with Jose at the police station earlier, but when he realized they were no longer alone, he and the doctor agreed to revisit the issue at later date, someplace else. They bid each other farewell and headed to their cars. Michael got into his car and headed towards his home.

Saturday seemed longer than usual for Michael Ashcroft as he drove his Lexus to his favourite wine and spirit shop on his way home. The throb in his head was getting more intense so he could hardly concentrate and it was causing haziness in his sight. Inside the shop, he hesitated before ordering a bottle of Jack Daniels, paid for it and headed back to his car. He did not even engage in the friendly chit-chat he sometimes enjoyed with the shop steward. He simply turned and headed back to his car without uttering a word. He flopped into the driver's seat, carefully manoeuvred the car off the side of the road, and headed home.

Camila was in the kitchen with her mother preparing supper for the family when she heard her father's unmistakable cough as he entered the house. The two ladies were enjoying an easy banter, talking about the latest in fashion and enjoying the juicy gossip they had heard floating around the neighbourhood when suddenly Camila's father strode into the house.

"Hey girls, is everybody okay?" Mr. Ashcroft greeted fiddling with his tie and trying to feign lightheartedness he didn't feel.

"You look tired and exhausted," commented Linda perceptively as she walked towards her husband to give him a traditional cuddle as he entered the hallway next to the kitchen.

"You bet. I need a shower before anything else," answered Mr. Ashcroft as he held her close to his broad chest. She always made things easier to cope with and it felt good holding her as the day had been draining and coming home always lifted some of the weight he carried from work.

"I think a cup of tea will make you feel better dad," said Camila still standing close to the kitchen.

"I know but I think that can wait too," he said releasing his wife gently and heading into the living room after giving Camila a peck on her cheek. She looked after him wonderingly as he reached for a small glass from the side cabinet.

Holding the glass with his left hand, Michael poured himself a generous portion of Jack Daniels and gulped it down neat before muttering some lame excuse at both of the ladies and going upstairs to the bathroom.

Although Camila had her own house not too far away from her parents, she didn't have any problem spending the nights with them whenever she felt like and especially at this moment when so much was at stake. The assault on her boyfriend was creating misunderstandings even between her and Fletcher and she had always turned to her parents as a sounding board when things were not going right with him. The fact that Jose Cameron was an employee of her father brought a lot of tension into the lives of the Angleton's as they tried to get an answer as to why and how the attack on Fletcher outside the Ogaden Night Club had happened.

Communication from Fletcher had dwindled of late and the usual romantic trysts seemed to have ceased as time went by because of the stress that was building up between the two families. Even within their work circles, the fractures were clearly showing however much they all tried to hide them from staff and their treasured customers.

After her father had come from the much-needed shower, Camila tactfully chatted about everything but what she sensed might be bothering him, until he had settled down enough to handle a discussion on Fletcher.

"Dad," she said, moving closer to him and sitting on the arm rest of his seat. "There's something I really need to know about Fletcher because the events unfolding of late are rather disturbing. Tell me, were you in any way involved in what happened to him?" Camila's voice was grave as she asked looking keenly at him with her usual unblinking and very unnerving eyes.

"I know you are all concerned about all this but I assure you that what happened to Fletcher had nothing to do with me," her father lied.

"And why are you wasting so much time and energy following up the case? Let the police handle the matter their own way and the culprits will be brought to book whoever they are. You shouldn't be bothered with trivial matters dad! You are above that," said Camila with a mix of irritation and sympathy in her expression. "I heard you went to the police station to see him, why?"

"I understand all that …but just like you, I need to know the root of the matter," answered Mr. Ashcroft evasively as he rubbed his chin and glanced quickly up at Camila.

His wife called out from the kitchen where she was arranging some dishes, "I stayed up late this evening waiting for you because I am very concerned about this whole thing you know." She waved to her side as though trying to wave the problem out the window. "We don't want this to blow out of proportion and if the Angleton's keep throwing a suspecting eye on you, then I don't know how this will eventually end with us as families, especially since we have been friends for so many years."

"Okay, if you want to know how far the matter has gone, wait until tomorrow after proper consultations with the authorities. You know that the suspects are already being brought to the station for interrogation, so let's let that take its course before we start worrying about anything okay?" Michael suggested defensively.

"It's okay to wait but before we get to hear from them, can't you just tell us what you know dad," insisted Camila with a tight expression on her face.

Realizing that he was been cornered, Michael tried to explain what had been going on since the fateful day but making sure that he omitted the most crucial bit about his involvement in the matter. He told his family of his meeting with Jose Cameron at the police station and how Sergeant Morgan Clifton was working hard to get the case resolved amicably and quickly so that they could all have the information that they needed on what really happened that night. He tried to sound as convincing as possible and as disinterested in the outcome of the investigations as any passerby, but Camila couldn't understand why, if he had nothing to do with it, he was so involved in the matter in the first place, or why he had a thin sheen of sweat forming over his forehead even as he narrated how the events were unfolding at the station. Camila just couldn't figure out what was going on so she finally gave up trying to glean any more information on the Fletcher case from her father and stood up to bid good night to him and her mother. She wasn't convinced that everything was okay but couldn't put her finger on what was bothering her. She walked out slowly after wishing them well for the night. Her mother watched her leave and sighed deeply from the tension that had built up in her chest as she tried to hide what her husband had shared with her earlier about the Fletcher incident.

The drive to her house took Camila almost twenty minutes. She had nothing planned for the following day so she took all the time she needed to relax on the sofa in her living room thinking about what her father had told them. She finally got up, took a quick shower and a shot of vodka to warm her up before slipping into her large and inviting bed. It had been a long tiring day for her and before long she was fast asleep.

Chapter Ten

The fury of the scorching sun was unbearable. The hot rays bounced off the tarmac in hazy mirages that disturbed Fletcher Angleton's eyes as he sped down the shimmering highway, defying all traffic rules. He was obviously frustrated and his stress showed in the way he negotiated the corners at a frightening pace. He had a mission, and only he knew what he planned as he wrenched the car around the twists and turns. He maneuvered his brand new Mercedes Benz Compressor like a frenzied rally driver.

On his trail, he had no idea of the speeding police car with its siren blaring and its blue lights flashing overhead. He had not noticed how fast he had been going, and now as he peered into the rear view mirror, he swore under his breath. He could see the angry policeman beckoning to him to stop. Crazed with a burning anger against those who had attacked him, Fletcher reflexively pressed harder on the accelerator, but his bid to get away was outdone in seconds and he gave up his short-lived run-away attempt after barely a minute, and screeched to a halt on the kerb.

"Are you out of your mind?" the elderly police officer said loudly and sternly as he stepped out of the car and strode over to Fletcher's open window. "You are driving like a maniac!" He said as he peered sternly at Fletcher.

"I am sorry, I didn't know it was me you were flagging down," Fletcher answered trying to feign innocence.

"Are you deaf that you couldn't hear the siren?" asked the police officer sarcastically.

"I happened to be concentrating on the road so much that I couldn't hear you, sir," Fletcher replied still sitting inside his car after switching the ignition off.

"You know you were driving over the speed limit, right?" the policeman asked him gruffly.

"I honestly didn't know that," Fletcher replied.

"Okay, well now you know why I stopped you?" the police officer continued, drawing a wad of tickets out of his back pocket and looking Fletcher up and down keenly.

Fletcher had learned over the years that placating a police officer after an offense was the only way out of a fix.

"You were over-speeding and disregarding the traffic rules and this is what you get for it," the officer cut enjoying Fletcher's discomfort.

"I honestly didn't mean to drive like a maniac, are you sure you want to give me that?" Fletcher asked scratching his forehead.

"License please?" the police officer ordered without hesitation.

"Sure," Fletcher Angleton answered dejectedly while reaching for his wallet in his left trouser pocket.

"So what's the hurry for young man?" asked the officer curtly.

He wasn't sure what it was that bothered him, but suddenly all the questioning by the police officer ticked Fletcher off.

"Just get on with it and let me go, okay!" he snapped, unable to hide his frustration.

"So, is that the way you want us to go?" the officer continued with a smirk on his face. "No problem, arrogance will not get you anywhere." He scribbled quickly on the tickets pad, and tore off the first leaf. He handed it to Fletcher as well as the license he had asked for earlier, and turned back to his police car without as much as a second look back. "You can never get away with that arrogance," the officer said over his shoulder as he shoved the ticket pad into his back pocket while heading to his blue and white car with the swirling blue and red light overhead.

Fletcher flung the ticket to the passenger seat, started his car and pulled carefully away from the curb mumbling expletives under his breath.

As expected, the private hall of the Sheraton Hotel was jam-packed with invited guests mainly from the Diplomatic Corps, and High Commissioners of different nations intermingling with each other. Men dressed in black suits with white shirts and coloured bow ties to match, and ladies displaying the best in fashion with long silky dresses and the gaudily coiffed heads as they all tried to outwit each other in beauty. It was a big farewell party for the outgoing Canadian Ambassador to the UK.

Standing by the side balcony of the well-decorated hall was a Polish lady. She sat alone holding a glass of red wine with her long, delicate fingers. On her side was a glittering blue hand-bag matching her frame-hugging blue and polka-dotted dress. From time to time, she would glance at the gold watch on her slim wrist and look around the large room questioningly. Samantha was her name and it took only the strongest willed man to keep from glancing in her direction every so often. She cut an image of a woman completely at ease with herself and with the expensive attire she donned and hour-glass, petite figure, it made it even harder for men to ignore her. Around her, the décor was stunning. The room was a large lounge area that accommodated a large number of invited guests without seeming too crowded. Samantha was about twenty-seven years old.

Entering through the side door with haste was Fletcher Angleton who almost collided with a hotel staff member who was carrying a tray laden with cocktails of different colours in tiny glasses. Fletcher had come by invitation and knew only Samantha in the room. Looking around the elite group of patrons, he saw a lone figure facing away from him. Running his eyes over her petite and exquisite figure confirmed to him that it was Samantha. He walked towards her confidently.

Samantha, a daughter of a high profile business associate of Michael Angleton, had known Fletcher for a while but had no idea he was engaged to Camila Ashcroft although she had met them together before. The first introduction from Fletcher on their first meeting in Camila's presence was casual and Fletcher had been careful not to even hint at a relationship

between him and Camila so Samantha had not the slightest idea of its exist-
ence. She came to this party through her connections to an uncle who was
a military attaché with the Polish Embassy. In an effort to avoid boredom
and enjoy the mingling, she had extended the invitation to Fletcher, the only
person outside her family she knew was fond of big parties. She had nothing
to worry about she thought; she was single with no regular boyfriend and
hanging around with Fletcher was something she was looking forward to.
Turning her head slowly and panning her eyes towards the entrance again,
she saw him and, despite her wait, she couldn't help smiling broadly when
their eyes met. He smiled back as he strode towards her.

Just a few feet from her, Fletcher's phone rang. He looked down at his
phone and cursed silently when he realized it was Camila. He put the
phone to his ear

"Hello," Fletcher answered slowing his step and hoping the call would
be over before he covered the few paces to gorgeous Samantha.

"I've been trying to get hold of you but no one seems to know your
whereabouts!" Camila said with an accusing and urgent edge in her voice.

"I am sorry love..." he answered.

He was guilty and Camila knew it immediately from her end; the way
he was talking and his sudden intake of breath made her sense that there
was something amiss. Samantha too saw the sudden frustrated look on
his face though she had no idea what was bothering him. She decided
not to ask him immediately as she was not interested in spoiling her party
mood. She watched as Fletcher turned to face the door so that she was
looking at his broad back as he spoke in an urgent, low tone into his cell
phone. He finally cut off the call abruptly and turned to her with a sheepish and forced grin. He bent towards her and kissed her gently on both
cheeks, making sure that he also ran his firm, long fingers down her side
lightly. She caught a whiff of his expensive cologne. He had struck her
as a refined and modern man when she first met him, and it was clear he
had not lost his touch. She could tell he was wearing an *Acqua Di Gio* by
Georgio Armani, a perfume she adored. She sensed immediately that this
was going to be a great night.

With more dignitaries coming in, they moved to a corner table reserved for two and sat down, looking intently into each other's eyes. Fletcher was eager to quickly forget Camila's call.

"So what took you so long to get here?" Samantha asked in a cool, affectionate voice.

"Traffic," he answered absentmindedly.

"You expect me to believe you, I drove through the same route and traffic was moving smoothly," said Samantha surprised.

"I know, it sounds crazy but I was stopped by a traffic policeman for over-speeding. Just my luck! He even gave me a ticket, the twerp! Here, look," Fletcher said after rifling through his coat pockets and removing the ticket for her to see.

"Oh my God I thought you were fibbing," she said.

"How could I lie to such a beauty queen?" he replied, his charming self getting back on track after running his eyes over her elegant figure and flawlessly made-up face.

"No wonder you looked disturbed sweetheart," said Samantha good-humouredly. Cheer up and enjoy the party. Does your flustered self have anything to do with who was on the phone?" she added perceptively, peering into his eyes.

"Yeah, I don't like it when people call me when I am trying to enjoy the company of a belle like you," he answered, keen to focus on more exciting things than the call. Their conversation digressed to other aspects of their lives as it had been a while since their last encounter.

"Last time we met you hinted to me that you would be in trouble if you didn't reach your sales targets," probed Samantha.

"Yes, I never did meet them but thankfully I didn't get into much trouble," answered Fletcher running his fingers roughly through his dark hair. They talked of his business experiences for some time for Samantha knew men enjoyed to have their ego stroked discussing their business successes. At one point however, as they lulled into an uncomfortable silence and sipped at their drinks, Fletcher's mind seemed to wander to more disturbing things. For a moment, he forgot she was there with him, and mumbled to himself, "Those fools almost killed me, you know!"

"What did you just say? Who almost killed you?" Samantha asked suddenly, her small frame tensing and perking up like the ears of a dog when it hears a sudden disturbing sound. Her surprised voice pierced through Fletcher's reverie.

He was shocked that he had spoken out loud, but it was too late to retract his words. He paused for a moment wondering if he should tell her what had happened to him at the Ogaden Night Club and about his hospitalization thereafter. Looking into her large, curious eyes, he realized telling her might relieve him of some of the tension that had built up in him. He decided to be open. "Some nitwits who mugged me when I was leaving a club one night; one of them is still in custody," he said wiping his mouth with a serviette he picked from the table in front of them, "they almost killed me…just attacked me and started beating the daylights out of me," he continued.

"Why? When did this happen?" Samantha asked obviously shocked. "I have known you as a decent person who wouldn't harm anyone. Why would anybody want to hurt you?" she asked drawing his large hand into her small, delicate one.

"I honestly don't know," he answered.

"Nobody can come from nowhere and assault you for nothing. What the heck was going on?" Samantha asked in consternation.

"I swear I have no idea what was going on. I was walking to the car park all alone from a pub and all I can remember is that I found myself in hospital bed not too long after that, badly beat up," he lied avoiding her direct gaze.

"Well, I don't understand," said Samantha "it honestly doesn't make any sense to me. So sorry about that darling," she said running her palm gently over his right cheek and looking deeply into his eyes with concern. "You should have called me; I would have come to see you in hospital at least."

Samantha looked enquiringly into his eyes, trying to get some answers to why this had all happened to him. He didn't seem willing to divulge too much about the incident, so she said, "I trust that there is nothing sinister about all this. I suspect this was someone who already had something against you from some past incident; otherwise it's rare that mugging like those take place in town nowadays. I feel bad that you didn't inform me of this when you were in hospital," she said pouting her shapely and well-glossed lips.

"I'm sorry darling," he said reassuringly "so much has taken place and I was in so much pain, I wasn't thinking clearly at that time. In fact, I was going in and out of consciousness the doctor says. It wasn't until just before I was discharged that I could even make sense of what was going on around me." Fletcher knew how to make a lady feel sorry for him and forgive any of his misdeeds.

"I suppose it is okay," said Samantha reluctantly. But now you are back to work?" she asked.

"I'm taking a short break from work to heal completely and also to try and find out what was behind the attack," Fletcher continued. He told her the details on the incident and he felt sorry that he had not told her about the ambush and all that he had gone through before meeting her. He had always had an eye on Samantha but she had only been interested in companionship and nothing serious. His cell-phone rang again.

"Hello," he answered turning away from Samantha slightly.

"You promised to call after a while and it's almost three and a half hours since! What's going on?" Camila asked angrily.

"Ooh I got tied up but it's alright now," he answered standing up and glancing around him to see where he could talk quietly to Camila without Samantha knowing who it was.

The noise in the hall was loud and live jazz could be heard in the background, as he took a step away. Samantha held him back deliberately talking in a loud voice so that the caller could hear that there was a woman companion with him. She suspected that this was his lady friend and felt a prick of jealousy in her chest.

"You don't have to go outside Fletcher or don't you want me to hear what you are talking about?" she asked knowing the woman on the phone could hear her. She guessed it was Camila and a jealous pang made her want to ensure Camila knew Fletcher was enjoying the company of another woman.

A slight pause as Fletcher indicated to Samantha to keep her voice down as he tried to manoeuvre around the seats and move a short distance away. The conversation resumed again on phone.

"Who's that? I knew you were lying to me Fletcher," Camila burst out on the other end. "Who do you think I am? Where is your common decency Fletcher?" Camila shouted furiously.

"I will explain when I get back," Fletcher said desperately trying to appease her and at the same time shield his eyes from Samantha's accusing look.

"Going to a party is ok, but surely taking another woman with you is the ultimate insult. I will not stand this nonsense Fletcher and I am tired of your lame excuses!" Camila continued feverishly.

"Calm down my love, it's not what you think, just listen to me," pleaded Fletcher Angleton.

"For how long do you think I will stand your fake excuses?" Camila demanded without pausing for breath.

"Look darling, I am serious it's all work-related," he tried to explain lamely.

"I don't know why you forget so soon. Fletcher, do you remember Angelina? You promised me that you'll never involve yourself with other women and here you are hiding from me to satisfy your selfish needs..." her voice broke as she tried to stifle a sob.

"Please my love, don't cry, I will definitely get in touch with you okay, when I am through with this meeting," Fletcher said in desperate tone continuing to fake that it was a business meeting. When she didn't stop sobbing, he hung up the phone, completely at a loss as to what else he could do to quickly sort out this mess.

Fletcher angrily strode towards the large windows in front of him and stared at the streets below. He didn't want to face Samantha when he was still feeling the heat of Camila's accusations. He swore under his breath. 'What a mess this is! I can't blame her though for being so mad with me.' He ran his palm over his forehead to wipe off the thin sheen of sweat that had broken out as a result of his embarrassment and frustration. 'She doesn't need to go through this!' Fletcher looked confused and short of words - the consequence of hasty and selfish decisions. 'Why do I find myself in crappy situations with women all the time?' he thought to himself staring at his cell phone. He tried to console himself that Camila was just being petty and that he would be able to appease her as soon as he got home later that evening. After all, he was an adult who could go out on his own business without having to ask her for permission. He loved Camila but he could sense that all that had happened over the past weeks, together with the mistakes he was constantly making with other women, were drawing them apart slowly. He had to admit, he was still young and handsome, with a constant flow of money and this made him a target of many beautiful women but he also knew deep in the recesses of his heart that he didn't want to lose Camila. He had come to realize that he loved her and that she had a stabilizing effect on him that he desperately needed as a man, not to mention that she was also strikingly beautiful and that any man worth his salt would not want to lose her.

Samantha could tell that Fletcher had blundered with the lady on the phone, whom she suspected very strongly now was the Camila she met him with one time, but she didn't want to be bogged down by the hang-ups she sensed they had. She was determined to have a good time so when he finally turned away from staring out the windows and came to sit with her, she concentrated on talking about anything else but what she had just witnessed. She was determined to have fun with Fletcher today and nothing was going to stop her. She ensured that the shots of Jack Daniels flowed freely; filling glass after glass for Fletcher to get his mind off Camila, and to soften him towards her instead.

It was eleven-thirty at night and despite the hiccup of the phone call earlier, after the free flow of drinks Samantha could finally see that it was turning out to be a lovely Saturday for both of them. The party went on without any further hitches. The food, music and service were delightful. Samantha was also determined that Fletcher would spend the whole night with her even though when she ventured to suggest this, he kept refusing, insisting that he had to go back and 'sort things out with someone'.

"I suppose you're right," she said reluctantly. She knew she was about to lose the fight to get him to stay with her and was quickly thinking of what other means she could use to detain him.

"It's only eleven-forty by my watch," she said looking at the golden watch on her slim wrist. She was not going to give up easily.

"Okay then, tell me what you have in mind," he asked as the warmth of the drinks they had enjoyed caused him to be less inhibited.

"If you are not happy in here, we can go to another club for a short while," she continued coyly as she rubbed her hand up his chest towards his face. Fletcher, I know you introduced me once to your girlfriend called Camila, so I am not trying to come in between you two. I just really enjoy your company and am glad you have spent today with me. Let's not end this too soon," she said huskily placing her small palm on his lap.

He felt torn because he was also attracted to Samantha and no one could deny that she was strikingly beautiful.

"Okay, let's hang around for another hour and then we can call it a night?" he said, the drink taking over the more sane part of his brain.

"Great!" Samantha said a triumphant smile on her full lips.

A slight movement across the room caught Fletcher. He panned his eyes across the room. A smartly dressed man was seated with three other equally smart men, in a corner. A bottle of vodka sat on the table in front of them. There were leftovers of snacks on a tray before them. One of the men turned and looked across at Fletcher. Their eyes met and Fletcher was aghast when he realized who it was. Oh my goodness! It was Dr. Carter of the Radcliffe Referral Hospital, a personal friend of Michael Ashcroft'.

Fletcher Angleton quickly turned his face away. He knew any information on his whereabouts, and the fact that he was in the company of another woman would not go down well with Michael Ashcroft. Frightening thoughts of what happened to him outside Ogaden Night Club not too long ago made him shiver slightly. He could not trust anybody and he suspected very strongly that the attack has something to do with Michael Ashcroft.

He had to leave, and quickly. Raising his head to face Samantha, he unceremoniously and hurriedly ushered her outside with his large hand cupping the small of her back and pushing her slowly to the entrance of the hotel to the camouflage of shadows cast by the flickering neon lights outside the expansive hotel.

"Wow! You are in quite a hurry now," said Samantha teasingly looking up at him. That was when she noticed he was no longer light-hearted and smiling, but actually looked stressed.

"I don't understand all this; what's happening?" she asked confused.

"I will explain when we get to the car," he told her quickly. "You remember I mentioned in there, when we were talking, that I had been attacked by gangsters outside the Ogaden Night Club some weeks back. Well, I just spotted two of the guys who attacked me that night," he lied.

"Why didn't you call the police, you can't let them get away with it?" Samantha asked trying to pull him back into the hotel.

"The case is already with the police and I didn't want to create a scene in front of all those dignitaries at the party," he replied with an element of truth.

"What! But, that's crazy!" she said incredulously.

"You would rather be surprised at what I am choosing to do my dear than hurt by ruthless men when I am around," Fletcher insisted still firmly leading her further away from the group he had seen. Don't worry I will not leave you alone, and in fact we can go wherever you want so long as we are out of this place," he said looking entreatingly at her upturned face.

"Okay, I suppose it's better if we get away from them, especially since you told me the case is still being investigated by the police," said Samantha with her mood lifted slightly by the thought that she would still be with Fletcher for a few more hours. She thought quickly and added, "I had hoped we could go to Gringos, it's about five minutes drive from here and it's a really lively and nice club; three different floors featuring all types of music," she said quickly before he could change his mind.

"Okaaaay," he said the relief bursting into his voice now that they had created some distance between them and the familiar faces he had seen at the hotel.

They soon settled at Gringos and continued with the free flow of drinks and playfulness. Fletcher was finally feeling relaxed. The night was long and the drink and dancing made all thoughts of Camila evaporate into thin air. Her persistent touches, the heat of their bodies and the drop in inhibitions the alcohol brought overcame them, and it was not long before they found themselves in a taxi, rushing to Samantha's.

Sunday started with slight showers and strong gusts of wind. Samantha opened the windows of her one bed roomed flat to let in the cool freshness of the morning before tip-toeing to the bathroom. It was ten o'clock. The fragrance from her floral-scented bathing gel floated out of the steaming shower cubicle and spread around the house. Twenty minutes later, she walked gracefully to her bed, wrapped in a pink towel. She quietly dressed up for the day.

Fletcher Angleton still reeling from the previous nights shenanigans slept on, his dark hair splayed around his eyes. He woke up with a hangover and without the slightest idea where he was. He blinked a number of times, adjusting his bleary eyes to the morning light. He looked around the room like a lost animal trying to determine from the scent around it where it was. He slowly wrapped a towel from the side table next to the bed around his waist and found his way to the bathroom, still feeling very drowsy. He was drawn to the small kitchen by the alluring smell of bacon and scrambled eggs and that is when it all came back to him. He looked over Samantha's tempting, petite figure as she smiled demurely at him as he stood in the entrance to the small kitchen.

"What time is it?" he asked rubbing his hair back and smiling sheepishly at her.

"It's ten forty-five," she answered.

"Oh my days! Why didn't you wake me up?" he said walking past her slowly and grabbing a bacon strip off the sizzling pan. He dropped it into his mouth with his head turned upward. He had suddenly realized how hungry he was.

"Are you late for church," she asked sarcastically.

He laughed nervously as he hugged her against him from behind, trying very hard not to think of what was waiting for him where Camila was concerned.

"Go get your shower and don't take the whole day in there," she told him lifting her arm and holding his cheek against hers so that his head rested on her right shoulder.

"Yup. That's the best thing for me right now," Fletcher said avoiding her searching eyes. "I need to find my way home after breakfast; I had a lot planned for today."

For the first time in his life, Fletcher Angleton felt stabs of regret after realizing how easily he had fallen into the one-night-stand trap. He couldn't understand how he had ended up in Samantha's bed, as last night seemed slightly blurry in his memory. She was beautiful and she knew how to make him happy but he had vowed to Camila, and to himself, never to stray and now he was faced with this blanket of guilt. He needed to get it off his chest. Letting this stray into something more complex would hurt Camila and she was his fiancée. He was already in hot soup for not getting in touch with Camila the whole night. He would have to face that nightmare when he got back to her. There was nothing he could do to undo last night. The milk has been spilt.

He turned towards Samantha before he left for the shower. "You know," he began with guilt and embarrassment creeping up his chest, "you are a special woman but …I am going to be scarce in future, I don't want to hurt you and I don't want to raise your hopes about anything that cannot take place between us," he told her haltingly.

"Come and have your breakfast and we will talk another day", she said shamefacedly, turning to continue with the bacon so that he wouldn't see what she really felt about him. She held his hand and led him to the table.

Fletcher sensed that she wanted to avoid a hurtful and deep discussion about anything. He pulled a chair around the small kitchen table and quickly settled down to try and enjoy the breakfast she had prepared for him. He decided they would have a serious discussion about Camila some other time. The tension soon dissipated and they chit-chatted about everything but what was really bothering him. After breakfast, he took a quick shower. He finally bade her goodbye and left in a taxi to the Gringo's Night Club where he had left his car the night before. He then headed off to see Camila.

Chapter Eleven

Maria Kosgei was the first to get to the office. Its large doors were locked and the concierge in charge of the building was no-where to be seen. For two and a half years she had worked for Michael Angleton with total loyalty and devotion and she was always one of the first to get to the office. It was seven forty-five in the morning and the weather was looking promisingly good.

Leaning on the hood of a parked van outside were three gentlemen and a woman; they talked in low tones while casting glances towards Angleton's office building. A uniformed security guard walked hastily past. He whistled his favourite tune as he disappeared through the open gate to the office corridors. A large bunch of keys dangled from his left hand. Appearing from the left wing, he strode to the main door of the office where Maria had been standing waiting for the office to open for the day. He turned the keys in the office lock and jovially swung the door open for Maria just as Janet Cooper walked in as well and headed to her usual seat by the reception desk.

The lights on the telephone switch board were flashing nonstop indicating that clients and associates of the company were constantly leaving voice messages. As was her duty, Janet Cooper started the day by listening to the messages while taking notes on different note pads, which she would then dispatch to the desks of the individuals they were meant for. She listened with her thick eyebrows slightly furrowed to one voice mail that was constantly repeated and sounded very urgent. It requested an immediate response from Michael Angleton and was from Sergeant Morgan Clifton.

Nine thirty in the morning, Michael Angleton walked into the office looking relaxed. Work had to go on despite all the goings-on surrounding his son. This had stressed him quite a bit over the days, but the night had been restful despite it all. He slowly flipped through the unopened letters in his in-tray as he absentmindedly listened to his voice messages. This was a routine he had carried out at this very desk for over two decades since he started his company.

"Good morning sir," greeted Maria Kosgei walking quietly into her boss's office. She was delivering yet another bundle of letters to his desk.

"Good morning Maria," he acknowledged.

"Tea or coffee?" she asked politely.

"Coffee please," he answered distractedly.

Within the next twenty minutes, people streamed in and out of his office with varying needs that he had to sort out. Sergeant Morgan Clifton entered the office about mid-morning and strode straight to Mr. Angleton's desk. It was clear from his stern demeanour that he had something serious on his mind. He was obviously disturbed by this case surrounding Fletcher. He sensed very strongly that one of the Michaels was guilty, although it was not clear yet who it was, and to what extent. A moment would present itself for him to know the truth and he knew he must wait patiently for it.

"Good morning Mr. Angleton?" Sergeant Clifton said extending his hand.

"Good morning Sergeant Clifton," acknowledged Mr. Angleton.

"Had a busy weekend?" the sergeant asked pulling one of the chairs close to Michael's table and sitting on it without waiting to be invited. He looked up at Michael.

"I can say I was busy because I had to travel to London for a meeting," answered Michael Angleton.

"Well, a few things have happened and I should keep you updated," the sergeant said.

"What's going on?" Michael asked.

"Well, we had to release Jose after our interrogation as, according to the law, we cannot keep him for too long without sufficient evidence. He's out on bail pending further investigations."

"Are you serious?" Mr. Angleton asked in disbelief.

"Yea, we had to let him go. It is the law you know, although I fear he might mess our investigations by contacting the other hooligans who may have been involved in this mess with him," the sergeant went on.

"Crazy mess!" Michael Angleton hissed silently. "Have you informed Mr. Ashcroft about it?"

"I thought it would be wise to let you know before spreading the word to the other party. Other thing is, I told Jose he still needed to report to the police station daily 'till the investigations are over. Also, told him to keep an eye on anybody else he thought was in that group and call me if he happens to see or come across any of them," said Sergeant Morgan, his voice hard.

"Other than Jose, have you found any of the other felons?" Michael asked.

"My officers are still looking for Henry Forbes who's gone into hiding but I understand there is a strong lead on his whereabouts," he answered.

"Okay, keep in touch and don't let that louse out of your sight!" Mr. Angleton said angrily.

"And by the way, do you mind if I call Mr. Ashcroft with the same information?" Sergeant Clifton asked as he turned back to quickly face Michael.

"Do as you wish. I think it's important he should know," Michael answered feigning nonchalance.

Sergeant Morgan Clifton turned slowly and walked towards the door. He left the Angleton office quickly, his mind already on other aspects of the case. The walkway was busy with clients entering and leaving the building, some with files in hand. Outside the door, two young men were having a heated argument. Their loud exchange drew a crowd of passersby. Sergeant Morgan walked past the crowd towards the car park where his unmarked police vehicle was. A soft wind blew and the sun still shone brightly. He got into his car quickly, and smoothly pulled out of the parking area, ignoring the small drama around him.

He scrolled through his contacts on his cell phone, looking for Michael Ashcroft's number. Sergeant Clifton believed in acting quickly when it came to his cases. He needed to inform Michael Ashcroft about Jose Cameron and latest developments. He dialed the number but it rang incessantly with nobody answering. He tried a second time and still there was no response.

Sergeant Clifton decided to give him a few minutes before trying again. He drove to a nearby café for breakfast. It was ten o'clock in the morning.

He had only sat inside the café a few minutes before his cell phone rang; it was Jose Cameron.

"Hello," said Sergeant Clifton as he flipped open his phone and placed it against his ear.

"I found him," replied Jose Cameron in a whisper.

"Found who?" asked the Sergeant mildly. He knew feigning ignorance and unconcern would encourage Jose to tell all. This always worked at the station when they were questioning suspects. He was sure it would work with a scared man like Jose as well.

"I have seen James walking in town with another guy, I think they've entered the big shopping mall by Oakwood Avenue," Jose went on excitedly.

"Who are you talking about, James, and another guy, who are they?" asked the Sergeant.

"James Wilcox, he is the guy who I think knows the whereabouts of Henry Forbes, remember the guy I told you about," Jose gushed with enthusiasm.

"Okay, and what about him, was he involved as well?" the Sergeant asked again.

"I didn't see him that night but I know him as a personal friend of Henry," Jose replied.

"Does he know you personally?" inquired the Sergeant.

"Yes, we know each other and I think he has met with Henry. I think he must know something about what's going on," Jose sounded conspiratorial; a man eager to get off the hook.

"Do this, keep an eye on them both and don't let them see you. Follow them at a distance and don't lose sight of them. I will be there in less than ten minutes. Remember this is to your advantage," the Sergeant said quickly, throwing his change into his pocket and getting up. He was using the carrot and stick technique on Jose this time.

"Okay Sergeant," Jose replied and continued, "But I don't know about the other guy."

"Just keep your eyes open and do not lose their trail, okay?" commanded the Sergeant.

"Okay sir, I will try my best," Jose answered.

It took Sergeant Morgan Clifton thirteen minutes to get to the scene. Two minutes later, James Wilcox walked out of the shopping mall alone, laden with bags of groceries and other goods for his family. Jose Cameron stood at a distance, camouflaged by the crowds of people walking in and out of the mall. He slyly kept an eye on James.

The unsuspecting James Wilcox got the shock of his life when Sergeant Morgan Clifton was suddenly standing before him, holding a police badge close to his face. "I'm Sergeant Morgan Clifton," he said "and I need to ask you a few questions. James had never been involved in any criminal activities, other than the odd drug purchase on a street corner, and under the cover of darkness, and he knew there is no way the sergeant could have known about such indiscretions. He knew he was generally a law-abiding citizen and had nothing to fear, but seeing this hefty, stern-looking Sergeant whip out a police badge and wave it in his face was still very unnerving. He tried to quickly recall and connect the dots regarding recent activities of his close friends to see if there was any shady deal he might be connected to, but nothing came to mind as he had completely forgotten about Henry Forbes. That is, until the name was finally mentioned by the Sergeant.

"I am sorry for the trouble Mr. Wilcox but I need to ask you a few questions about Mr. Henry Forbes, do you know him?" enquired the Sergeant drawing James closer to his car with a firm grip.

"Henry Forbes, I think I know somebody by that name, what about him?" James asked unable to hide a slight tremble of his lips.

"He is wanted by police for questioning in relation to a recent attack on someone, any idea where I can get him?" Sergeant Clifton asked.

"I don't know where he is because it's a long time since I last saw him," James lied.

"What about his home address, care to give it to me?" Clifton asked.

"No idea, never been to his house."

"I have information that you are his closest friend and I have a feeling that you could be lying," said the Sergeant.

"I am telling the truth sir," James said looking around him nervously and noting the questioning glances that shoppers leaving the mall gave him.

"Do you understand that if I find that you are not telling the truth you'll have put yourself in trouble for nothing? You would be considered guilty of obstructing our investigations on a case he might be a suspect in," continued the Sergeant.

"I know that sir," James replied.

"If I find that you are obstructing our investigation by lying, you will find yourself in deep trouble," said the Sergeant again, more ominously.

The exchange was brief, but it was enough to tell Sergeant Clifton that Wilcox was not being straight with him. His many years in the police force enabled the sergeant to pick up on body language that spelt suspicion and guilt. He watched from a distance as James hurried to his car, dumped his groceries quickly onto the back seat, and jumped into the driver's seat. He drove off at a rather high speed. It was clear he was no longer the calm man who had walked out of the supermarket in the mall a short while back; something had triggered this sudden flustered behaviour. A quick thought and Clifton also jumped into his car and sped after Wilcox. He kept a safe distance but did not allow himself to lose sight of James. Before long, Wilcox parked outside his apartment. He however did not go in, but instead walked a few blocks ahead to a public phone booth by the kerb side. His mind was still churning after his meeting with Clifton that he did not even notice the policeman a short distance away from him. Clifton had guessed that if Henry Forbes was in the house, it would take them only a short while before they communicated and planned what they would do if they were summoned to the station. He was right. Henry Forbes was in the house enjoying a bottle of Budweiser in the company of Pamela Wilcox who was listening sympathetically to his tales of woe. Little did they know that the sergeant had made a few quick calls and shortly after they had gotten to James' neighbourhood there was already a back-up team in place - a search warrant at the ready. The telephone in the house rang and Pamela Wilcox answered; it was her husband calling from the nearby telephone booth.

"Hello," Pamela answered the phone.

"Hey it's me dear; is Henry still in the house?" Wilcox asked his wife, trying to sound as if nothing disconcerting had happened.

"Yes he is here, do you want to speak to him?" she asked.

"Give him the phone please my love," James replied quietly so as not to get her suspicious.

"What's up man?" Henry asked holding the receiver against his ear.

"No questions; just try and get out of the house as soon as you can; police are looking for you and they think I know where you are," said Wilcox, stammering from the effort of trying to warn his friend quickly.

"But how did they know I am here man?" Henry asked in shock.

"I told you no questions, I was stopped by a plain-clothed police officer at the mall a few moments ago, and he was sure that I might know of your whereabouts," James replied.

"Okay but where do I go now?" Henry asked worried. "Let me get my stuff and I will let Pamela know where I have decided to run to," Henry said putting the phone down and swivelling to face Pamela.

Before he hung up the door bell rang and since Pamela was close to the door, she flung it open thinking it was someone James had sent.

Three uniformed police officers entered flashing their badges. One was holding out a search warrant, and in an instant they were reading Henry his rights. It all happened so fast that Pamela and Henry just stood staring in shock -- like deer in the glare of headlights. The atmosphere was tense and the action by the policemen swift. Pamela and Henry barely had a second to think of what to do. In an instant Henry was handcuffed, read his rights, and being bundled into a police car.

It was now evident that the war was on; a caution message was left for Mr. James Wilcox to report to the police station the soonest possible to record a statement. As the boys in blue left, Pamela Wilcox was left alone in the house crying. It was too much stress for her in her pregnant state and she felt totally violated by the way the police had barged into her house to arrest Henry. Her heart was beating wildly long after the police had left, and she felt slightly dizzy.

The light wind outside belied the scorching summer sun. People went about their business and children cackled and ran about oblivious to the drama that had taken place in Wilcox' house. An ice-cream van was parked nearby surrounded by children screaming out their choices to their sweaty, disgruntled parents. The Asian vendor had been at this same corner for decades and demand for his multicoloured ice lollies, scoops and cups was still booming. His perpetual grin and high-pitched "you want this one no?" attracted one pound after another from the children's chubby and eager fingers. He smiled as he dropped each coin into the dirty, back pocket of his overalls.

Brighton was known to be a quiet city where people went about their business without much ado. Family feuds were unheard of, especially among the high and mighty families in the houses that peppered the affluent area. Politicians and civil leaders were respected by the society and even the younger generations knew that families kept their dirty linen well hidden from other families. Societal divides, such as between the Muslims and Christians did not affect the fact that they did business with each other without a problem, and whenever there was a community activity, all the people worked towards its success. Of course, there never lacked a few disputes here and there, but every aspect was resolved harmoniously by the respected leaders in the neighbourhood.

The way the police cars had surrounded Pamela's home therefore, and barged in waving their badges, had embarrassed her greatly as she had seen that a number of people had stopped to watch the peculiar drama. She decided to lie down on her bed after the incident and wait for James to explain what was going on after he got home from the mall.

Mr. Ashcroft was sitting in his office when he received an intercom message from his secretary,

"Sergeant Morgan Clifton is on line two," she said respectfully and hanged up the phone.

"Michael Ashcroft speaking," Michael said as he put the phone to his ear.

"It's Sergeant Clifton, I need to see you urgently," said the Sergeant.

"Is it about the case?" Michael asked.

"Yes, by the way we need to meet on this; you know it's not good to speak on phone regarding case details. I think I have told you this before, you never know who's listening," the Sergeant said quietly.

"What do you suggest sergeant?" Mr. Ashcroft asked.

"Let's meet at the Italian-owned pub off Victoria Road opposite the Shell petrol station, preferably after five-thirty," proposed Sergeant Clifton.

"Okay five-thirty on the dot."

There was a faint knock on the office door before it swung open and Linda Ashcroft walked in followed by her daughter Camila. Typically they did not need any clearance from the receptionist; their visits were assumed to be part of official business. Feeling at home, Camila moved about her father's big office, tidying up files and dossiers that lined the cabinets, and gently wiping any dust hidden in the shelf crevices as she waited for her father to finish with the phone.

Linda sat opposite her husband. After his phone call, they began to talk in low tones on business and domestic chores that needed her husband's attention. As usual, Mr. Ashcroft listened patiently without interrupting. He simply nodded from time-to-time to let her know he was listening; something he had learned from many years of his marriage to her. His mind was elsewhere however, and today he wished they would just leave him to attend to his affairs. As time went by, Linda pulled out from her handbag a cheque book. She handed it over to her husband.

"I need to pay for the last months supplies," she said pushing the cheque book across the shiny, mahogany desk.

"Come on sweetheart, this figure is too high, what was that you bought? Twenty seven thousand pounds is quite dear you know," Michael said smiling temperately.

"These are old debts; I was too busy I forgot", she replied.

"That's okay, where is the invoice?" Michael asked.

Linda rifled through the many pockets and crevices of her handbag; they had agreed many years ago that her husband could not sign any cheque without the supporting documents, which he would file in the office. It was an unspoken understanding now, a family's governing policy. Yet here she was, totally unable to find the darn invoice in the handbag. It was not there, she finally had to admit, clicking her tongue with frustration, and it was all her mistake, and she couldn't remember where it was.

"So?" asked Mr. Ashcroft.

"Well, I don't have it and I can't remember where I put it," she said feeling foolish as this was something she always tried to avoid.

"If you find it, bring it to the house and I will sign the cheque for you. Meanwhile call the suppliers and tell them you'll settle their bills tomorrow," Michael said matter-of-factly reclining on his swivel chair and taking a deep breath. Linda nodded understandingly and stuffed the cheque book back into her bag. She understood he was just trying to avoid trouble with the auditors in future, and she had come to respect him for insisting on such issues. She turned and removed a file from the cabinet above him and started to leaf through it slowly. There was a document she needed in order to respond to another customer's request adequately and she decided to focus on that for now.

All this while Camila was reading a tabloid she had bought downstairs at a newspaper stand close to the office building. The headline had grabbed her attention and she couldn't resist buying it although she wasn't really a tabloid lady. She preferred the more serious and analytical journalistic pieces in the Guardian and the New York times. She had been standing by the window a distance from her parents turning the large pages slowly. She had come with her mother because she had a few things to talk about with her father, but she realized that it was not the right time to do so. She noticed the look of frustration on her mother's face, and one thing she had learned from an early age was never to interrupt her parents when they were having business discussions. Fletcher was constantly on her mind though. She knew that he had lied to her when he came to her house yesterday to explain where he had disappeared to the night before. She didn't believe the yarn he told but unfortunately it was his word against hers because she had no evidence to implicate him in anything shady. Not yet anyway!

After Linda had finished with the file and had found the document she had been looking for, she turned back to her husband. He sat forward and pulled a seat closer to her, patting it slightly so that she could know he wanted her to sit down and listen. He felt he needed to tell her about Jose Cameron.

Linda sat down and they continued to talk in low tones. Michael told her of the fact that Jose had now been released from custody, and he also told her about the meeting with Sergeant Morgan Clifton and what they had discussed. She could tell that he was not at peace about their meeting or that Jose was no longer at the station. He also let her know that he was expecting to be late getting home that evening.

It was normal for Mr. Ashcroft to inform his wife whenever he had other activities he needed to attend to other than his official work. Linda knew her husband would not rest until the whole Jose case was resolved. She could see this whole business was stressing him, what she didn't know was that he was also struggling with a lot of guilt and it was taking its toll on him. He needed to think of a way of getting Jose Cameron to come to a meeting, and he needed to know how to go about this by the end of the day.

Linda Ashcroft and her daughter finally left the big office as quietly as they had come. They left Mr. Ashcroft to ponder the burning issues alone. The drive back home didn't take long as the Range Rover roared through the streets with ease. They both enjoyed the soft music from the stereo in the large dashboard. It was also getting warmer as the day got older. The time was one o'clock.

———————

Pamela Wilcox sat alone on the sofa set with tears of anger uncontrollably rolling down her face. Several attempts to get hold of her husband proved fruitless because his cell phone was switched off. A stomach cramp sent spasms through her swollen belly. She writhed helplessly in pain, craving a glass of water. Forcing herself to stand up slowly, she walked a few steps towards the kitchen before her weak legs gave way. She fell with wide frightened eyes near the kitchen door. She looked frantically at the phone hanging on the wall but it was out of her reach. The images around her started to fade and became like distant stars and the little energy she had left in her frail body finally slipped away. With a gasp, her raised head fell to the cold floor and she lost consciousness.

Thirty minutes later, James Wilcox walked through the back door of his two bed roomed flat hoping nobody would see him entering the house. He had never lived with fear because he had not done anything terribly criminal in his somewhat mundane life. He was only afraid because of his association with Henry. That was a reality he had to grapple with and it had definitely gotten him into a lot of trouble already.

With his grocery bags well tucked under his arm, he passed through the unlocked back door leading to the kitchen. He called out to Pamela in a loud voice but there was no response. Wondering about the silence, Wilcox placed the grocery bags on kitchen table and walked towards the sitting room. His heart stopped when he blindly stumbled upon his wife lying on the floor, unconscious. "Oh my goodness!" he said in a loud voice, staring at his wife lying helplessly on the floor.

"What happened here?" he shouted kneeling down next to his wife.

He was shocked and afraid. Pamela was pale and cold, her clothes clang to her shivering body after sweating excessively. She was highly dehydrated and there was some blood between her legs. Her breathing was slow. Something serious had happened and James could tell that she had been hurt. He quickly called for an ambulance. Gently, he lifted his ailing wife from the floor and placed her tenderly on the sofa before placing a wet towel across her forehead. He was worried and scared and the possibility of her having a miscarriage was too terrible a thought for him to think about. He sat down next to her as he waited for the ambulance and rubbed her limp hand gently.

'Why did I allow this man to stay in my house for crying out loud?' Wilcox wondered to himself. 'This is why all these terrible things are happening to us. But, surely somebody had to be there for Henry, and he has always helped me before whenever I was in a fix. But I don't deserve this. It's too much to bear. Why my wife for goodness sake?' he thought to himself angrily as he waited for the medics who seemed to be taking a lifetime.

Tears of hate and dejection dripped down his face; he knew he was dealing with double tragedy. His fate was unclear, but caring for Pamela was his first priority, regardless of what the future would bring their way. He was jolted out of his reverie seven minutes later by the sound of a siren as an ambulance approached their house. It was approaching at an incredible speed towards their front door. James placed Pamela careful back on the sofa and flung the door open as he waved at the ambulance driver and directed the medics to his doorstep. As it stopped, two of them jumped out of the back and pulled a long stretcher that they held between them as they rushed in through the front door. They quickly strapped Pamela onto the stretcher and lifted her into the ambulance just as fast. This was something they had been trained to do in two minutes flat. They strapped an oxygen mask onto her pale face and allowed James to sit in the back of the ambulance with them as they rushed to the hospital. They drove fast to Radcliffe Referral Hospital where a team of Emergency Unit personnel rushed to meet them and wheel Pamela inside for emergency treatment. James watched helplessly as they waved him away from the doors of the accident and emergency room.

Chapter Twelve

Dr. Carter was off duty and was therefore spending most of the day on the golf course. He loved every minute of it when he had the upper hand. Golf was a pastime that helped him deal with any stress he had from work. Monday was also a good day for him to play as the course was not crowded; most people preferred to start the week in the office. There were therefore few players around.

He was alone with a middle-aged Asian man who seemed to have a knack for golf too. Dr Carter wanted to enjoy a good round with him. Though Mr. Singh was an excellent player, Carter gave him a run for his money at every hole.

"I have been playing golf for a while now and I feel euphoric anytime my ball finds its target. It's the most exciting feeling in the world! By the way, we've been playing together but I didn't introduce myself, my name is Manjitt Singh".

"I am Dr. Carter, work at the Radcliffe Referral Hospital," replied Dr. Carter offering his hand.

"Is this your regular course?" Manjitt asked bending down to retrieve his golf ball from the hole.

"I do come here quite often, but mostly on weekends," answered Dr. Carter.

"You seem to be a good player. One of these days we should link up and have a proper challenge on this course, what do you think?" Manjitt proposed.

"Sure enough, I will be here on Saturday with a colleague and if you can avail yourself that would be brilliant," Carter replied.

"That sounds good, I will bring my business partner along to make it more exciting," Manjitt said.

Dr. Carter had been distracted throughout the game. His mind seemed elsewhere and he had this niggling feeling that something was very wrong, but he couldn't put his finger on what it was. He couldn't seem to concentrate on the game as enjoyable as it always was to see that he was assured of a win. In the past, whenever such feelings crept over him, he would find that something bad had happened to a friend or to a family member. He wondered whether this was some sort of premonition. He wanted to call it a day on the golf course and wondered what excuse he would give Manjitt. Walking on towards the sixteenth hole, he pretended everything was normal as they talked about political issues. It was approaching four o'clock when his cell phone rang.

———————————

Michael Ashcroft sat on his desk waiting for his meeting with Sergeant Morgan Clifton. His work at the office was starting to slide because this case was distracting him and taking a lot of his time to try and sort out. This frustrated him as he always liked to be focused while working at the office and wanted to set the highest standards possible. This distraction with Jose meant that his performance at work was also affected. He pursed his lips as he swore to himself that he was not ready to let go of his business empire because of an error that simply magnified itself due to the carelessness of Jose Cameroon. 'What do I do now', he thought 'I need to know how to deal with this psychopath son of a mongrel,' he thought to himself angrily as he took off his gold-rimmed spectacles. His meeting with Sergeant Clifton was fast approaching and he had no idea what he was going to tell the Sergeant. He needed more time to think about this with a friend, but whom?

'Yes!' He remembered his good old friend Dr. Carter. Every time he had a problem where a solution was not forthcoming, he would turn to him for advice. This was definitely one of those moments when they had to put their minds together. Dr. Carter was the way to go. Michael hurriedly picked up his cell phone and dialed the number that was etched in his memory.

"Hello," Dr. Carter answered.

"Don't tell me you are busy today," Michael started.

"Is that Michael, Ashcroft?" Dr. Carter asked waving his hand to Manjitt Singh to give him a few minutes before he got back to the game.

"Yup, it's me," Mr. Ashcroft answered. "Tell me…what's up?" Carter asked walking towards the hilly edge of the golf course.

"I need to see you today at about six o'clock," Michael said without being too assertive.

"Is everything okay?" Carter asked with curious tone.

"Well, generally everything is okay but there are a few things I need to sort out with Sergeant Clifton," Michael said.

"Well, I am having a round of golf with a local gentleman down here but I think that time will be appropriate for me. Today is my day off and I don't mind a few drinks later," said Dr. Carter.

"Okay, let's meet at the Italian-owned pub off Victoria road," Michael suggested.

"Which one is that?" Dr. Carter asked.

"That's the one opposite the Shell petrol station up the hill."

"Yes, I know it. You said around six o'clock?"

"Exactly," Michael said and hanged up.

After this brief conversation with Mr. Ashcroft, Dr. Carter stood on the golf course with different thoughts going through his mind. He knew about Fletcher from the hospital, and that Jose was one of the suspects taken to the police station for interrogation. After Michael's call, Dr. Carter could not help thinking about Jose Cameron and how he had served Mr. Ashcroft with devotion. He couldn't understand what had gone wrong between Jose and his boss, and he couldn't for the life of him decide who among the two was responsible for the mishap on Fletcher. Being Michael Ashcroft's close friend meant Carter was biased against Jose. He and Michael went a long way and they had done all kinds of deals together. They were used to covering up for each other, even when some of their deals went awry. He didn't know what to expect from their impending meeting. Mr. Ashcroft was highly unpredictable and could be impulsive at times.

Looking at his wrist watch, Dr. Carter raised his hand to beckon to his companion who was also busy talking on his cell phone. Manjitt raised his head and looked up to the bright skies while shielding his eyes from the sharp sun rays. A cool, gentle wind cascaded from the hills across the horizon bringing with it some energy that boosted their desire to continue with the game. Dr. Carter shrugged the thoughts of what was happening between Michael and Jose and picked his golf club to continue the game. The two had really nothing to do with him and whatever they decided to do with each other was honestly none of his business. He needed to enjoy this free time with his newfound friend before his meeting with Ashcroft later on at the inn.

Manjitt Singh suddenly brought on his teeing proficiency and started to dominate in the wins, leaving Dr. Carter looking like an amateur in the field. Manjitt found it hard to conceal his joy. He had a permanent smile on his face.

"I see the big smile on your face," teased Dr. Carter in a rough voice.

"Don't try and distract me," replied Manjitt smiling all the more.

"I can bet this will be my round, just wait and see," Dr. Carter said swinging his golf club.

"Never count your chicks before they hatch, look at that, the worst shot you've had in a couple of rounds," Manjitt was pointing at a thicket nearby into which Dr. Carter's golf ball had drifted. There was no denying he would continue to win this game.

"Oh my God, did you see that? I tell you what! You caused that," Carter rebuffed chuckling as he walked towards the thicket.

The two gentlemen had already developed a good rapport with each other, so they promised to meet for another game soon. It was getting late so they parted with a handshake and headed in different directions.

There was still an hour left before the scheduled meeting with Michael Ashcroft so Dr. Carter decided to drive home for a quick shower and to change his golf outfit for something more casual. As a divorced man, his expansive house, though impressive from the outside, had different items scattered all over the seats in his living room. He dashed upstairs undisturbed by the mess. The meeting with Ashcroft was important.

Michael had arranged two meetings at the same place; he needed to kill two birds with one stone.

Sergeant Clifton was the first to arrive at the Italian pub seven minutes before the time agreed. He sat in a secluded corner and asked for a bottle of Budweiser from the waitress who was walking about the lounge attending to different patrons. It was a popular joint and free seats were hard to come by. The lights were low and the shadowy ambiance made it difficult to see the faces of the other patrons. He wondered whether Ashcroft would be there on time.

Five thirty on the dot, Michael Ashcroft strode majestically into the pub heading straight to the low-lit bar. He turned his head in every direction looking for the Sergeant.

"Double Jack Daniels please with coke," requested Mr. Ashcroft.

"Do you need ice on it?" asked the bar tender.

"Yes please," he replied glancing into the dark corners of the spacious lounge.

He handed a five pound note to the bartender. Holding his drink between his fingertips, he moved aside to create space for other patrons. The place was as packed as it was every evening. From the corner of his eye he spotted a sizeable figure sitting down in a corner reading and taking notes in a pocket diary with a sleek ink pen. He blinked to sharpen his vision. It was Sergeant Morgan Clifton.

With his hand extended, Mr. Ashcroft walked to the table and sat directly opposite the Sergeant. They shook hands

"Need another one like that?" Michael asked pointing to the almost empty bottle of Budweiser.

"Well, my shift is over for today so who am I to say no?" answered the Sergeant.

Michael Ashcroft looked around for a waitress to send for Clifton's drink but they were all running around, busy serving the other patrons. He decided to concentrate on the Jose issue with the sergeant.

Their conversation started on the mundane issues of the day before they got down to the business that brought them to the table. Sergeant Morgan Clifton was sceptical about the idea that was being floated by Mr. Ashcroft. His many years in the Force made him cautious about agreeing with any plans that encouraged an evasion of what was lawful. The idea of dropping the Jose case was not something he would agree with easily.

Jose Cameron, his most valued witness, had finally told Clifton about Ashcroft's involvement in Fletcher's debacle. He had also mentioned that he had not told anyone else about this until he had mentioned it to Clifton. It was obvious Ashcroft was afraid of the outcome of the case. Just talking about it made a light sheen of sweat break out on his forehead as they continued with their talk. Clifton refused to budge despite Ashcroft's persistence.

"I don't think it will be fair for us to dismiss this case without the involvement of Mr. Angleton," insisted Sergeant Clifton firmly.

"I know but what do you think his reaction will be if Angleton gets to know of my involvement?" Michael asked.

"Well it's not going to go down easy, but you have already involved us at the station, so you can't change that".

"That's true but it's not too late to think of what to do," Michael replied.

"The only thing I can do is to delay the investigation and hopefully we will eventually lose track of witnesses and some important details on the case, but don't forget we have Henry Forbes in our custody," said the Sergeant.

"Who is Henry Forbes?" Michael asked.

"He is one of those guys who assaulted Fletcher Angleton," the sergeant replied.

"You mean you've gone that far with the case?" Michael asked surprised.

"Yeah, that's why I told you it will be very hard for me to throw this case out of the window," retorted the Sergeant.

"But he doesn't know anything about me?" Michael asked in a hoarse voice.

"I don't know yet, I will interrogate him tomorrow and that's when I will gather as much information as possible," Clifton answered honestly.

"Please keep in touch with me and don't disclose this to my friend Angleton," Michael said wiping his spectacle lenses.

"Let's keep this between us," Michael curling two fingers up and down to show the quote sign before beckoning to a passing waitress for the bill.

They had talked at length evaluating all facets of the Jose case. All this time Michael did not mention Dr. Carter to the Sergeant because he hoped he would be gone by the time Carter arrived. But, they had gotten carried away talking about the case and all the other things going on in their lives that it got to seven o'clock before they knew it. Fortunately, the lounge area was large enough, and dark enough for him to meet with two different people, without any of them being the wiser.

The sergeant finally left promising that he would see how to help Michael Ashcroft out of the fix.

Michael turned and slowly walked around the bar looking for Dr. Carter. He knew it was way over the time they had agreed to meet and he wasn't even sure that the doctor would still be waiting for him this late. How did he know that he would take that long with the sergeant anyway? He hoped the doctor hadn't given up. As he rounded the final dark space in the bar lounge, he spotted the doctor waving down a harried waitress for a drink.

"Hi doc," said Michael "I am sorry to have kept you so long, too many people I have bumped into today. I am glad you didn't give up on our meeting. I really needed to talk to you and it's great to see you," said Michael patting the doctor on the back apologetically while pulling a chair quickly closer to him.

"Well, you definitely have taken a long time," said the doctor gruffly. "If I didn't know that this was important to you I would have left a long time ago".

"I know…sorry about that, let me buy you the next few drinks to make it up to you," said Michael in a conciliatory tone.

After a few drinks and a few more apologies the doctor finally relaxed and they settled down to talk about what was bothering Michael. The music filtered incessantly from the speakers that were strategically placed around the corners of the lodge, together with the increasingly loud chatter from the patrons. It was enough noise to hide what they talked about in low tones as they tried to figure out a fool-proof plan of how best to eliminate the evidence from Jose Cameron without raising any suspicion. Leaning closer to Dr. Carter who was seated directly opposite him, Michael Ashcroft expounded his plan without missing out any detail, while watching his friend's face tensely to see what his reaction would be.

"Michael, you'll never cease to amaze, why on earth would you think of that for goodness sake?" asked Dr. Carter astonished.

"Ever since I was a small boy, I always loathed the idea of ending a feud in this kind of a set-up and thank God I never said a word about it to the Sergeant, I know it's not one of the best things to do but I also need to protect my social standing," Michael Ashcroft's said defensively.

"Only two things I will assure you of, first of all, you don't have to worry about me because what you have just shared will never leave my mouth, and secondly you are my friend, but please count me out!" Dr. Carter was determined not to be part of what he had just heard.

"I need you in on this Doctor," said Michael before adding conspiratorially as he glanced up and about him, "remember what happened to George Franklin three years ago, a very successful entrepreneur who was a pain in the ass to your cousin, the guy who was trying to harm your business?" Michael could see immediately that this was not a memory the doctor liked being brought up, so he took advantage of the doctor's discomfort. "If you've forgotten I can refresh your mind a bit," said Ashcroft. "He came to see you at the hospital for a simple medical checkup and what happened, the poor guy never woke up the following morning. He was as dead as a dodo and you remember the cause of death huh?' Michael continued peering into the doctor's eyes accusingly. "Do you remember an overdose of some concoction that you administered Doctor?" Michael continued, "Do you remember how you got away with it? We had dinner with the investigating officer at the Hilton Hotel and of cause you know what happened because you were there, money exchanged hands and that file was closed, case over." All this time Michael Ashcroft was speaking in a whisper looking directly in the eyes of Dr. Carter without blinking.

"What do you want me to do?" Carter asked unable to push away memories that inundated his mind. The nightmares had never stopped after that incident but Dr. Carter had kept this to himself. Michael's bringing it all up again made it all the more difficult.

"Well, that louse must be silenced," Michael insisted while placing his spectacles on the table.

The idea was simple and devious. They both knew it could be done but neither of them was prepared to deal the possible repercussions. This was murder they were talking about. They talked with their heads close together, urgently trying to weigh the pros and cons of their scheme. They wondered how to bait Jose Cameron to meet with them. Carter knew he had to help Michael; there was too much to lose if he didn't. They decided to meet after two days at Hotel Trefontana, eight o'clock on the dot, with each coming up with a plan that they could get away with. They vowed to keep this to themselves. The doctor was also eager to bury the ghosts of the past. They had agreed that Michael would never bring up the Franklin incident again after getting rid of Jose.

The idea weighed heavily on Dr. Carter's mind even as the dew fell lightly on the grass when he awoke the next morning. He remembered the events of three years back. He could never forget what happened and he hated himself for being such easy prey to his cousin, who lured him into poisoning George Franklin for the sake of protecting somebody else's business interests. No matter how hard he tried to move on with life, he was always haunted by what had happened that fateful night. He would feel a toxic mix of guilt and shame for he knew what had happened had been driven by someone else's greed. Tossing alone on his double bed, he hated the fact that Mr. Ashcroft was now using the same nightmarish event from his past to get him to deal permanently with Jose. He hated the fix he found himself in but he knew he had no means of escape until the deal was done.

Michael Ashcroft got to his house some minutes past eleven o'clock that night. His wife Linda had just gone to bed leaving Camila downstairs glued to the television set. She was watching a wildlife documentary on the National Geographic channel, about the sprawling Masai Mara Game

Reserve in Kenya. She had been there a number of times on holiday and watching the documentary also reminded her of the times when her parents used to visit the resort when she was a young girl. She turned when her father opened the door to the house and came in.

"Hi," he greeted his daughter.

"Hi dad," she acknowledged with a smile.

"It's quite unusual for you to be alone in the sitting room, where is your mum?" he asked after taking off his coat and hanging it on the hook next to the main door.

"She went to bed a few minutes ago. Can I warm some food, you hungry?" she asked him modestly.

"That will be kind of you my dear; I haven't had anything to eat the whole day. I'm starved," he replied.

"You look a little tipsy too today dad. Today's Monday. It's rare for you to be drinking early in the week," she commented perceptively as she walked towards the kitchen.

"Sometimes it happens when everyone you want to see asks for a meeting in a pub," he answered evasively as he tried to laugh off her curious question.

After the meal, Mr. Ashcroft and his daughter chatted on different topics before she suddenly asked him about the thorny issue of Jose Cameron and the progress of the investigations.

"I understand Jose is out on bail?" she started.

"How did you know," asked Mr. Ashcroft surprised.

"Come on dad, I have friends around," she said without naming names.

"I think you should have been a detective. Okay, how did you come to know about it?" he asked smiling.

"A friend of mine bumped into him in town," she replied.

"Anyway, it's true. He's out because according to the law the police are not supposed to hold a suspect in custody for more than two weeks without charging him with a crime, so they couldn't keep him in there any longer without hard evidence that proved he was involved with what happened to Fletcher," he answered. "No wonder they say the Law's a donkey,...or something like that."

"And any idea what will happen next?" she asked again.

"I understand he will be reporting daily to the police station until the case is determined," her father replied.

"So they still have not established the person who assaulted Fletcher?" she continued.

"Their investigations are quite spread out now and Sergeant Morgan Clifton told me they've got another guy by the name Henry Forbes in custody and I think he is the main suspect," Michael Ashcroft answered while trying to keep a straight face.

"I spoke with Fletcher this afternoon and he told me that he was going to see Sergeant Clifton at the police station," Camila said innocently to her father.

"Oh…really? Well, let's wait and see what happens. The matter is with the police, so there is nothing we can do, and there's no need to speculate," her father said as he made to get up and head to his bedroom. He was trying to discourage Camila from prying too much about Jose and the case. However, Camila was reluctant to let him go so he sat down again as she went on.

"But dad, something is a bit fishy here, why is everyone so concerned with this case. It's hanging around everyone's neck like an albatross. What's really going on dad?" she probed inquisitively.

Michael deftly changed the subject at an opportune moment and it wasn't long before he noticed she was getting sleepy.

It was well past midnight when Camila stood up and bid her father good night promising to see him the next morning before he left for work. Although he tried to persuade her to stay on and spend the night with them in their house she declined and left for her apartment. She left her father deep in thought as he sat alone on the sofa. It was a safe neighbourhood so he was never afraid when she insisted on driving back to her own apartment even late at night. He finally decided to go upstairs and join his wife in bed.

Though he tossed and turned thinking of how he was relying too heavily on his staff to carry out his business because of the attention he was paying to the Jose case, he finally fell asleep totally exhausted and pressed against his wife's warm back.

Chapter Thirteen

Dawn was breaking as Michael Angleton, his wife Lesley, and their son Fletcher Angleton sat quietly at their dining table having breakfast. The curtains on the large windows facing the large and scenic backyard were drawn. Outside, the sky was grey, embracing dark clouds that threatened to unleash a downpour. As usual, the weather guys were wrong, having predicted sunny spells. It was going to be a gloomy day, and even the sparrows' search for insects proved futile due to the frequent showers. The plan was to visit the sergeant today, and none of them were looking forward to the meeting.

Sitting alone in his office, Sergeant Morgan Clifton was busy scrutinizing the statement Jose Cameron had written at the station earlier, about the incident outside the Ogaden Night Club. It was puzzling because Jose did not mention, even once, that his boss had anything do with the ambush on Fletcher.

Yet, Clifton, could distinctly remember Jose saying that Mr. Ashcroft had asked him to punish Fletcher Angleton for his unbecoming behaviour regarding Camila. He had said that Ashcroft was incensed by Fletcher's habit of propositioning harlots in the dark Brighton streets, especially because Fletcher seemed to show no remorse.

According to Jose Cameron, the actions of Henry Forbes and his cahoots was regrettable and whatever actions they took was beyond what Ashcroft had asked for. As Clifton mulled over the statement, he found himself in a predicament because, though this case could lead to rivalry between two powerful families, each of the men involved was growing more trusting of

Clifton. It was this growing friendship that was increasingly disturbing. He was in a tight corner indeed.

The door leading to his office was not closed, the receptionist's desk was clearly visible and he could see a man leaning over the counter talking with a police officer there. Clifton's desk phone started ringing; it was from the reception.

"Sergeant Clifton," he answered.

"You have visitors here who would like to see you, can I send them in?" asked the woman at the reception desk.

"Do you know who they are?" asked the Sergeant.

"Yea, Mr. Angleton, with his wife, and son," she replied.

"It's okay, you can send them in," the sergeant said and hanged up the phone.

The expectations were high from the Angleton's family; neither of them knew that Jose had been released on bail pending investigations, and in their minds, they were expecting a hearing in court would have been arranged by the Sergeant by now. That was not to be. The Sergeant slowly and carefully brought them up to speed, and explained what had happened regarding Jose's case.

Michael wondered quietly to himself how Sergeant Clifton could have released a prime suspect in the Fletcher case knowing that Jose could very well disappear completely. What exactly was going on between the Sergeant and Jose? Henry and the other louts were only accessories to what had transpired that night at Ogaden Night Club, so how could the prime suspect be let loose so easily. Michael Angleton wanted all these questions answered but following the straight and narrow didn't seem to be helping him get to the bottom of the case. He needed revenge and the Sergeant was not the one to help him get it he thought to himself. A lot of time had been wasted already trying to let the law take its course. He was becoming surer by the minute that another route had to be taken to ensure that those who had tried to harm Fletcher would not get away with it. He decided to keep what he was thinking to himself.

"I think you are now all updated on the developments of this case," started the Sergeant clearing his throat in slight embarrassment as it was clear his visitors were not satisfied with the steps that the police had taken so far.

"Have any of those two guys told you the motive of the attack?" asked Fletcher Angleton who had been listening attentively.

"According to Jose, he personally didn't know why those guys attacked you and he seemed both remorseful and very sorry about it all," explained Sergeant Clifton with a lot of reservation.

"But you are sure about this other guy, what did you say his name was?" asked Lesley Angleton.

"His name is Henry Forbes and I am sure he was involved, that is why we had to get him before he thought of running away, or of warning the other culprits," he answered nodding his head with confidence.

"One thing I don't understand Sergeant is that if you are that sure about it, why have you not taken this Henry to court since you arrested him?" the expression on Michael Angleton's face was stern as he asked.

"There are some things that we still need to do before we can take him to court. I haven't had time yet to interrogate this Forbes guy to the extent that I wish because we only got him yesterday. He is one fellow I believe will give us the names of the other three guys who were involved in this crazy act," Sergeant Clifton responded without giving too much information.

"Have you informed Mr. Ashcroft about these new developments?" asked Michael Angleton.

"We haven't met so far but I will let him know if he calls," the sergeant lied.

"Let him not know that we were here following up the leads," Angleton suggested.

"I need to see this louse called Henry," hissed Fletcher quietly.

"You don't have to curse," his mother who was sitting next to her son reminded, prodding him with an elbow as she gave him a disapproving glance. As his mother, his age didn't matter when it came to discouraging foul language.

"Sorry mum, I am just so frustrated by this whole mess!" he responded scowling.

"Is there any chance we can see this Henry, or whatever his name is?" Lesley asked.

"At this stage it is a bit early for that," Clifton answered.

"So according to you, Jose Cameron was not involved, he just happened to be there with those hooligans and now he is a free man. Don't you think he can try to get in touch with the rest of them and warn them of imminent arrest?" Fletcher Angleton asked.

"He vowed to cooperate with us by reporting here every day until otherwise advised," replied the Sergeant and we don't have anything to show that he will not keep his word. We always have to be careful with detaining someone at the station for longer than the law allows; the stipulated two weeks, unless we have hard evidence to prove that his release will lead to endangerment of others, or escape of the culprit.

"That means I will have to stay indoors because those louts can attack me again," Fletcher retorted angrily.

"You don't have to worry, I warned him if anything was to happen to you, he will be considered the prime suspect and that is enough to deter him from trying anything funny," replied the Sergeant.

The exchange was not ending. Michael Angleton felt that the case was not being handled properly by letting Jose loose despite the fact that he was definitely around during the attack on Fletcher. He wondered whether Mr. Ashcroft was involved in the latest turn of events, especially since Jose had been his employee. Fletcher was dating Camila but this had never led to any animosity between the well respected families. The more he thought about it, the more strongly Mr. Angleton determined to have his way with this case, no matter the dirty tricks he might have to resort to. Justice had to be done, for his sake and for Fletcher's. Whoever was behind this would be punished. He sensed very strongly that the sergeant had been compromised in some way, but there was no way he could prove it.

It was thirteen minutes past ten o'clock when Michael Angleton arrived at his office. The tray on his desk was stacked with letters and internal memos. Maria Kosgei came into his office about five minutes after his arrival to hand him an additional memo. She stopped suddenly and stared at him in astonishment. She had never before seen her boss slumped over his desk with his eyes closed She turned and rushed to Janet Cooper's desk.

"Janet, I don't know whether to panic, but it's quite unusual for Mr. Angleton to be slumped over his desk in such a manner, and definitely not at this early hour of the morning. Come and have a look." There was concern etched on Maria's face.

"Is his breathing okay?" Janet Cooper asked.

"I never went close enough to check. I was passing by his desk and thought it was unusual that he should be sitting in that manner. I just turned around immediately to come and call you," Maria replied.

"It's less than ten minutes since he came in, that is strange," said Janet.

"You know he trusts you more than anybody else in here. Let's not waste time Janet," Maria's insistence persuaded Janet to get up and walk with her to Michael's office quickly to check what could be up.

"Let's go and see what is going on," she said.

Janet Cooper was shocked to find Michael Angleton slumped over his ornate desk with sweat dripping from his well-shaven face; something was terribly wrong. He didn't move an inch even after they had entered his office.

"Call Mr. Bailey quickly, I am sure he is at his desk," commanded Janet Cooper as she rushed over to her boss and started to quickly loosen his tie.

"Okay," answered Maria hurrying out obediently.

It didn't take Maria Kosgei long to locate Bailey, as the only employee with some background in nursing within the department. Bailey swung into action as soon as Janet told him what she had seen in Angleton's office. He rushed with them to Michael's office and immediately lifted his torso off his desk and reclined him gently against the back of his orthopedic seat, after unbuttoning his shirt, to ensure his breathing wasn't constricted in any way. They kept it quiet so no one else in the office knew what was going on. Bailey knew that his boss was a diabetic and suspected he had low blood sugar that had suddenly caused him to lose consciousness.

"Give him time and he will be okay, no need to panic. This is common with diabetics," said Bailey with assuring tone.

"Shall I call an ambulance?" Maria asked.

"There is no need Maria, he will be alright, let's give him a few more minutes," Bailey answered mopping Michael's forehead with a damp cloth.

The atmosphere within the office remained tense as they waited for their boss to come round. Michael Angleton didn't know what had happened to him. He slowly came to and was surprised to find Bailey sitting close to him. Bailey who was trying to explain what had happened in a low voice. Michael was still reeling from the faint. He slowly checked his coat pockets for his usual tablets and luckily for him, he found a strip of Diamicron, an oral hypoglycemic that was used for Type 2 diabetics like him. He needed to take two tablets. This was all he needed to feel better.

"Can you get me a glass of water," he requested with a weak voice while trying to shift his weight and sit more upright.

Without saying a word, Mr. Bailey walked away, coming back with a glass of water after only one minute.

It was one of those bad days. Michael remembered a similar occurrence about six months ago when he fainted and collapsed at a seminar. He had been fortunate because already he had delivered his speech and very few of the conference participants noticed what had taken place. He started to feel a bit more energetic after taking his medication, but he still felt the need to go back home and relax for the rest of the day. He knew of late he'd been thinking too much, overworking his brain, defying his doctor's directives; He needed to slow down and let his son do most of the office work, he thought to himself as he slowly found his way out of the office with Janet watching him and wondering to herself why he seemed so disconcerted of late.

With his head still besieged by thoughts of all the things he needed to do, Fletcher Angleton sat alone in a restaurant sipping a warm cup of coffee. Looking at his diary he realized there was a lot of his office work he had put on the back burner. His employers expected a lot from him, and his work entailed travelling, especially within London. The Jose case had been a distraction these past weeks. Camila was also feeling taken for granted and he didn't want to lose her by focusing too much on the case. He was in a catch-22 situation and he needed to take some time out to think alone. He had chosen this restaurant because it was hidden from all the hustle and bustle of town centre, and he was also trying not to meet anyone he knew. He sipped his coffee thoughtfully.

———————

From the police station, Lesley Angleton went back to her house. Luckily for her, there was not much she had planned to do that day. The sun was finally coming through and warm air drifted into her compound by the trees lined behind her well tended back garden. With a woman's magazine tucked under her arm, she walked through the large sliding doors to the alluring back garden with a warm cup of coffee. She picked up an old Victorian stool and placed it squarely on the lush green grass and sat down to bask in the warm sunshine. When she needed some peace and quiet, this was always the best place to get it.

It was eleven forty-five when the front door swung open unexpectedly. It was Michael Angleton, his coat hanging on his left arm and his tie loosened around his neck. The top three buttons of his light-blue shirt were undone. He walked despondently to the kitchen thinking there was no one else in the house. The back door of the house was partially closed making it difficult to see anyone in the back garden.

He stood at the fridge wondering what to do. Sighing, he opened it and took out a packet of milk, pouring a small amount into a cup. He reached for the kettle and that is when he noticed the kettle was still warm. That meant someone else was in the house. He peered out the large glass doors to the back garden and saw his wife Lesley reading a glossy woman's magazine. She sensed some movement and looked up

"So you decided you also needed a breather did you?" he asked her after pulling the sliding doors open.

"I've told you I don't hear you sometimes, you walk so quietly like a cat, I didn't expect you at this time," she answered turning around to face him.

"I know. I've decided to take a day off because I collapsed in the office and realized I urgently needed a rest," he said.

"What happened darling?" Lesley asked perturbed, I am sure it's that sugar level issue again, you should have called me dear," she said.

"I was really very bad before at the office, but now I think I am alright," he answered looking at his watch.

"Let me make you a cup of tea," she offered "that usually gets you back up and chirpy," Lesley said rising to go to the kitchen.

"The kettle is on and I have poured some milk into a cup," he said walking with her to the kitchen.

"So what happened, you didn't have any problem in the morning when we parted?" Lesley Angleton continued.

"Immediately after sitting down on my chair in the office, I just lost it and fainted, slumping over my desk like an idiot. I felt embarrassed when I finally came to and there was poor old Bailey sponging my neck and forehead with a damp cloth, but there was nothing I could do about it," he said grudgingly as he sipped his tea slowly.

"Don't you think it's wise to go and see Dr. Rudolf," Lesley suggested.

"No, I don't see the point as I feel better now. All I need is to rest for a day and I will be okay," he replied. "I'll go take a nap as soon as I am through with this cup of tea. I think this case with Jose is what has been getting me down. I will be so relieved when it is all over," Michael said rolling his eyes.

"You do that darling, don't let something that you can't change much stress you," Lesley said as she rubbed his broad back slowly with the palm of her hand.

Camila finally joined Fletcher for an early dinner. Fletcher Angleton didn't mind spending his time with Camila Ashcroft that afternoon but felt torn between being here with her and going to the office to try and catch up with his work as he had so much work still left to do. Although the dinner was good, their conversation was sometimes strained. Sipping from her glass of red wine Camila determined not to let her fiancée get away with all the lies he had been telling her. She knew he had lied about his last trip away and she was determined to get to the bottom of everything.

Fletcher Angleton could not hide his anxiety either. He wondered how he was going to get out of this fix he was in. He loved Camila and she was obviously a catch, but the guilt of his choices over the past few days ate at his heart. His temples pulsed and small veins stood out on his hairline. He knew she was going to make it difficult for him today

In his mind, he knew that she would have given up on him long ago, except that she loved him. Many were the times they had quarrelled and though he loved Camila, he sometimes felt trapped into being monogamous and domesticated, which ran against his old character's grain.

He was tense and his stomach muscles were tight with anticipation. He had to woo her today. He reached out and held her hand to appease her, and kissed it gently.

"You win, I am not going anywhere else today," he said hesitantly.

"You need to tell me the truth Fletcher. Don't think that sweet nothings alone are going to make things good between us. Let's not pretend there is nothing wrong between us. You know I don't like that. Tell me how we can strengthen our bond if you keep leaving me out with what's going on in your life," Camila insisted, not moved by his overtures.

"Today I will do anything you ask of me and this is from my heart," said Fletcher quietly. I know it is important for us to meet more often and we shouldn't let anything else take priority," he said remorsefully.

He was lucky the bar they were in was not busy on Tuesdays. With time, and after a thousand apologies and promises that he would change for the better, Fletcher was finally able to appease Camila. She finally relaxed and talked of other less stressful issues of their lives. But the thoughts of the case were still at the back of her mind.

There was too much going on. She didn't know what the plan was. Her father was skeptical about the case and was not opening up to her. It was taking too much time to sort everything out and this bothered her. She wanted to be told the truth. She knew her father well to know that there was something he was hiding and that this was something that would affect the family.

She did not know exactly what had happened and several times she had tried to gather information from either Fletcher or her father but both were always finding an excuse to avoid her probing questions. Camila's diligence in convincing Fletcher to stay with her today was an attempt to get to know why there was a gridlock on his case. She wanted to know the truth.

"I don't want to be too nosey but I feel I have every right to know what's going on with the case. It seems that a lot has been hijacked by this heinous act and your parents and my parents are drifting farther and farther apart as friends. Please love, tell me the truth about what's going on," Camila urged Fletcher.

"I know you're concerned sweetheart but other than what you know I don't think there is anything else to tell," he answered.

"You can't expect me to believe that. What is it that you are hiding from me?" she asked pointedly.

"Look here Camila, I don't know why you think I am hiding something from you, we are all waiting for the investigating officer to finish his work," Fletcher replied evasively.

"Were you not at the police station today meeting with Sergeant Clifton or whatever you call him?" she persisted.

"I will explain everything that transpired at the meeting this morning. I promise," he said while trying to think quickly what would be safe to divulge without worrying her too much.

It took Fletcher Angleton more than two hours to convince Camila that there was nothing more he knew other than what he had already mentioned to her about the case. At times he wondered how he could explain that he had some suspicions that her father was involved in some way. If Jose Cameron had acted on his own, why was her father dragging himself into the case so much, especially given his standing in society? Okay, so Jose had been Mr. Ashcroft's employee but that didn't mean her father should follow the case up so keenly as if Jose were his son. Something was amiss somewhere. His effort to hide what he was thinking while at the same time trying to give Camila the impression he was divulging everything about the ambush and developments at the police station caused Fletcher's heart to palpitate and a small trickle of sweat formed on his face, like the early morning dew on a lawn. Despite his suspicions, he could not tell her exactly what he thought was going on.

It was true Michael Ashcroft had something to do with it, but nobody from outside knew about it except Dr. Carter and Sergeant Morgan Clifton. With the arrest of Henry Forbes, the likelihood of ending the feud out of court was not possible any more, except by some miracle.

But the one-million-dollar-question still remained. How was Michael Ashcroft tangled up in this whole mess! And what did Fletcher Angleton do to deserve this uncalled for humiliation! There was no answer yet; only time would tell.

Chapter Fourteen

The High Street in Brighton was busy with compulsive shoppers crisscrossing from one shopping mall to another in a bid to take advantage of recently advertised sales. The sun overhead was shining brightly so James Wilcox hung his jacket loosely over his left shoulder as he walked away from the police station. Seated on a public bench, next to a news vendor, was a one-man-guitarist entertaining a crowd of passersby with his well-rehearsed snippets of rock music, which reverberated from his acoustic guitar. The walk from the police station to the town center took Mr. Wilcox twenty-five minutes, enough time to reflect on his predicament.

At the police station, Sergeant Morgan Clifton had listened keenly to what James had said about his relationship with Henry Forbes and it had been clear to the sergeant as he listened that this was just a friend who had naively helped another without knowing what had taken place, and without even being near the Ogaden Night Club that fateful night. James had come across as obviously innocent so no charges were made against him. He was released after a tense time of interrogation by officers at the station. His request to see Jose and have a word with him was categorically refused and he was firmly ushered through the station exit after the interrogation was over.

Although his head was filled with worrisome thoughts of his wife, at least he knew one problem was out of the way. He didn't have to worry about Jose and his cahoots. He vowed to himself that he would never make such a stupid mistake of housing a crime suspect again. Even though Henry was a personal friend, his wife's comfort and protection had to come first.

He remembered with concern how Henry Forbes had helped him in times of need in the past and felt a stab of guilt that he had been unable to help him as well this time around. But at least, he had tried to help him, and had hosted him in his house, so he couldn't really be blamed for anything Henry went through after that. He would not regret trying to help his friend even though what eventually happened to Pamela was stressful and unfortunate.

The image of his wife Pamela lying in pain on a hospital bed tore at his heart and he vowed to be more careful about causing her stress especially during her pregnancy. He loved her desperately and the more he thought of what she was going through, the more his legs felt like jelly. He walked weakly down the street, and finally slumped down on a bench not too far from where the solo musician was having his funfair.

He was sweating and felt nauseated and he hoped desperately that Pamela would not have a miscarriage because of the risk he had taken.

Time moved fast; it was one o'clock on Wednesday afternoon. The visiting hours at Radcliffe Referral Hospital were between 2 and 5 in the afternoon and James realized he had no time to waste. He wanted to be by his wife when that time reached. He had not eaten for the last twenty-four hours. He wondered what to do to make things better for her, and he was worried she had gotten worse when he was away from her. The Henry incident had pushed her blood pressure up and that is what had caused her sudden bleeding. She was very lucky she had not lost the baby. Every time James thought of what had transpired as a result of his welcoming Henry into their home, he felt extremely stupid.

Shaking his head, he finally stood up and walked slowly towards the bus stop feeling miserable and weak. His house was not far from town centre and after fifteen minutes he was unlocking the main door to his house. The towel that he used to wipe his wife's face was still lying on the floor in the living room. He walked on to the kitchen and found the groceries still in the plastic bags as he had left them on Monday after he had come from the supermarket at the mall.

Then he remembered.

After spending the fateful night at the hospital, he hadn't gone back to his house the following morning because he feared the police would return to look for him or for Henry. Instead, he had gone to his wife's brother's house where he stayed for the day. On Tuesday afternoon, he recalled going to his work place to explain his absence the day before. It was after this that he finally headed to his house. He had been so exhausted from all that had taken place that he had gone straight to bed and slept without noticing the mess around him.

James decided to take a quick shower and head to the hospital to see his wife and make sure she was okay.

Lying in the hospital bed and facing up, Pamela Wilcox opened her eyes. Standing by the bedside was her husband holding a bouquet of beautiful flowers. She looked tired and haggard but she managed to smile weakly upon seeing him there. James massaged her face and hand, whispering lovingly into her ears.

"What happened?" Pamela asked her husband with a confused look on her tired face.

"Everything is okay," he answered.

"I want to know what happened to me," she asked alarmed.

"It was a small accident in the house but I will explain when you get better," answered James placing the bouquet in her hands.

"How is my baby?" she asked with a prick of fear in her heart.

"Our baby is okay and is right here with you," he answered touching her small protruding tummy.

"I am feeling weak; the doctor told me I lost too much blood," she said.

"I know how you feel, but I don't want you to worry because tomorrow I know they'll let you go home," James said.

The long curtains hanging around the bed swung open and a female doctor walked in holding a file in her hand.

"You must be Mr. Wilcox the husband if I am not wrong," she started.

"Yes," he replied.

"Come with me for a minute," she requested.

Standing by a small cabinet in the corridor, a few feet away from Pamela's bed, and after a short introduction, the doctor explained what was going on with Pamela.

"I am Rebecca, Dr. Rebecca but you can call me Becky," she said and continued, "by the way I am the one taking care of your wife while she is here at the hospital and I can assure you there is no cause for alarm."

"Hi, I am James, and yes, I am her husband," James answered nodding towards Pamela's bed.

She nodded and continued, "You were very lucky because it was just by the Grace of God that she did not lose the baby after the trauma she went through. The bleeding was intense and it was triggered by panic. What she needs to do now is rest for a while before resuming her daily chores, do you understand that?" she asked.

Without speaking, James nodded his head in affirmation.

"By the way, the circumstances that lead to this, although you did try to explain to me earlier, should be avoided at all costs. On several occasions, we have tried to warn the police and let them know that the number of miscarriages women are having due to panic attacks, or sudden trauma are increasing, but they don't realize how serious the situation is. It's actually very serious," the doctor went on, frustration lining her voice.

"I feel partly to blame," said James hurriedly. The person the police were looking for was in my house at the time. They raided the house to catch him and my wife was there. I should not have welcomed a suspected criminal into my house because it lead to the sudden police search in the home; especially seeing the state my wife is in now," said James Wilcox sheepishly. "I should have known better".

"It's terrible. Sometimes, I wonder if there are any married policemen, or whether they know what it's like to have a family," said Dr. Rebecca closing the file she had been holding open in her hand, with a grave look on her face. "The way they barge into people's homes...anything could be happening in one's house when they come crashing in like that!"

James and the doctor finally turned and walked back to Pamela's bed. By the time they got back to the little cubical, she was already dozing off. She was woken up to take her medication. She was obviously tired and took some time before opening her eyes. James spent a few more minutes with her, then kissed her lightly on her forehead before he quietly left.

The meeting was scheduled to take place at Hotel Trefontana eight o'clock on the dot. Dr. Carter was on call that night with a meeting planned with his interns at ten o'clock. He would have to squeeze his meeting with Michael Ashcroft in as he had promised that he would make it. Even if he didn't turn up for his hospital meeting, some medical colleague would cover up for him.

Located five miles outside the city centre, Hotel Trefontana could be seen from a distance because of its luminous neon lights flashing aloft the balcony of its third floor. Built on a hill, the hotel boasted one of the best landscapes. It was surrounded by century-old oaks and a variety of wildlife walked about freely a safe distance from the hotel patrons. It was a hot spot for wealthy American tourists who sometimes liked to frequent out-of-the-way places, to grab some quiet outside of the heavily polluted metropolitan cities of California, New York, Manhattan and other capitals they hailed from.

Driving alone down the hill from the hospital, Dr. Carter speedily navigated his automobile down the road. His mind was so fixated on the meeting before him that he did not even consider his blatant breach of the traffic rules. A lone fox limped across the road narrowly missing a direct collision with the speeding car and forcing Dr. Carter to skid and almost lose control of his car. He cursed under his breath and sped on up the hill towards the hotel.

It was fifteen minutes to eight when Dr. Carter eventually drove through the gates of the hotel and after going through the formal security checks, he drove round the winding lanes to the back of the hotel where he parked his car.

On the second floor of the hotel, Michael Ashcroft sat quietly on a high stool by the bar drinking his favourite Jack Daniels and occasionally engaging in light conversation with the man serving at the bar. Those around him were relaxing and minding their own business as time passed slowly. A young couple danced to the lazy jazz tunes floating softly from the well-camouflaged speakers. The wide bar-room was air-conditioned and Michael savoured the peace and quiet as he waited for Carter.

It didn't take Dr. Carter too long before he spotted his friend at the bar. With his cell phone on his left hand, he walked steadily towards Michael, his arm outstretched to greet him. Michael stood up and reached out to welcome Carter amicably. He asked for another drink.

"More to drink pal?" Michael offered.

"I will take an orange juice," Carter said.

"An orange juice; come on man, you can do better than that this evening," Michael teased.

"I know, it's only because I am on call tonight. I have a meeting booked for ten o'clock," Carter replied looking at his watch.

"You mean you are going back to work?" Michael asked.

"Yes, unless I get somebody to cover for me, otherwise I will be left with no choice but to go back," answered Dr. Carter.

"You must have somebody stand in for you?" Michael queried, not convinced.

"That's why I have to keep my phone close, I am expecting a call from Dr. Rajesh Patel to confirm if he is going to stand in for me," replied Dr. Carter.

"So this doctor is at least aware of your absence?" Michael Ashcroft continued.

"Well, I told him I am attending a meeting somewhere and I might be late, so he is aware and I am sure he will confirm in under ten minutes whether he can stand in for me," Carter said.

"Fingers crossed," replied Michael taking a sip from his glass.

"Fingers crossed indeed," Dr. Carter said with a forced smile.

Passing a glass of orange juice to Dr. Carter, Michael Ashcroft led the way to an empty table in a secluded corner of the hotel. Neither of them wanted to start a serious discussion on Jose at that early stage so they talked about politics for a while changing their focus to business and other inconsequential topics. Dr. Carter's cell phone rang; it was Dr. Patel. Dr Carter picked the call and listened. It was obvious that Michael was getting increasingly tense and frustrated as the conversation with Patel seemed not to end, because he sat upright in his chair, his face turning slowly red like someone who has been exposed to the unpredictable summer sun with no sign of a shade to protect him.

He tolerated the conversation as he stared at Carter, his eyes unblinking. Finally, the conversation came to an end and Michael was unable to hide the relief he felt when Dr. Carter told him that Dr. Patel had agreed to stand in for him at the evening meeting with the interns. Dr. Carter had deliberately extended his conversation with his workmate long after Dr. Patel had agreed to cover for him at the hospital. He had enjoyed watching the consternation on Michael's face. After telling Michael that Patel had agreed to assist, Dr. Carter stood up and walked to the gent's toilets.

"I think this time I will have double vodka mixed with ice and coke," Dr. Carter said upon returning to his seat.

"Why are you trying to be funny doc?" Almost ten minutes on phone then another fifteen minutes at the gents and you haven't told me the most important thing yet!" Michael said anxiously.

"Relax pal, we have all the time we need now," Carter replied.

Another round of drinks and the two men settled down for serious business each laying down his plans on how best to embark on the Jose case. At times, there was heated debate when they couldn't seem to agree. Dr. Carter was determined to protect his reputation as well; he didn't want to leave any loophole that would have him linked to this shady plan.

"If you involve a third party in this it will compromise your position and we don't want that to happen," Dr. Carter emphasised.

"I know, I know but I am not convinced it's the only way to go on this," Michael replied.

"I have an idea you might agree to," said the doctor.

"What is it then?" Michael asked.

"Leave it with me pal and I will get in touch soon on it. Remember George Franklin," Carter said with a tinge of sarcasm in his voice as he stood up.

"Where are you going?" Michael asked.

"Do I need a permit to go for a pee?" Carter asked laughing loudly.

"You need to see a doctor, you pee too much," commented Michael joining into the relieving banter.

"I am a doctor too you know," said Dr. Carter laughing.

"Doctors don't treat themselves medically; do I need to remind you of that?" Michael said feeling slightly lighter hearted now that he seemed to have the doctor on his side regarding the Jose plan.

Carter left Michael alone in the dark lounge. Michael sensed strongly that despite the doctor's apparent confident air earlier, there was something he was not being honest about. Michael knew Dr. Carter had an ace up his sleeve but he determined to broach that issue later.

Outside the big compound, trees surrounding Hotel Trefontana swayed from side to side as a gust of westerly winds swept across the English Channel to the Main Land. A draught of fresh air blew through the slightly open windows of the bar lounge pushing off the curtain of thick cigar smoke hovering in its dark corners. It was getting late and the noise inside the hotel increased with time as the patrons ordered fresh rounds of intoxicating drink.

Dr. Carter finally came to the lounge and Michael got up. They both walked towards the car park which was increasingly busy with taxis coming in and out with all manner of customers. Leaning on a railing surrounding the car park Dr. Carter listened as Michael urgently whispered some last minute instructions on what more they should consider regarding their plan on Jose. He felt increasingly harassed as Michael spoke but he held his true emotions in check. He was too tired to encourage an argument with Michael. Finally, they both called for their cars from the valet and headed to their different homes.

The drive home was lonely and slow for Michael Ashcroft. He felt tired and exhausted. As draining as his discussions with Carter were, they had ended on a hopeful note and Michael felt that Carter was going to ultimately help him sort out the Jose fracas. It was not until he got to his house that the reality of what was just about to happen started to dawn on him. A sudden quiver ran down his spine, followed by a migraine headache.

He remembered how Jose had been such a loyal member of staff for over three years, and wondered how he could actually be planning his death just to avoid the public embarrassment of being named in the Fletcher debacle. He knew that this whole mess was not Jose's fault; he had simply done what Michael had ordered him to do as his boss. Jose had always worked devotedly in Michael's office, and for those years he had worked without complaining. Yet, here was Michael with a heinous scheme up his sleeve all because of a stupid mistake he had instigated. He felt like the politicians of medieval times who eliminated their adversaries by decree without remorse. A haunting feeling crept up his heart when he also recalled that such politicians always paid for their heinous acts in one way or another or those choices came to haunt their children for generations.

Mr. Ashcroft realized that no matter what guilty feelings he was struggling with now, things had already gone too far and were not reversible. The plan had been laid and there was no turning back now. There was still one problem they would have to contend with however --Sergeant Morgan Clifton. The Sergeant was Jose's closest contact at the moment and Jose's sudden disappearance would definitely raise eyebrows. Michael feared this could trigger an all-out feud with the Angleton's. 'Would it be advisable to involve the Sergeant in this scheme?' he thought to himself. He felt miserable because the answer eluded him. This was his own problem and he had to find a way of winning despite the odds.

His wife Linda was asleep when Michael walked quietly into their bedroom. He undressed and wrapped a towel round his waist. He looked at his watch before removing it and placing it on the sideboard. He then walked slowly and as quietly as possible towards the bathroom. He needed a shower before going to sleep. He felt this might wash off the layer of filth he felt had slowly grown on his heart as a result of this scandalous plan with Carter.

Chapter Fifteen

Seeing him there in the periphery of his vision made Fletcher Angleton's eyes brim with tears of hate and anger. He felt like a wounded lion when it suddenly espied its attacker. He felt breathless and weak like a hunted gazelle when trapped in a corner, about to have its life snapped away like a dry twig. The panic attack had come suddenly, and the rage rising in him caused him to breathe hard and clench his fists. He felt like a mad man about to pulverize his enemy but frustration rose up in his throat when he realized there was nothing he could do without getting into trouble with the law. He could only stare in shock.

It was outside the national library at the town centre where he saw Jose Cameron leisurely leaning on a wall, and talking on his cell phone. Jose was facing the opposite direction but kept turning to look around him like a confused person. Fletcher Angleton was coming out of a chemist across the street where he had gone to pick up his father's high-blood pressure medication when he saw the unmistakable figure of Jose. He thought of getting closer to him but something kept holding him back. He felt like a coward, even though he knew that if he and Jose were to take each other on, Fletcher would crush him and totally humiliate him.

Overcoming the tumultuous emotions that bubbled up to the surface as he considered whether he should approach Jose, Fletcher Angleton walked closer to his nemesis and stood strategically close enough to make his presence felt. Even though he was now shoulder-to-shoulder with Jose, he failed to draw the man's attention. Jose was so taken by his conversation on the phone; he was laughing hysterically with the handset tightly clamped to his left ear. Whoever it was he was speaking to was not in a hurry to end the chat. After a few minutes Jose finally slid his cell phone into his pocket. A faint tap on his left shoulder made him startle and swivel around in consternation.

"Do you remember me, or maybe you thought I was dead?" Fletcher Angleton was full of rage as he faced Jose Cameron. Sweat now dripped profusely from his face and his chest heaved with fury as he looked intently into Jose's scared eyes.

The approach made Jose Cameron jerk backwards. This was the last thing he expected. He stared at Fletcher without saying a word. He felt like a rat caught in a trap. It took him a few seconds to control his feelings.

"What the heck is wrong with you Fletcher?" he blurted.

"Are you crazy?" Fletcher yelled back. "You dare ask me what's wrong with me?"

"Just leave me alone and go," said Jose fumbling nervously in his pockets for a cigarette.

"Listen! When you and your stupid gang of rascals attacked me outside the Ogaden Night Club, you thought I will never breathe this air again. What is it that I did to you to warrant that attack hey? Okay, here I am now and if you want to kill me, do it now you wretch," the pitch of Fletcher's voice was sharp and rising.

"I don't want any trouble Fletcher; I had nothing to do with what happened okay! That's why they let me go…that's why I am free," Jose stuttered defensively.

"It was you and your gang of cowards. Did I do anything wrong to any one of you to warrant such a beating, or you think I have forgotten what happened?" Fletcher's verbal onslaught was getting louder and attracting a group of passersby.

"My friend, don't try to create a scene here, I told you I had nothing to do with it," Jose continued trying to back away and looked around nervously.

"You think I am stupid? And don't call me your friend again because I am not! What you and your scoundrels did to me, don't think you can get away with it," Fletcher continued inching closer to a quaking Jose.

"Leave me alone," Jose Cameron hissed in frustration.

"If you think you are man enough, face me now and prove your worth you louse!" yelled Fletcher shoving Jose hard in the chest so that he stumbled backwards.

"I told you before, it was some other guys and I wasn't involved," stammered Jose hurriedly taking a few steps back.

"Some other guys, huh? You keep talking of some other guys. Who are these other guys you coward?" Fletcher asked angrily.

"Okay then, do what you want to do because I am not going to hang around here arguing with you for nothing," Jose was looking around him wildly now.

"Look at you, you can't even kill a mosquito you coward. Where's all the bravado you had that night at Ogaden hey? I will make sure you suffer the same way I did and I don't care what happens to me after that," Fletcher said prodding Jose Cameron's chest provocatively.

With both of his fists clenched; Fletcher Angleton moved swiftly towards Jose throwing an incredible uppercut that narrowly missed its target. Realizing Fletcher was after a physical confrontation, Jose Cameron quickly dashed behind the crowd vanishing like thin air, out of his adversary's sight. Although he was also angered by the actions of Fletcher, he knew a fight would not serve him well. Walking behind buildings, he followed an alleyway that led to an open area; part of a recreation park, where he sat down under a tree, happy to be out of Fletcher's reach. With trembling fingers he took his cell phone out of the pocket and dialed the all important number.

"Sergeant Morgan Clifton here," was the answer from the other end.

"Hello, it's Jose Cameron and I need to see you," Jose said hurriedly and in a shaky voice.

"Is it urgent?" asked the Sergeant.

"Well, I think it's very important," Jose answered.

"Okay, you will need to make it to my office in less than forty minutes because I will be going for a seminar in an hour's time," said the Sergeant.

"That's okay with me Sergeant," replied Mr. Cameron breathlessly.

"See you shortly then," the sergeant concluded and hanged up the phone with a quizzical look on his face. He could tell that Jose was in a panicked state.

Not too long after, Sergeant Clifton was sitting on the edge of his desk when a knock on the door startled him. Without coming inside, a tall uniformed policeman leaned into his office still holding the door with one hand.

"Your man Jose is here, can I send him in?" asked the officer.

"Is he alone?" asked the sergeant.

"All by himself sir," replied the officer.

"Send him in then," Clifton answered.

From the look on his face, Clifton could tell that Jose Cameron was apprehensive about something. His hands were trembling and his face was sweating profusely. He did not have any jacket on and the T-shirt he was wearing was visibly wet under the armpits. Fearing something serious has happened, Sergeant Morgan gave Jose some time to cool down and turned on the air conditioner before showing him a seat opposite his. He strode quickly out of his office, leaving Jose Cameron on his own for a while, and returned with a glass of cold water.

"Take some water, you seem to need some," offered the Sergeant.

"Thanks," Jose answered gulping down the contents.

"Do you need some more? I can get you some more if you want," asked Sergeant Morgan Clifton.

"No thanks, I feel better now," Jose replied.

"You look troubled, what's the problem this time?" Clifton asked after realizing that Jose was composed and not as tense as before.

"It's about Fletcher Angleton," Jose started.

'What about him?' Sergeant Clifton asked leaning forward in curiosity.

"Well, I was standing outside the National Library talking on my cell phone when I felt a tap on my shoulder. Standing there behind me was Fletcher Angleton. I don't know where he was coming from but, out of nowhere, he started shouting at me in front of everyone! He was spoiling for a fight, and even threw a few punches, but luckily I was too fast for him and ducked. He missed knocking me off my feet I tell you. A large crowd of curious onlookers was gathering around wondering what was going on. I felt embarrassed and left him there shouting at me," said Jose like a commentator at a wrestling match.

Sergeant Morgan Clifton was a seasoned law-enforcement agent and his many years in the force had taught him to listen keenly to people without interrupting; he noted every word Jose said on a notepad.

"All this time you say he was shouting at you challenging you for a fight is that right?" he asked.

"Yes sir that's right," Jose answered like a schoolboy reporting a bully.

"Did you exchange abusive words with him?" Clifton asked.

"No sir, the only thing I remember telling him is that I had nothing to do with what he was accusing me of," Jose blurted out.

"Was there anybody within the crowd of onlookers who recognized you and can bear witness to your testimony?" continued the sergeant.

"No sir and even if anybody recognized me I didn't notice,"

"Okay, my advice to you is to try and keep away from any member of the Angleton family until this case is fully resolved. Everything you've told me is well recorded and I will summon Fletcher to the station to see me. I will see whether he will deny or accept what you've told me and I hope to solve everything amicably so leave it to me okay?' said the sergeant.

"Yes sir and please if you get in touch with him, just tell him to leave me alone okay, just that," requested an obviously ruffled Jose Cameron.

"One more thing before you go, tomorrow your friend Henry will be released on bail pending further investigations. He told me a lot about you, and the reason why he tried to run away from his house was because you also threatened him. I am only trying to deal with you in a civil manner Jose because you look like a nice chap. I don't want you anywhere near Henry at all, and don't forget he is our main suspect. He has been advised to stay at his home if he is to be assured of our protection, so do not jeopardize your own case by doing something stupid, is that clear?" the sergeant said stone-faced.

"Yes sir," answered Jose Cameron meekly, relieved that he seemed to have the sergeant on his side.

"You may go now and stay out of trouble okay," the sergeant concluded shaking Jose's hand.

Walking slowly up the hill from the police station, Jose Cameron felt dehydrated. He had planned to do a number of things today but his unexpected encounter with Fletcher Angleton had knocked the air out of his sails. He removed his wallet from his trouser pocket and checked its contents. He only had forty pounds but he decided to spend it at the nearest pub so he could quench his thirst and think of what his next move would be.

The sky was mainly clear except for patches of grey clouds forming and slowly obstructing the sun.

Camila Ashcroft was in her back garden reading the latest novel by Danielle Steel. The smell of freshly-mowed grass was still in the air. Along the trimmed fence, a squirrel moved about digging small furrows in the soil then covering them up. It would dash for cover at the slightest sound. Camila enjoyed watching the innocent creature.

Not to be outdone, a small flock of birds hopped about chirping happily as they competed for the worms that had been exposed in the low grass. Camila enjoyed relaxing in her garden and watching the small creatures scampering about. She took refuge here when she found it hard to concentrate on her work or when she was stressed. The weather was warm enough. She looked at her wrist watch and was shocked at how fast time was moving. It was already half past six!

'What was that?' Camila thought to herself, 'did I hear something or am I day dreaming,' she mumbled.

The sound of tyres against the gravel outside her front door caught her attention. She remembered Fletcher Angleton had promised to come that evening for dinner; they had talked about it over the phone the day before, but she had forgotten all about it until now.

The tap on the door persisted, followed by the constant buzzing of the door bell. Music played softly in her living room muting the sounds coming from outside. She had also been so lost in her thoughts that it took Camila some time to hear the door bell. She walked slowly to the main door, peeping through the pigeon hole. It was Fletcher Angleton standing outside and whistling as he waited.

"I've been standing here for ages," he said hugging her tightly against his chest when she had opened the door.

"Imagine I was outside in the back garden and I was enjoying myself so much I didn't hear a thing," she said hugging him back and looking lovingly up into his handsome face as she led him into the house by one hand.

"And you did not hear the sound of the buzzing door bell?"

"I was not alone that's why," she replied.

"What do you mean you were not alone?" jealousy stealing up his heart even though he knew Camila would never cheat on him.

"Come and meet my companions if you think I am joking," she teased leading him to the back yard.

Without saying a word, they walked together to the back garden and to her amazement there were even more birds of different plumage all over the garden. Along the fence she noticed a swift dashing movement and out emerged a small brown fox from the hedge.

"I hope now you'll believe me," said Camila almost in a whisper not to disturb the creatures.

"Oh my goodness!" Fletcher Angleton said astonished.

"Look at that…did you see that?" she asked pointing at the fox.

"And it's not alone, did you see the squirrels moving to the other side of the fence?" he said grinning.

"It's so beautiful," she said sighing softly.

"Yea, just like you, so amazingly beautiful," he said looking at her seductively.

Camila looked up into his face and smiled youthfully. They both laughed heartily.

They sat down and chatted quietly, watching the little animals. Camila was relieved that her fiancé seemed relaxed and able to chat for a long time with her despite the pressure he had been under of late. As time passed by, neither of them cared about anything else, other than being together and listening to the chirping of the birds around them.

The sun faded behind the merging of clouds in the sky and a slight chilly breeze swept across the enclosed garden as dusk set in, forcing even the most stubborn squirrel to scurry away from the yard.

"Your friends are all gone so let's get inside my love," said Fletcher helping Camila up.

"It's even getting cold now," replied Camila picking up from the ground the novel she had been reading earlier.

Leading the way, Fletcher Angleton walked to the kitchen and quickly heated two cups of instant coffee in the microwave before joining Camila in the living room. He settled down on the sofa. He handed her a cup and they sipped the hot drink thankfully and in comfortable silence. After some minutes, Fletcher started fidgeting. He felt the urge to tell Camila what had happened during the day. The encounter with Jose Cameron in town, although not welcome, was something that he couldn't keep to himself and the best way to relieve his mind of the burden was to talk it over with his fiancée.

Fletcher slowly narrated the whole episode with Jose, embellishing the details so as to emphasize how he had scared the hell out of Jose so much so that in the end Jose had scampered away like a small child. He told her of how he almost allowed himself to be drawn into an all-out tussle with Jose in front of a large crowd that had gathered around. He hoped he would impress her with his macho reaction and lack of fear. But, Camila was not amused by the story. She shook her head bewildered and after he finished his narration, she looked at him and blurted in hurt and frustration.

"That was not a clever thing to do, what if you had gotten hurt?"

"What was I supposed to do, I am sure he was part of the group that tried to kill me," Fletcher replied defensively, embarrassed that he had failed to impress her with his heroics.

"If anything was to happen to this guy, don't you think it can backfire on you regarding your case with the police?" she shot back.

"Okay, no need for you to get so uptight about it. I was just determined he and his louts would think twice the next time they try to hurt me in any way," Fletcher said gruffly.

"Have you told anybody about it?" Camila prodded.

"No, I didn't see the need," he replied.

"Not even your father?" she continued.

"No," he answered.

"Let's hope Jose will not report the matter to the police," Camila said frowning.

"Let him do whatever he feels like, I don't care anymore," Fletcher said, "furthermore those guys wanted to kill me."

They finally sat in sullen silence listening to the music that was still playing in the background. Fletcher's story of bravado had fallen flat on its face. He had not wanted to frustrate or scare Camila. Outside, through the drawn curtain, the full moon was visible with specks of stars dotting the skies as tall trees swayed in unison changing direction with the flow of the gentle wind. Despite the small hiccup, Fletcher Angleton felt at ease in the comfort of Camila's spacious house. He always felt relaxed when he was around her. After a few minutes, Camila got up and went to the kitchen.

She stood by the sink and found that she felt she was in a dilemma. She had forgotten she had nothing in her pantry with which to prepare supper. There was nothing in the fridge and there was only a packet of spaghetti in the side cabinet. She tried to remember the last time she shopped but couldn't recall a date. This was because she spent most of her evenings at her parent's house where she had her meals.

She had to come up with a plan that would go well with both of them. Two choices: either to go and have a meal in a hotel or order a pizza from the local outlets. They had agreed to have supper at her house and this was something they enjoyed but today she had not remembered as she sat in her back garden and watched the little creatures playing around. She had also forgotten that she had nothing in her pantry to prepare a meal with for Fletcher when he came to visit her. Unfortunately, though she loved cooking for Fletcher, today she had not stocked up.

Camila knew Fletcher well. He liked to go out especially on Fridays and especially when there was something bothering him. She had to think of a way out of this mess. She strode purposefully from the kitchen, and sat by him smiling demurely.

"You know what my sweetheart," she said stroking his hair.

Fletcher looked up and sensed immediately something was up her sleeve. "What is it this time, dear?" Fletcher asked smiling.

"Why are you looking at me suspiciously, you don't even know what I want to tell you," she chuckled stroking his hair.

"With that smile on your face I am sure this is something good," he said.

"I want to take you out for dinner," she said looking at her wrist watch.

"That sounds good to me but how come you changed your mind about cooking for me today?" he asked. "I remember you wanted to very much.

"I wanted to surprise you," she lied before she hurriedly excused herself to go to the bathroom.

Fletcher didn't need too much persuasion to go out with Camila anyway as long as it meant he would still be with her. He didn't mind the change of plans. He got up and turned to grab his coat that was hanging by the door. His cell phone rang and he pulled it out of his shirt pocket and looked to see who was calling him. It was his father.

"Hello dad," he answered,

"How are you doing?" his father enquired.

"I am okay, how about you?" Fletcher asked.

"I am fine but something has come up," said his father.

"What is it dad?"

"I received a phone call from Sergeant Morgan Clifton and what he is telling me is not good at all if it's true," his father continued.

"What could it be?" Fletcher asked pretending not to know.

"Is it true you had a confrontation with Jose Cameron this afternoon in public?" his father asked before Fletcher could breathe in.

"It was not a big deal dad," Fletcher replied evasively.

"That's where you go wrong. You know too well you have a case against these rascals and without thinking, you go ahead and look for a fight with Jose! Are you out of your mind?" said his father angrily.

"No dad. Jose started provoking me by showing me his middle finger, you know what I mean?" Fletcher lied.

"It doesn't matter; he reported to the police and made a statement with Sergeant Clifton, if anything was to happen to him you could find yourself in real problems," shouted his father at the other end.

"I am sorry," Fletcher capitulated.

"Listen and listen very carefully, you are not a child. I have been told by the Sergeant to tell you to keep away from those guys. Whenever you see them, you must avoid them. We don't know why they assaulted you in the first place and even now everybody is trying to get to the bottom of the act. Who knows, they might try to attack you again. Do you under-stand?" Fletcher's father was livid, and he hanged up the phone before his son could respond.

Thankfully, Camila had not heard the conversation although she must have heard the phone ringing, as she had dashed to her bedroom to change once Fletcher agreed to go out for a quick dinner with her. She was gone for nearly an hour. When she came back she was sparkling from head to toe. The elegance of her dress and make up made her time spent upstairs justifiable and her perfume filled the air in the room with a sweet scent. Her hair fell back over her slender shoulders and she looked regal standing there in front of him expectantly in her stilettos.

He smiled feebly at her as she turned to look at her reflection in the mirror on the wall of the corridor to her sitting room. She could see Fletcher behind her in the reflection. He was sitting thoughtfully on the sofa. She wondered who had called him when she was in the bathroom.

Turning her head to face him, she realized something was not right. He looked gloomy and in deep thought. Unable to hide her curiosity, Camila walked closer to him and asked.

"Are you okay?"

"I am fine, by the way you look great," he answered trying to hide his true feelings.

"You don't look okay, is there something wrong?" she asked him again.

"It was my father on the phone and he is not happy," he told her.

"What's the problem then?" she asked.

"It's this headache called Jose; he reported the confrontation to the police. The louse!" Fletcher said angrily.

"I told you what you did was not wise at all! I hope you now agree?" Camila said without empathy.

"I know it was bad but why run to the police station? He's a coward, he is," Fletcher retorted visibly disgusted.

"All said and done, accept your mistake," said Camila laughing.

"Some people are dumb for real, or what do you reckon my dear?" he asked.

"You are very right, some people are truly dumb indeed," she replied sarcastically.

"Are you mocking me Camila," Fletcher asked incredulously.

"Why do you think I am mocking you? You said some people are dumb and all I said is that, it is very true some people are very dumb," she said mockingly.

"Okay, I am dumb and you are very clever, is that what you mean my love? He asked her bemused and trying to draw her to him as she continued to tease him.

Fletcher led her towards the door, "Let's go my dear, it's getting late."

It took them forty five minutes to get to the small hotel where she knew they could enjoy the grilled Red Snapper he enjoyed so much. Stepping out of the car, they walked hand-in-hand to the restaurant. There were a few familiar faces here and there as they looked for an empty table; the hotel was almost full as it was a popular place. A Hispanic couple was sitting at a table for four with two empty seats. They beckoned to Fletcher and Camila, who moved towards them and sat down relieved.

———————————

Thinking of how it all began, Michael Angleton called his wife Lesley who was in the kitchen cleaning up the utensils after the meal. He explained his concerns about what Fletcher had done that day. He also wondered aloud if it was right for them to drop the case and let bygones be bygones. They decided it was better if they waited for the outcome of the investigations.

It was becoming more difficult for Michael to concentrate on his work at the office. His sugar level was getting worse and his doctor had told him to take a long vacation if he didn't want to get worse. However, he didn't know what was going on with the Ashcroft's family. Of late, their communication was not like before and no one could tell how bad this Fletcher issue had made things. They talked about it with his wife and they both agreed to invite the Ashcroft's family for a meal soon.

"I am going to sleep, have a good night," said Mr. Angleton stretching his arms.

"Good night dear, I will catch up with you later," replied his wife.

"But don't take too long," Michael said turning his head to face her.

"Don't get any funny ideas," she said with a twinkle in her eyes.

"Good night love," he said and walked upstairs to sleep.

Chapter Sixteen

What they planned boggled their minds for more than a fortnight. Michael Ashcroft and Dr. Carter knew it would not be easy to persuade Jose Cameron to meet them at the racecourse, unless they made the idea sound very attractive. It was a gamble because there was bad blood now between Jose and his former employer; the Fletcher issue had poisoned their relationship.

Dr. Carter managed to trace Jose Cameron at the Ogaden Night Club without making his presence known. With his car parked at a distance and armed with a pair of tiny binoculars, Dr. Carter could easily monitor the movements of regulars walking in and out of the club. The idea was to get Jose and lure him away from the club before he entered it.

It was Friday afternoon and Dr. Carter was getting jittery. Unaccompanied, he sat in his car feeling impatient and hoping that he would shortly be able to spot Jose and convince him to go some place with him for a chat. He was hoping Jose would believe that Michael wanted to make amends with his former employee, and let bygones be bygones. This was his third visit to the club with this plan in mind. He had already failed to spot Jose the last two times, but this time Dr. Carter vowed to stay put and wait until he spotted Jose, no matter how long it took. The sound of music from the car stereo and the warmth drifting from outside sometimes caused him to unwillingly doze on and off for a fraction of time. He felt frustrated because he would startle from dozing wondering how much time had elapsed. At times he thought it wise to sit on his car bonnet and keep an eye out for Jose from outside his car, but as they say 'the guilty are afraid' so he opted to endure the wait from inside his car so that no one would be able to recognize him, or see him leaving with Jose.

The musical chime from the Big Ben sounded from a cathedral a few kilometres away; it was already six o'clock in the evening. Dr. Carter's endurance was waning fast and the more he thought of Jose the more frustrated he felt because of not being able to spot him. 'I hope this is not another of those wasted moments in life,' he hissed to himself in a whisper as he adjusted the volume on the car stereo. The vision from outside was clear and apart from occasional obstructions from the busy crowd moving about on varied business, most times he had a clear view to the Ogaden Night Club entrance.

Albeit reluctantly, Dr. Carter felt he'd had enough and didn't want to spend more time waiting for somebody he wasn't sure would turn up. He started his car, then he switched it off again, not sure whether he wanted to leave. He started it again and engaged the first gear but switched it off again. The throbbing in his groin was intense and increased with time. He could no longer ignore the need to go to the gents. Finally, he got out of the car and walked straight to the Ogaden Night Club, quickly passing by the security guards without uttering a word. He dashed up the stairs to the gents toilets. This call of nature turned out to be a blessing in disguise.

A fragment of a familiar face reflected from the large mirror on the wall above the hand washing basin. Dr. Carter glanced sideways at Jose Cameron and watched him return to the bar lounge. Without wasting time after quickly relieving himself, Dr. Carter walked swiftly down the stairs to the main bar, looking around to make sure that Jose hadn't left. Standing by the corner with a bottle of Budweiser in his hand was Jose Cameron. Bingo! Dr. Carter walked to where he was standing and immediately started to chat with Jose after a brief greeting. After a short exchange; Jose agreed to meet him outside the club, in Carter's car. That's all Carter needed anyway, a few minutes with him, away from the public.

But something kept bothering Carter's mind; first he didn't understand how Jose got inside the club without being spotted and second he wondered what would happen if Jose brought a friend over to introduce to him. That would change the situation to a more precarious one. He could not control that and just hoped that luck would be on his side and that Jose would come alone. The doctor went back to his car and waited with his mind racing. Finally, the stout figure of Jose Cameron emerged from the main door of the Ogaden Night Club. Jose swaggered down the lane to where Carter's car was parked. It was clear he suspected nothing and had no reason to fear as he had known the doctor for some time. With a smile on his face he opened the side door of the car and got inside making himself comfortable on the passenger seat.

"It's been a long time since we last met," started Dr. Carter.

"I know, by the way how's Mr. Ashcroft getting on?" Jose asked.

"He is doing fine," replied Dr. Carter not surprised that Jose should ask about his former boss.

"I felt bad after what was supposed to be a small matter exploded beyond my control," Jose said. He had also briefed Jose a little on what he knew about the case when they were in the lounge bar.

"Never mind, Mr. Ashcroft is already dealing with it and according to what he told me yesterday it's like the case against you had been thrown out," Carter answered.

"And how come Sergeant Clifton hasn't told me about it?" Jose asked a confused look on his face.

"As far as I know they still had an arranged meeting today with the Sergeant to finalize the deal," Carter replied.

"So are you now telling me not to bother reporting on Monday as I always do?" Jose Cameron asked.

"Of course you'll still have to go there on Monday but I am sure it will be your last time to report at the station," assured Dr. Carter.

"That sounds good to me although it's quite unusual for Mr. Ashcroft to make such a move," he commented.

"I know it's a bit unusual," Carter replied.

"If I may ask, what made him decide to do that?" Jose asked looking at Carter on the driver's seat.

"The truth of the matter is that he had a number of reasons: one was because he felt guilty because he knows at the bottom of his heart that he had everything to do with what happened to Fletcher, and second, because he felt that you don't deserve the humiliation that came with what happened to Fletcher, and finally he felt the need to protect his friendship with the Angleton's, remember Fletcher is the boyfriend of Camila his daughter," Dr. Carter said as he thought quickly on his feet.

"So in short, you've been sent by Mr. Ashcroft to pass this message to me?" Jose asked again.

"Sort of, but that's not all," Carter replied reclining on the driver's seat.

"I hope it's nothing alarming, what you are about to tell me," commented Jose Cameron.

"It's nothing to worry about," assured the doctor.

The silence that followed seemed to last for eternity as both men struggled with a hidden unease. With a baseball cap slightly covering his forehead, Jose Cameron tried to analyse what Dr. Carter had told him, 'why couldn't his former boss call him on his cell phone and explain all this without sending an emissary, or was there something sinister going on?' he wondered to himself. Jose kept these troubling thoughts to himself.

For the years he'd been working with Michael Ashcroft, there was never a time when they had quarrelled or had disagreements of any kind. He remembered how he had run all kinds of errands for Mr. Ashcroft for a generous reward. There was no doubt in his mind about Michael's integrity. But Jose also knew that Michael was cunning and a hardworking man who could sacrifice anything to protect his social standing and business. Jose reclined on his seat with an expressionless look on his face. He didn't want to give the doctor the impression he was worried about anything.

Jose's apparent trust in Carter caused the doctor to turn his head away from Jose to hide the smile forming on his lips. He rubbed his chin thoughtfully. The thought of his case being thrown out was good news to Jose and he believed the immense influence of his former boss was enough to silence any of Jose's detractors.

The window on the driver's side was lowered and warm fresh air blew from the outside. Dr. Carter realized that he had won the first round of persuading Jose that there was no animosity between him and his former boss, so without wasting more time he continued with his plan.

"The most important point here today is not that your case has been terminated. What really made Michael Ashcroft send me over to you was that he wants you to go back to working for him as you did before," Carter said and kept silent again for a while.

"Are you serious, or is this some kind of big joke?" Jose asked incredulously, turning his head to face the doctor.

"That's the way it is," Carter answered nodding his head slightly.

"I can't believe it; he wants me back at work?" Jose asked genuinely amazed.

"With full pay and compensation from the last time you left." Dr. Carter realized that he was divulging too much and sometimes when a deal sounded too good, it was usually suspicious, so he continued cautiously, "that's what I heard him telling his wife."

"Telling his wife?" Jose asked curiously.

"Yes his wife Linda, that was three days ago," Carter said.

"Oh my! I just can't believe it!" Jose exclaimed excitedly.

"So, are you busy tomorrow?" Dr. Carter asked trying not to lose track of their plan.

"No, not at all," Jose blurted hoping that Dr. Carter was planning on getting him to meet Ashcroft, his former boss and put all this debacle behind them.

"Then you should try and see him tomorrow afternoon, that's what he told me," Carter said.

"I will give him a call and request for a meeting," Jose was still smiling as he replied.

"Tomorrow is Saturday and all you'll have to do is to join us at the Racecourse, you don't have to bother calling him, I will tell him that you'll be coming and he will be expecting you," Carter said.

"I am trying to think of what to tell him because I feel I am also to blame for what happened to Fletcher that night, even though I didn't really go with the guys to beat him up," Jose told Dr. Carter, as if such a confession would give him a better chance with his boss.

"Don't worry about that Jose; Michael is a gentleman but the only thing you should not forget is to tell him that you are very sorry for what happened to Fletcher that night at the Ogaden Night Club. That's all he needs to hear from you."

"So, tomorrow afternoon, at the Racecourse?" Jose asked opening the car door and sticking one leg out lazily.

"Don't get too drunk and if there is something you'll need from me, I will be at the hospital until quite late today."

"No problem doctor," Jose said flinging his other leg onto the tarmac. He got up slowly and left. Dr. Carter watched him ambling off for a few minutes before driving off with a smirk on his plump face. It had all finally worked out as he had planned.

Dr. Carter had nothing he needed to do at the hospital that night and he needed to regroup his thoughts after his encounter with Jose. Thinking of the task ahead, he drove his silver VW through the High Street and on to the parking bay of an Indian restaurant he liked that was along the main road. They served chilled beer and authentic Oriental Cuisine; just what he needed right now.

On entering the restaurant, Dr. Carter sat at a corner table. He grabbed the menu that was propped up on a wooden stand to the side. A lit candle flickered on the stand. He felt hungry. He raised his hand to get the attention of a uniformed waitress, who nodded and came over holding a small pad and pen. Without reading the menu, Dr. Carter asked for his favourite meal of Butter Chicken, and cheese cubes in spinach known as *Palak Paneer*, served with rice. He also asked for a glass of chilled white wine.

A lot was going on in his mind as he enjoyed his meal. There was Mr. Ashcroft to notify about his encounter with Jose Cameron and this had to be done quickly as time was not on their side. Things could go wrong at the last minute so they needed to tie this plan together quickly to avoid any mistakes. After a few hurried bites of the delicious meal, he decided that he needed to call Michael.

Looking around slowly to make sure there was no one paying attention, Dr. Carter took out his cell phone and called Michael Ashcroft who was having dinner at home with his wife Linda. Michael's cell phone was in his jacket that was still hanging on the wall behind the door to the living room. It rang five times with no one answering it. Mr. Ashcroft had a habit of not having his cell phone with him when he was having his meals at home because he wanted no interruptions during his time with the family. He normally called back anyone who had tried to get to him after he had eaten and relaxed with the family members for about an hour. So, he only managed to return Dr. Carter's call about two hours after dinner.

"Hello doctor, you called me earlier but I was a bit busy, any news?" Michael Ashcroft asked.

"A lot has happened and I wish to see you urgently," replied Dr. Carter.

"We can't meet tomorrow?" Michael asked.

"I am afraid we don't have much time," answered the doctor.

"Is it that urgent?" Michael asked again.

"Very urgent," Carter said.

"Very well then, where are you?" Mr. Ashcroft continued.

"I am in a restaurant having my dinner," Carter replied.

"Shall I say in thirty minutes?" Michael suggested.

"That's alright, let's meet by the left wing parking bay of the Indian restaurant you know I like in the town center. I am eating there now," said the doctor.

"That's ideal," Michael answered.

"Be here on time please, we need to iron out a few things concerning what we had talked about the other day," Carter said firmly.

"Ok, thirty minutes and I'll find you there," Michael said and hanged up the phone.

Linda Ashcroft was watching her husband carefully. She had known him long enough to know from the eager look on his face that something important was up. She resisted the urge to ask any questions. She listened as he said he needed to dash off for a few minutes to meet a client, and wondered quietly what was going on.

"I know this could be an important meeting but please don't take too long before coming back home," she said stroking the thick mane of the cat on her lap.

"Don't worry my love, I will be back within no time," Michael replied.

Camouflaged by the dancing shadows of the tall Acacia trees lined along the perimeter walls of the parking bay, Michael Ashcroft's sleek Lexus was parked alongside the fence. It was hard to spot. This was a good place to meet Carter as they needed to keep a low profile. Other than the twinkling of the stars in the sky above, the night was dark and chilly with tree branches swaying from side to side as the wind picked up.

It was well past the thirty minutes within which they were supposed to meet at the parking bay but he still couldn't see Dr. Carter. Suddenly Michael's cell phone rang.

"What's happening Michael, I've been here waiting for you for the past I don't know how long and I can't see you anywhere. This is important you know." It was Dr. Carter. He couldn't see Michael's car and he was getting frustrated.

"Calm down man, I am here already, just drive around the fence on the southern side of the restaurant and you'll see my car," Michael replied.

"Okay," Carter said and hanged up the phone.

Both men were eager to fine tune their plan regarding Jose. They needed to be sure that what they discussed in secret today would work. It was the only way forward if they were to save their reputations and get this thing over with as quickly as possible, and without any mistakes.

Dr. Carter didn't know until now of the confrontation that had occurred a few weeks back between Fletcher Angleton and Jose Cameron. The fact that Sergeant Morgan Clifton had the knowledge of what transpired was a fact that made their scheme even better because if anything happened to Jose, Fletcher would be the first suspect. Their final plan was simple and fool proof.

Michael Ashcroft had the financial muscle to manipulate things to his advantage but he needed people on the ground to execute the plan. All that was needed was for Dr. Carter to make sure that Jose was at the right place, on the appointed date and time. It would not be easy to make sure all this worked out, but it had to, and there were not to be any loose ends.

"This might sound utterly ridiculous but it is the only way we can do it," said the doctor when Michael finally got to him.

"Let me hear it, I know you can do it," answered Mr. Ashcroft.

"And don't blame me if anything goes wrong. I have talked to Jose and he is willing to meet with you tomorrow," said Dr. Carter.

"Let's hope the boy will show up," Michael said doubtfully.

"Why not, he is desperate and wants this behind him," said the doctor.

"Ok, let's be positive and believe that nothing will go wrong," Michael replied.

"Okay shall we call it a day?" asked the doctor after they had gone over the plan at length.

"Tomorrow at two o'clock as agreed," Michael answered.

"I will do most of the talking because you know he fears you. All you'll need to tell him is that everything has been taken care of and since he had been a loyal worker, you are willing to take him back to continue with his duties just like before," continued the doctor.

"Okay, deal!" Michael Ashcroft replied.

With the scheme sealed and understood, the two men finally parted company.

Dr. Carter drove his VW Passat blindly within the town center not sure which way to go. His mind was in turmoil as he thought of the task ahead. Sometimes he wished he had nothing to do with it. But, he was already head deep in the mess and there was nothing he could do to extricate himself from it. His dream of a quiet life as a doctor in a respectable hospital seemed more elusive over time because of these experiences he kept having with Michael Ashcroft. First, there was the George Franklin thing, and now this.

'What a life for goodness sake?' he wondered to himself angrily. 'Why couldn't he be left alone to live his life? His mind raced with a million thoughts so that he didn't realize he was driving like a maniac.

It was not until he negotiated a sharp corner, and narrowly missed an oncoming Mini Morris that he realized he was not himself. He regretted how far he had gotten himself mixed up in Ashcroft's mess. It was too late to pull out now. He felt guilty and wanted to assuage his conscience but the job had to be done.

Tossing from side to side alone on his bed, Jose Cameron found himself in a disturbing dream. The events of the day had been disconcerting and he kept turning his conversation with Dr. Carter over in his mind. Slowly his mind drifted to more appealing thoughts of reconciliation with Michael, as he savoured the idea of returning to his former position within the Ashcroft Empire and getting back into their good books and all the benefits that came with it. This was going to be exciting. He couldn't wait for it to happen.

It was a welcome moment for Michael Ashcroft. At last, he was drawing close to the end of the disarray that the Fletcher incident had caused. He felt calm for the first time in a long while after his meeting with Carter. He settled on his sofa in the living room and with his feelings of accomplishment, he leaned his head back and dozed off.

Chapter Seventeen

Pamela Wilcox on leaving Radcliffe Referral Hospital did not understand why there had been an invasion in her house. There was no recollection at all in her mind as to why it had happened. She had been careful to do all that the nurses and doctors wanted to make sure she and her baby were safe, but still she felt somebody owed her an explanation. It was three weeks since the police raid at their home.

———————

Henry Forbes knew he was the cause of all this trouble, and he had to gather the courage to face the Wilcox's family and make things right. His conscience niggled at him even when he tried to deny what had befallen them. He was personally responsible for Pamela ending up in hospital. Thoughts tumbled through his mind of all that he had gone through with Wilcox; perilous times together that led to this bond they now shared. He felt isolated and vulnerable most times however, like an animal giving birth alone in the forest. 'I have no choice but to face Jose Cameron in the end,' he thought to himself.

———————

What had happened in their home was difficult for Pamela to ignore. They had gone through their ups and downs in their marriage but nothing could be compared to what had taken place the past few days. She wondered at the future she had with James Wilcox. She loved him, of that there was no doubt. She decided to surrender her worry and bewilderment to whatever was coming their way. She chose to maintain her usual calm despite the confusion and heartache she felt. She needed to protect her baby and stressing would not help.

Events were spiralling out of control it seemed. Jose Cameron's debacle seemed to hold everyone at ransom.

The time was twelve noon and the weather was becoming gloomier. Jose Cameron was determined to face whatever he had to in order to have the meeting with Michael Ashcroft. He was not going to let any excuse keep him from getting his old job back.

It took him one hour fifteen minutes to get to the Racecourse. Public transport was slow due to some road repair to a section that connected town centre with the suburbs. A slight drizzle made progress slower with every driver struggling with poor visibility as they meandered along, but nothing could dampen Jose's eagerness to get to his destination.

Michael Ashcroft was having a quiet, last-minute discussion with Dr. Carter before Jose arrived, as they tried to ensure that their plan was water-tight. They sat in a small cubicle in a bar at the Racecourse. Most of the seats were vacant because most patrons were busy following the horse racing events on the field. It was quarter past two and there was still no sight of Jose Cameron.

"Are you sure he understood what you told him?" Mr. Ashcroft asked.

"There is no doubt about it," replied Dr. Carter.

"I know him to be a very punctual fellow when it comes to time-keeping," Michael said.

"It's quite a distance you know, let's give him some time," answered the doctor.

"By the way did you place any bets?" asked Michael squinting to look the big television screen on the wall.

"I don't gamble," Carter answered.

"What do you mean you don't gamble? Is this the first time we've been here together?" Mr. Ashcroft asked bemused.

"But I don't," Carter countered defensively.

"Just say that you're not doing so today because I know you gamble," Michael continued.

"Okay, today, no gambling for me," Carter said sheepishly.

"Exactly," Michael Ashcroft was smiling in reply.

"So how much have you put down today?" asked the doctor.

"A thousand pounds and I think my horse is going to outrun the rest," Michael said.

"How do you know that?" Carter queried.

"You talk with the right jockey and everything falls in line," Michael smirked confidently.

"That's cheating," Carter retorted.

"So what, they do it all the time," Michael said peering curiously at the big television screen on the wall opposite them.

"If they know you are doing that my friend, you'll will find yourself in a real fix," warned Dr. Carter warily looking around him.

Twenty five minutes past two o'clock; the flamboyant figure of Jose Cameron came out of the shadows. He walked slowly like someone who was not sure of where he was going. He was dressed in a black jeans and a white checked shirt. He walked straight to the bar and looked around in anticipation. Was it the drizzle outside or was he sweating? With a handkerchief he wiped his face before asking for a bottle of Budweiser from the bar tender.

Michael Ashcroft was the first to spot him and he nudged his companion with his foot.

"Leave everything to me; from now on I will take charge," said Dr. Carter standing up.

"Okay he is all yours," replied Michael in a whisper quickly picking a tabloid from the table.

Pretending not to have seen him, Dr. Carter walked past the main bar to the gents toilets across the lodge, he made sure Jose Cameron didn't see him walking past and within two minutes he came back again heading straight to the bar. Their eyes met and like old friends meeting after a long time, they hugged each other smiling widely and thumping each other on the back. They sat and exchanged pleasantries and after a while Dr. Carter bought a round of drinks for all of them and led Jose to where Michael Ashcroft was seated.

"It's been quite a while now Jose, how are you getting on?" Mr. Ashcroft greeted extending a firm hand and trying hard not to look his usual formal self.

"I am trying to keep my head above the water," replied Jose struggling to maintain his cool before his former boss.

"Sit down and relax," welcomed Michael pointing to an empty chair next to his.

"Thanks," Jose said, pinching his trouser legs up by the knees slightly and raising them an inch before sitting down.

"You need to place your bets before the race is over," said Michael Ashcroft, a slyness slipping into his voice.

"Not today," Jose replied none the wiser.

"How come nobody wants to place a bet today?" Michael asked not referring to anyone in particular.

"Don't worry about us, you never know, it could be your lucky day today," said Dr. Carter just as slyly.

"Well it looks like I am the only one who is greedy for money here," said Mr. Ashcroft concentrating on the television.

"I am feeling hungry already; shall we ask for some food?" asked Dr. Carter looking enquiringly around at his companions.

"Oh that's a good idea, drinking on an empty stomach has never been good," agreed Michael Ashcroft.

The talks began with apologies from Jose Cameron for being late. He took time to expound on his reasons for being late, all of which were not relevant to the two gentlemen. Their main concern was he had made it to this meeting. It was going to work out as they had planned after all. The noises from outside were getting louder as the now tipsy patrons cheered for their favourite horses as the races continued. The food was brought steaming on plates, which were placed on the table. The three men talked at length about business and the difficulty investors were having with the high level of bureaucracy, red tape and decadence in high offices; anything but what brought them to the Racecourse in the first place.

Timing was crucial, Dr. Carter turned to Mr. Ashcroft with the query of his intended trip to Istanbul laying the ground for Jose Cameron to be cited as a possible employee.

"I have tried to get a person whom I feel I can trust to work for me but it's difficult to get someone like Jose," said Mr. Ashcroft.

"I mentioned that to Jose yesterday and I don't think he has any problem coming back to work for you again," said Dr. Carter.

"It's good we have him here with us and of course he will need to tell me himself if he is willing to come back and work for me," said Michael turning with a raised eyebrow to Jose.

"I believe all human beings make mistakes and what ultimately happened was not Jose's intention, the problem was caused by those other guys going overboard," Dr. Carter cut in feigning defence for Jose.

"I would love to come back and work for you," Jose said hurriedly to allay any fears that he was in doubt about getting his old job back, or any other job for that matter with Michael Ashcroft. Then he added hesitantly, "My problem is that, I am still not free to do as I choose. I need to be reporting to the police station daily until my case is concluded."

"I think that issue has been put to rest," said Dr. Carter.

"Yeah, that's done away with. However, you'll still have to go there on Monday as usual and Sergeant Morgan Clifton will formerly tell you himself that your case is now dealt with and that you are now free and have no need to keep reporting at the station," added Michael quickly, exuding confidence.

"The ball is on your court Jose; it is up to you to decide," said Dr. Carter.

"And by the way Jose, we both need to forgive each other for what happened and move on with our lives you know," said Mr. Ashcroft giving Jose a fake grin.

"I feel very sorry and partly take the responsibility because I failed to tame the boys and make it clear to them when they were leaving me behind to keep an eye at the Ogaden Night Club, that they were not to hurt Fletcher much. Very sorry about it all," Jose Cameron said timidly.

"Let's forget about the past, it's all up to you to decide now whether we all move forward or not," was his former boss' rejoinder.

"So long as this case is off my back I don't see why not," Jose said unable to hide his obvious relief.

"One thing I request of you Jose is that, do not discuss this with anybody including Sergeant Morgan because that would ultimately compromise me. So when you see him on Monday pretend we haven't met; we haven't said a thing about this," said Michael Ashcroft urgently.

"No problem. Great that you have chosen to overlook everything I did and start afresh," Jose went on feeling encouragement welling up in his chest.

"Good, lets enjoy the drinks then; we must toast to a new start," said Mr. Ashcroft quickly, glancing at Dr. Carter with a knowing look.

"Did you say you'll be traveling to Istanbul?" Jose Cameron asked radiantly.

"Yes, I have some business to sort out there," Michael replied avoiding any eye contact with Jose.

The first hurdle was over; Jose Cameron was confident that his case was a concern of the past, and now that he was being offered a new lease of life, there was no turning back. Filled with dreams of freedom, he indulged himself in celebratory frenzied drinking. He chugged one bottle after another to the delight of his two companions who were keenly making sure that Jose's glass was never empty.

After about an hour, Jose Cameron's demeanour had transformed to that of a crazed drunk. Dr. Carter realized his time to act was approaching. Well-secured in his jacket pocket was a concoction of a lethal combination of noxious odourless chemicals secured in a fifteen-millimetre syringe. The mix could kill even a large bull within twelve hours. The idea was simple; mix the contents of the syringe in Jose's drink at the right time, and the miserable bloke would never wake up to see the sun again.

Dr. Carter didn't waste his time when the opportunity presented itself. Jose Cameron had downed so many drinks that he needed to rush to the gents. Looking around to make sure nobody saw his actions, Dr. Carter retrieved the syringe from his jacket pocket, plucked off the protective plastic covering that was over the syringe with his left hand, grabbed the half-full bottle that Jose had been downing, and injected the contents into it in one smooth move. As quickly, he returned the bottle to the spot it was on when Jose left for the gents. Even Michael Ashcroft didn't see anything. Dr. Carter had done everything swiftly, with the highest level of dexterity.

"It's done," he said turning to Michael with a gleeful yet fearful look on his sweaty face. He looked like a boy who had just stolen his mother's pearls.

"What's done?" asked Michael.

"The job is done, just wait until tomorrow," Carter replied.

"I don't understand," Michael said quietly looking around guardedly.

"Just stay quiet," Carter said firmly.

Innocently, like nothing has happened, Dr. Carter engaged Mr. Ashcroft with stories and myths from Egypt's history as Jose Cameron came back from the gents. He resumed his position at the table and joined in the interesting discussion on mummification of pharaohs and the hidden treasures many say are buried deep in the tombs of the Egyptian pyramids.

Like a thirsty camel, Jose held the already laced drink with his left hand and gulped the contents down intermittently as he spoke to the two older gentlemen. He was enjoying the idea of making up with his former boss, and especially the free drinks that came with this meeting. There seemed to be a never-ending supply of drinks available that night and Jose was in no hurry. He was determined to enjoy this night.

"So when are you going to Istanbul?" he asked his former boss again.

"Thursday of the coming week," Michael Ashcroft lied.

"Any idea for how long you will be gone?" Jose continued.

"It will depend on a number of things I need to tie up there. Probably five to six days."

"I am working tomorrow and I think I have had enough," interjected Dr. Carter not addressing anyone in particular and trying to cut off Jose's prodding.

"Let's have one more then we can call it a day," replied Mr. Ashcroft feeling slightly light-headed at how smoothly their macabre plan was moving on.

"By the way, how are you guys getting home?" Jose asked.

"I can drop you in town if that's okay with you," offered Dr. Carter.

"That's fine with me," Jose replied.

"When you are ready, we call it a day," Carter said.

From the Racecourse, it took them forty minutes to get back to town. Dr. Carter dropped Jose off at a bus-stop in town before he drove off to his own house. The effects of Dr. Carter's concoction were lethal but not meant to be immediate. Jose therefore felt that he could still handle one more drink before going to sleep that night. However, by the time he got home, he was surprised at how warm he was feeling. He was dizzy with the idea of getting his job back and thought it must be the excitement of this new beginning he had been promised that made him feel so euphoric. He staggered up to his bed a happy and a relaxed person.

Michael Ashcroft on arrival at his house, and after greeting his wife and chit-chatting about non-important events of the day, went to the bathroom to take a shower. He left her coddled by the warmth of the smouldering embers at the fireplace in the living room. Her cat was by her side purring and in deep sleep. The events that took place at the Racecourse Club left Michael slightly bewildered especially when he recalled Dr. Carter's quiet but firm statement 'it is done' without further explanation.

He felt he needed to get things straight with the doctor before getting off to bed as soon as he had taken a shower. His mind raced over all that had taken place a few hours before. He turned up the heat in the shower as though to match his racing heartbeat and the swirling thoughts burning up in his mind. The whole bedroom was engulfed in steam by the time he was through with the shower. He suddenly realized he had been there for more than twenty minutes.

He finally turned the steaming stream off, put on his pyjamas and walked downstairs to a warm welcoming cup of tea that had been prepared by his wife Linda who was impatiently waiting for her husband to come downstairs.

"That's an unusually long time you've taken in the bathroom my dear," she said.

"It is this neck pain that keeps recurring," he lied touching the back of his neck as if in pain.

"And you take thirty minutes in the bathroom for that?" continued his wife.

"You know whenever I get this problem, the best therapy is self-massage with hot water and that's what made me stay longer than usual in the shower," Michael replied evasively.

"So how are you feeling now?" she continued.

"Much better now but wait until we get to bed, you'll know I am as fit as a fiddle," he said with a cheeky twinkle in his eye.

"What are you driving at Mr. Ashcroft?" she asked giggling.

"Wait until we get to bed, it is part of the therapy you know," he replied laughing.

"And your day was okay darling?" she asked more seriously.

"It was alright," he answered.

"You don't look like everything is fine; is there something wrong other than the neck problem?" she queried perceptively.

"Not at all my love," he lied.

Linda Ashcroft had always been inquisitive in nature. She walked to the kitchen and placed a portion of lasagna in the microwave for her husband, but she was carrying on her domestic duties on auto-pilot as her thoughts were focused on how her husband's business was dwindling because of the lack of consistency on his part over the past few weeks. Of late, there had been continuous complaints from the subcontractors. Late payments were delaying the supply of materials to various construction sites and this created anxiety among junior staff as well.

As husband and wife sat enjoying the warmth from the burning embers in the fireplace, they talked in low tones about the issues affecting their family life; the ever widening gap between themselves and the Angleton's, and the weakening of their relationship with their daughter Camila because of what had happened to Fletcher Angleton. They didn't know what to do to end the feud amicably. What had happened to Fletcher Angleton meted by the Cameron hit squad had turned all their lives upside down.

Confined in his house alone, Dr. Carter had no doubt of what was about to happen to Jose Cameron. He knew from his medical background that, the toxic concoction administered to an unsuspecting Jose would be effective. It was only a matter of time before Jose felt its deadly power.

Dr. Carter shuddered as he thought of what would happen. He fought hard to suppress any fear or regret for what he had done. It was too late to entertain thoughts of guilt. He had made a choice and he had to live with it.

Tossing from side to side on his bed, Dr. Carter could not find sleep. He was haunted with thoughts of Jose in his final dying moments. All efforts to fall asleep failed. He felt he was not all to blame and kept reassuring his heart that Mr. Ashcroft was actually the one to blame for the decisions he had made over Jose. However, the smell of blood engulfed him. The memory of George Franklin filled his mind menacingly taunting him. He had to deal with Jose, or with George Franklin's death and the part he had played in it. Either way, he lost. Dr. Carter had to accept the fact that he had become a cold-blooded murderer.

The wind was blowing intensely outside. It was a quiet night with occasional sirens from the cruising ambulances passing by. James Wilcox was sitting on his bed singing love songs from Kenny Rogers to his wife Pamela. He was feeling rather romantic that evening and seeing his wife perking up on a daily basis after the horrible incident, made him quite happy.

However, he was getting increasingly worried about the recurring nightmares he was having. They all started after Pamela was admitted in hospital and he guessed it had everything to do with her frightful experience with the police. When he would close his eyes he had strange thoughts of a unicorn with its sharp horn piercing through a mammoth elephant and gouging its heart out. The unicorn had no mercy and would rip the elephant's flesh apart with extraordinary strength.

The images kept appearing in James' mind. The last time he had struggled with such disturbing thoughts, his friend Gerald was gunned down by unknown assailants. That was seven years ago. James wondered to himself 'Was there something wrong taking place with one of his friends?' His wife had finally fallen asleep as he sang to her and James glanced at her beautiful face beside him.

The disturbing images made it difficult for him to sleep. He walked out of the bedroom to the sitting room. It was ten o'clock, 'not too late to call a friend' he thought. He felt that if he could speak with Henry Forbes, he might be able to get rid of the tormenting images.

With his wife sleeping soundly James was feeling a bit lonely and to make it worse, it was Saturday, his favourite day of the week for socializing. He put on a windbreaker and headed for Henry's.

Chapter Eighteen

The preaching was going well in the church. The Rt. Reverend Crisple Wilson conducted the ceremony basing his sermon on a book he had written 'Maintaining Unity in the Community'. The church was half full. Singing with their voices raised high, the congregation's collective joyful harmony rose high up to the ceiling and the melodious chords vibrated through the walls of the large church and descended again with soothing notes to the worshippers below. The touched believers raised their open palms in the air as if reaching for the invisible Holy Spirit. After the worship session, the Reverend shared some additional thoughts from the Scriptures.

Sitting on the third pew from the altar with his head bent in tranquillity was Michael Angleton. On his left was his wife Lesley and Fletcher Angleton was a few rows behind them. The music from the choir continued as an elderly woman hammered the big piano placed in a secluded corner, and as people swayed their heads to the rhythm.

Coming to the church for Sunday service was for some a habit developed over the years without much meaning attached to it, but for others, the true believers, this was the only day to put aside the week's distractions and to bequeath their souls to God while seeking forgiveness for past misdeeds.

Not a single Sunday passed without the Angleton family attending church service, and Lesley, who happened to be the Chairperson of their church's Women's Guild made sure of it. As they sat quietly listening to the sermon, they had no idea that Michael Ashcroft and his family were also in the same church service. They were seated several rows towards the back of the church. Unlike the Angletons, Mr. Ashcroft and his wife were not regular attendants, but only came when they felt like it. What surprised Linda the most today was that her husband was the one who had initiated the move this morning as she was preparing breakfast.

"I like the way the weather is looking today sweetheart," Mr. Ashcroft had said to his wife as she whisked the eggs in the kitchen.

"It looks like it will be a nice and sunny one," she answered.

"Any commitments today?" he asked her.

"No why?" she asked.

"Why don't we go to the church then? What better way than to start a new week," he said.

"Oh that's a brilliant idea," she said placing the ready bacon and scrambled eggs on the table.

"They normally start the sermon at eleven o'clock isn't it?" he wondered aloud.

"We still have enough time," said Linda sipping her coffee.

"I will call Camila and ask if she will join us as you get ready," Michael Ashcroft said.

"You can try but I don't think she'll be available," Linda replied.

"Why do you say that, how do you know?" he asked looking surprised.

"She was to attend her friend's birthday party and you know with girls when they go out on their own, but you can still try her," Linda said.

"Yes, let me call her and see," her husband said.

Michael Ashcroft found it difficult to hide the sense of frustration he felt that day. He was obviously unsettled and found himself moving about in the house pretending to be busy, doing even the most unusual chores, and although his wife didn't ask any questions she wondered what was really bothering him.

Finally, she decided to probe a little.

"You don't look okay dear, what is it?" Linda asked him before going to the bathroom.

"I told you yesterday about my neck, I think the problem is getting worse," he lied.

"If it's getting worse you should go and see a doctor," she said.

"I still have the Diclofenac tablets I am taking to ease the pain," he said.

"Will you be going anywhere else after church?" She asked.

"I was thinking we could all go to the Royal Pavilion Inn afterwards," he suggested.

"That will be great!" she said and walked upstairs to the bathroom.

As predicted by her mother, Camila was still nursing a hangover and could not join them for the church service that Sunday but after her father's cajoling, she promised to join them at home after the service.

The parishioners passed through the exit in a line like newly recruited cadets and shook hands with the clerics as they left. Standing in small groups outside were some elderly citizens discussing parish development projects, and next to the overgrown flower garden opposite the parish entrance was a group of women from the Mothers' Guild talking about the flower arrangements needed for the wedding of the Mayor's daughter that was coming up.

As they walked hand-in-hand, Michael Ashcroft and his wife heard the unmistakable voice of Lesley Angleton as she gave her views on the overgrown and withering flowers clinging to the church walls. The church bell chimed loud and long over the mingling crowd made up of sanctimonious hypocrites and genuine believers.

In a bid to thaw the tension that had built up between the two famous families, Michael Ashcroft tried to reach out to Fletcher after the touching sermon.

"I hope you'll come with us to the Royal Pavilion Inn for lunch today," said Mr. Ashcroft to Fletcher after forced pleasantries.

"The Royal Pavilion Inn, I am not sure right now but will let you know soon enough," replied Fletcher.

"It is a nice place to have lunch or dinner especially on a warm day like this", Michael Ashcroft said.

"I've been there once and that was a long time ago," Fletcher replied.

Camila was sitting inside her car, which was parked at her father's compound; it was about one o'clock in the afternoon. The mid-day sun that had been there during the day was slowly fading away and a steady breeze continued to blow softly. There were some grey clouds in the distance. She didn't have to wait long before her mother's Range Rover negotiated the sharp hilly bed leading to the compound.

Camila stepped out of her car smiling and went to greet them.

"I was thinking we could all go to the Museum Art Gallery then we can all go to the Royal Pavilion Inn after that for lunch. The Art Gallery is not far from the Inn anyway," suggested Mr. Ashcroft.

"I can't even remember where it is," said Camila.

"It is along the Old Stein road," Michael answered.

"Not too far away then," added Linda.

They all agreed to go along with the new idea, and the day passed quickly as they moved from one exhibition area at the gallery to another spending more time where the ancient artifacts were displayed. Reminding his wife and daughter about the historical events of the past, Michael Ashcroft found consolation for his troubled mind as he reflected on the myths and realities of the Medieval Ages in comparison to the modern world.

To Camila's great disappointment, Fletcher Angleton did not join them at the house even though they waited for him for more than an hour before they left for the Royal Pavilion Inn. She kept trying to call him on his cell phone without success. They were glaring cracks in their relationship, but she was determined to protect what remained of it.

By the time they were through with viewing all the Gallery's exhibits, they were starving and ready for the scrumptious servings the Royal Pavilion Inn was famous for.

Serving from the buffet lined along the side walls of the large dining area, the group selected small portions of mouth-watering chunks of roasted beef that were sizzling inside hot-pots, together with some portions from a range of authentic cuisines from Arabic and Oriental countries. They were spoilt for choice

The group settled down to a quiet lunch in the Inn before finally driving home. The meals at the Royal Pavilion Inn were always great and helped even the most uptight aristocrat to relax after a difficult week.

———————

That evening, James Wilcox left his wife alone in the house to pay a visit to his friend Henry Forbes. The perplexing visions that kept haunting him during the nights were too much to deal with on his own and he thought it would be better to sit down with a friend and talk about it. He couldn't make sense of all the ethereal imaginations rushing in and out of his mind. Henry was in his back garden smoking pot -- 'the green stuff' as he called it -- when James approached from the back gate.

"What's up, long time no see," greeted James.

"I am cool man, how about you?" Henry replied.

"I am cool," James said.

"Any more troubles with the boys in blue?" James asked.

"No man, no more troubles," Henry said looking up at the skies, and trying to blow circles of smoke upward.

"Something strange has been bothering my mind and keeps coming back to me all the time, I couldn't even sleep", explained James.

"What's the problem man?" Henry asked.

It took him thirty minutes to tell Henry of the nightmares that had been haunting him and Henry didn't interrupt him. James was clearly disturbed and felt that something was not right somewhere.

"Have you been in touch with your friends of late?" asked James.

"We speak all the time and if I need to see them I just go to the Pasaras Night Club. That's where I am sure to find them all," Henry said in a matter-of-fact voice.

"Will you be going there tonight?" James asked again.

"Maybe," Henry replied.

"Okay."

"I have learned a lesson you know," Henry said.

"I know," James said.

"It's a matter of protecting my skin man," Henry said laughing, "and that guy is roaming freely," he said referring to Jose Cameron and clicking his tongue in frustration.

Passing time with Henry Forbes was a good idea and James felt better after their chat. He recalled the moment Henry Forbes came to his house. He had been running away from Jose Cameron and James wondered if he should ask Henry how his relationship with Jose had been since that time, but thought better of it. He felt he needed to be less involved with what was going on for the sake of his wife Pamela. He finally excused himself and left his friend to head for home.

It was late in the evening when Dr. Carter called Michael Ashcroft. Having spent the whole day in the hospital, he felt tired and uneasy as he tried to put together the events of the previous night. The image of Jose Cameron sitting with them, cracking jokes without knowing what lay ahead of him caused a cold shiver to run down Carter's back. Every time he thought about what had transpired, sweat ran down his armpits.

Dr Carter was alone in his house when he remembered the syringe with the venomous mix. He sat upright suddenly when he realized that he didn't remember where the syringe was or how he had disposed of it. It had been the last thing he wanted someone else to find and he couldn't remember where he had put it after emptying the contents into Jose's drink.

Dr Carter jumped up and started turning everything upside down in his bedroom as he sought the syringe. With sweaty face, he turned out wardrobe drawers and even shook out the clothes he had worn that night but he did not find anything. He checked the pockets of the jacket he had on but realized it wasn't the one he had worn on Saturday. He looked everywhere but couldn't find the syringe anywhere. He panicked after remembering the syringe was in the same jacket he had worn the night before, but that it was not in the house.

'Did I leave my jacket at the Racecourse Club for goodness sake?'

Dr Carter wondered aloud to himself. He decided to drive back to the Racecourse Inn to check for himself. It was not until he got to his car that he thought of checking for the syringe inside the car as well. To his relief, the jacket he had worn that night he was with Jose and Michael was lying on the back seat of his car with the empty syringe securely concealed inside the pocket. He breathed a sigh of relief and smiled to himself as he wiped the sheen of sweat off his brow. It was then that he decided to call

Michael Ashcroft to tell him how he had panicked and how he had finally found the syringe in his jacket.

Michael Ashcroft listened keenly to the phone conversation, nodding his head in affirmation at what the doctor was narrating. They talked at length and vowed to each other never to let anyone know what had taken place that night with Jose. The conversation ended with them promising to see each other the following day.

Chapter Nineteen

Amanda Walter's schedule remained the same for the one week holiday from campus. Her visit to her mother Natasha, in London over the weekend, went on without a hitch. At twenty four, she was a jolly blonde, full of life, and determined to excel academically. Amanda was a fashion enthusiast with unique taste.

While walking through the Greater London High Streets, she noticed men's leather jackets displayed in one of the shop windows and decided to buy one as a surprise gift for her boyfriend Jose. It was a Monday afternoon, her last day with her mother, and she planned to spend the rest of her holiday in Brighton with Jose as they had agreed.

One thing kept bothering her though; from the day before, the silence and lack of communication from Jose was worrying. She had been trying to get a hold of him but his phone would ring and nobody would answer the calls. It was unusual but Amanda tried to comfort herself that maybe Jose had forgotten his phone somewhere. The day ended well. It had been sunny throughout. Watching the EastEnders with her mother in the sitting room, Amanda mentioned that she wanted to stay in Brighton for a few days before going back to Oxford.

"Sometimes I get bored staying here all alone," said her mother.

"I know how it feels to be alone," Amanda said.

"I feel like leaving this job and starting my own business," Natasha continued.

"But you are better off because at least you are busy during the day," her daughter said.

"It was better when I had you here with me," said Natasha pulling at strands of her daughter's long hair between her slim fingers.

"By the way mum, I will be going back to the campus next week on Monday but I had a plan to stay with Jose for a few days," Amanda said.

"You are an adult now, it's your choice you know, and again it's good to know your partner well," her mother Natasha answered.

"Next time I will come with him mum, I would like you to meet him."

"That's a good idea and I hope he is as good a person as you describe," said Natasha smiling.

Natasha had never struggled financially in her adult life. Her husband, a senior military commander with the Royal Armed Forces, was deployed in Afghanistan where he was busy fighting. She hadn't seen him for the last eight months. With her son also in the military, she was used to being alone and it was only Amanda whose presence made her feel less lonely and restless. Amanda also made a point of visiting her mother every time she was on holiday from campus. Natasha had no doubt that her daughter tried to behave and make decisions that were respectable even as she tried to enjoy life as a young woman. She also knew that Amanda worked hard to excel in her studies. She was ambitious and enjoyed the freedom of living alone. It was good having her over for a visit.

Before Amanda Walters boarded the twelve o'clock train from London Paddington to Brighton, she had to make sure she finished carrying out the chores her mother had asked her to do: the laundry and ironing, and cleaning up the house before embarking on her journey. It was to be another month before she returned to see her mother again and she liked to leave her happy by tidying up. Her mother was a stickler for cleanliness. Even at twenty four, Amanda still felt passionately attached to her mother and always wanted to impress her.

It was one thirty in the afternoon and Amanda Walters, on arrival in Brighton, decided to pass through the local fish and chips shop for a take-away. She was feeling hungry and was certain Jose would be at work so she would need to buy something for them to eat that evening.

Across the street, two uniformed police officers were patrolling the streets, and beyond them were young children playing about as their mothers watched over them. Small tricycles lay about on the lawn in the large park a few metres away as the children ran about squealing in delight. Pigeons lined up on the telephone cables atop the houses along the street. They cooed noisily as Amanda Walters passed below their peeping eyes. She walked slowly until she arrived at Jose's gate

The door bell rang for the third time without any response. She tried again for the fourth time but still there was no answer. She bent to check if Jose's spare key was still under the small potted plant in front of the main door. Since he knew she would be coming over, he may have left it there. She scrounged around under the small pot and was relieved to find the solitary key. She picked it up and quickly inserted it into the lock of the front door and pushed the door open. She was hit by a pungent stench that filled the air as she entered the one bedroomed house. Nothing looked out of place except for a pair of jeans oddly spread on the carpet near the kitchen door. Amanda placed the take-away fish and chips container on the kitchen work-top and quickly crossed over to open the only window in the sitting room.

With the main door still open, and even after opening the window to let in fresh air from outside, the unspeakable stench that was almost suffocating still hung in the air. The door to the bedroom was slightly open and some sunlight shone through a gap in the drawn curtain into the bedroom. Amanda was trying to determine where the horrendous smell was coming from as it was not too overpowering in the kitchen, so she turned and headed to the bedroom.

On entering the bedroom, the stench was overwhelming and Amanda stood shocked and just stared. Jose's swollen and partly decomposed body lay across the bed. His head was hanging grotesquely over the side of the bed. His whole body was rigid and cold.

Amanda Walters dashed out of the house screaming and wailing loudly for help. A young man passing by the house was the first to respond to her cries. He held her small frame tightly against his chest as she screamed hysterically. He tried to understand her babbling and frightened glances into the house she had just left. The uncontrollable screams and sobs continued for some time before subsiding into desperate gasps for air. Amanda collapsed in a confused, frightened heap on the pavement before her former lover's house. She could not believe she had just seen Jose dead, and with rotting flesh.

The few neighbours and passersby gathered in small groups near the entrance to Jose's house with those bold enough venturing inside to get a glimpse at his lifeless and contorted frame. The young man continued to comfort Amanda and managed to call the police using his cell phone. It was not long before the group of people that had collected around the entrance to Jose's house heard the loud noise of sirens from the police cars and ambulance approaching in the distance.

Tuesday two o'clock in the afternoon. Detective superintendent Victor Griffins was the first to arrive at the scene followed by other homicide detectives. An ambulance with its lights flashing was parked near the steps leading to Jose Cameron's house, and across the street, a hysterical Amanda Walters was being comforted by a female police constable in her mid-thirties.

At the scene, forensic detectives were busy taking pictures and picking samples of nobody-knows-what with their gloved hands, various tongs, and other odd-looking instruments. Curious onlookers were now being discouraged from getting into the house so as to avoid any tampering with the crime scene. It was an hour later that a calmer but obviously dazed Amanda was whisked to the police station to record a statement. She had to go through this rigorous questioning, painful as it was, because she was the first person to have arrived at the house to find Jose's contorted and decomposing body on his bed. This was a painful procedure but it had to be done. Amanda felt like her heart had just broken into a thousand pieces!

She remembered how she had looked forward to seeing Jose and the shock of finding him dead and cold in his bedroom was hard to bear. She would never forget that horrendous image. With tears of loss flowing uncontrollably on her cheeks, Amanda Walters decided to go back to London after she had recorded the statement at the police station. She needed to seek solace from her mother Natasha. She could not bear going back into Jose's house. The mere thought of it made her whole body tremble uncontrollably. She knew only her mother could understand the devastation and shock she felt, and this alone gave her the strength to hail down a cab and find her way there without passing out altogether.

Jose's macabre death was the breaking news from the main broadcasting channels. 'A man in his mid-twenties has been found dead in his house in Brighton.' The news broadcaster went on to state that the victim's name was being withheld until the next of kin were informed. He added that the cause of death remained unknown. The particular story was repeated every fifteen minutes as a news flash. Bad news was always good news; this is how the world turned from day to day. It was this kind of story that drew throngs to their TV screens. Apart from the few people living within the neighbourhood and who happened to be around during the grisly discovery, and also because the victim's name was still not known, very few knew who the dead person was.

Michael Angleton received a call that evening from Sergeant Morgan Clifton requesting a meeting in his office the following morning. The Sergeant did not divulge the reason for this urgent meeting. After receiving the information from detective superintendent Victor Griffins that afternoon, Sergeant Clifton recalled the moment when Jose Cameron reported the confrontational incident with Fletcher Angleton and wondered if Jose's death had anything to do with that incident. There was no strangulation or struggle at the scene and the most probable cause of death was either an overdose of drugs or poisoning, but the factual details would have to come from the coroner.

The news had startled Michael. He turned and stared at the TV screen. The news broadcast continued on Jose's grisly death. Lesley Angleton asked her husband if he had heard the news.

"I heard about it from the car radio as I was driving home from work," he replied. "I wonder who could have carried out such a heinous act," Lesley said, concern etched on her forehead.

"Have you spoken to Fletcher?" Michael asked.

"A few minutes back, and he is alright," she answered.

"Sergeant Morgan Clifton has called requesting a meeting tomorrow morning and he sounded very concerned," said Mr. Angleton.

"Any idea what it's all about?" Lesley asked.

"I haven't any notion," Michael Angleton said.

"I think it's all to do with the case," she said placing a hot cup of tea on the table for her husband.

"I wish this was all over and done with, I don't have time to waste on stupid and trivial matters," Michael said removing a diary from his coat pocket to jot down the time for the meeting with the sergeant.

"You might think it is over, but until the case is concluded, this matter will continue to haunt us," Lesley said matter-of-factly.

"I will pass by the Sergeant's office before going to work in the morning," Michael said taking a sip of tea from the steaming cup and wondering why the sergeant was asking for a meeting.

"I can't remember the last time a person was found dead in their house. Normally, if it's not suicide, you expect that if someone has been attacked that maybe a neighbour would hear or see what is going on and quickly call for an ambulance," commented Lesley Angleton.

"Let's not jump to conclusions on this issue my dear," said her husband.

"Anyway it's none of our business," Lesley said walking towards the kitchen.

Amanda Walters fell into her mother's arms and narrated her horrific experience as soon as she got in through the door. Her mother listened mortified and finally burst into tears as well. Both women wept unashamedly for some time and finally settled into a disturbed silence. There was nothing they could do and their hopes and prayers hinged on the truth coming out as to how it all happened.

For the time they had been together, Amanda never had any doubts about Jose's character. He had come across as an honest and straightforward individual and Amanda had never heard him complaining about any person he interacted with. She also knew most of his friends and none struck her as murderous. She couldn't recall Jose ever complaining of any health problems either. She wondered quietly to herself; 'Was it a heart attack? What could have caused his death?' An answer eluded her and she didn't have the courage to ask what had really happened when she was being grilled at the police station, after Jose's body had been taken to the morgue. Amanda was scared and troubled.

The news spread like wild fire within the neighbourhood and there was great concern among some residents especially those who witnessed the work of the investigators and medical team at the scene after the incident. When James Wilcox saw the news broadcast on TV, he called his friend Henry and asked him if he had heard the news broadcast and whether he might know who the person was. James had a disturbing feeling in his heart about the news clip. However, unlike James, Henry Forbes was not aware of what had happened as he had not watched the news yet. He was hearing it for the first time and wasn't really bothered about it. Strangely for James, he kept having butterflies in his stomach. He had been on edge since he had watched the news that afternoon.

———————

Pamela Wilcox was busy filling in a crossword puzzle in the sitting room. She leaned on the low coffee table as she sat on the carpet. Sometimes, she would glance at the twenty-four inch television in the corner of the room. The broadcast was hard to ignore as grisly pictures of a dead man kept being flashed on the screen. She looked across at her husband who was seated on an armchair; his eyes glued to the broadcast and wondered what was going through his mind. When she asked him to change the channel, he flatly refused, leaving her wondering what connection he had with what was being aired on the television.

"You know I like watching the EastEnders, can you change the channel for me please?" she asked for the umpteenth time.

"Just a moment, I will change it shortly," he told her.

"But they have been repeating this sordid story for the last two hours," she pleaded.

"I know but they still haven't named the victim, maybe it's a person that we know," he replied.

"You are only being selfish," she continued.

"You know whenever I get this disturbing feeling, there is always something to it," James replied trying to justify his keen interest in the broadcast.

"It doesn't matter to me, so long as you are not the victim, who cares who that is?" she retorted.

"Okay you win," said James switching channels so as to avoid the nagging that he knew was coming his way if he refused to watch something else. He threw the remote onto the sofa after changing channels and tried to act like he was not disturbed about anything.

"Thanks darling," said Pamela with a smile, relieved that she could finally watch her favourite series.

The fine dust blowing from the construction site was too much for Michael Ashcroft. His workers were busy with earth-moving machines shovelling tonnes of gravel and sand nonstop to beat a client's construction deadline. The building site was a beehive of activity with manual labourers striving to ensure the work did not delay. Michael's company had bid for and won a tender put out by the Local Council to construct a new housing estate. They needed to complete the construction on time; otherwise it would cost his company a fortune, a thing he was keen to avoid. As usual, to ensure there were no delays in jobs for important clients, Michael decided to supervise the work himself.

It was quarter to five when he got the news from Dr. Carter. The heat from the blazing summer sun forced Michael to seek some shade from which he could observe the construction work. It was important to focus on his business. He was determined to work up to six o'clock that evening, weather permitting. Dr. Carter's call was expected and lasted only for a second. The doctor only said two words -- 'it's done'. The message was clear. Michael understood and didn't ask any questions. He turned to his workers and slipped the cell phone into his shirt pocket. He continued to work as if nothing had happened even though his heart was racing and his hands were damp and shaking.

He wanted to meet with the doctor for more details but this could only be done after work, somewhere very quiet. From the time Dr. Carter put the noxious concoction into Jose's drink at the Racecourse Inn, Michael had not talked to him about what had happened thereafter. The die was already cast; there was no turning back. He knew he owed the doctor a lot, most especially silence.

It was time to go home and everybody was eager to escape the scorching sun. Michael Ashcroft felt relieved when he finally drove out of the construction site. On the way to his house, he listened to music from the car radio. It helped him calm down after the heart-stopping bit of news from Dr. Carter, and soon he was driving through the gate to his compound.

The house was empty; his wife Linda was nowhere to be seen. Normally she would leave the office at five o'clock and drive straight home unless she had other arrangements and she would inform him of such plans. It was not too late and maybe she had gone to the shops or passed by Camila's. Michael Ashcroft went upstairs and had a shower. After he dressed, he decided to call his wife.

"It's now half past six and I am in the house wondering where you are," he said on the phone.

"I am with Camila and Fletcher; we're watching the news," she said.

"Something interesting?" he asked.

"Yes, I think you will be surprised by the news although no one is sure. We are waiting for more information on it," she answered.

"I was very busy today. I was at the construction site, remember? It was back-breaking. There's no way of keeping in touch with what's on the news out there," he said.

"I understand how hard it must have been, especially with this hot sun," Linda said.

"Anyway I will catch up with you later," Michael continued.

"Are you going anywhere?" Linda asked.

"I need to get some fresh air. I don't want to stay in the house all by myself, but I will be coming back soon," he replied.

"I will see you later then," Linda said and hanged up the phone.

Driving out of the compound again, Michael steered his Lexus through King's Road and parked outside the Northern Lights Restaurant where Dr. Carter was waiting impatiently. It was still bright outside with sun rays fading away behind the tall buildings around them. The restaurant was not crowded and there was enough room to enable them to sit away from the few people inside. A double shot of Jack Daniels for both of them and their sullied business commenced.

"I told you it was easy, just like A, B, C," started Dr. Carter.

"I can't believe it is actually done…that you actually did it," replied Mr. Ashcroft as he looked about the low-lit restaurant furtively.

"I was confident because I knew I had administered the right dosage of the deadly mix. Even a prized bull wouldn't have lasted more than twenty-four hours after downing that," said the doctor pompously.

"Are you aware that it's all over the news," asked Dr. Carter. "Although no one cares about such news for too long; the interest in the incident won't last I can assure you," he continued.

"Okay, so that's what Linda was referring to? We spoke on the phone before I came to see you," said Michael.

"The pathologist might find traces of the stuff in his body, but there will be nothing to tie us to it so we need not worry," said the doctor.

"Okay, tell me how you did it," Mr. Ashcroft said, curiosity and urgency lining his voice.

"I had everything in a fifteen millimetre syringe, in liquid form. There is no problem because the liquid had no odour," so Jose could not suspect anything the doctor said.

"And then what?" Michael asked again.

"Relax, I am getting to that part of the story man," the doctor sounded slightly exasperated. "When Jose went to the toilet, I quickly squeezed every drop of the poison into his drink. Even though you were right there, I did it so fast you didn't even notice," continued the doctor.

"That was amazing," commented Mr. Ashcroft. "I don't know how I will ever repay you for helping me out in this thing."

"You don't owe me anything. We are now equal, remember. I paid for what we did to George Franklin. You knew about it but you kept your mouth shut. That's all I need from you, your silence as well," replied the doctor looking at Michael in the eyes meaningfully.

"Okay," Michael agreed. "In fact, let's drink to that," he said standing up to go to the bar.

"Only one thing I feel that I must tell you," continued the doctor.

"Since getting home on Saturday from the Racecourse Inn, I haven't been feeling very well; it must be nerves," Dr. Carter said with a disturbed expression crossing his brow.

"If it's something serious you might need to get some treatment," Michael ventured.

"I thought the same but I am a bit reluctant and I don't know why," said the doctor.

The two gentlemen sat talking quietly with their heads close together about what they had done. The flat screen television hanging on the adjacent wall was airing a football game that was of no interest to them. Then at exactly eight o'clock, the news headlines started with the identification of Jose Cameron as the man who had died in his house. The next of kin had been informed and the probable cause of death said to be an overdose of unknown illicit substances. Nothing was said about Jose's death being a possible homicide.

A look of relief registered immediately on the faces of the two friends when the broadcast came to an end. Dr. Carter's face broke into a wider grin and revealed, for the first time, two pairs of gold-plated molars, to the surprise of his friend. Like two schoolboys relieved that their truancy had not been found out, they dissolved into a frenzy of downing one Jack Daniel's after another and vowed they would never again do such a thing.

Michael Ashcroft, although he felt relieved, couldn't shake off what Sergeant Morgan Clifton had told him about Jose. The sergeant had warned him that if anything happened to Jose that Michael would be considered a prime suspect because the sergeant had gotten wind of Michael's involvement with the assault on Fletcher Angleton. So, even as he celebrated with the doctor, Michael knew that he was still not completely in the clear.

"Remember when Jose was in custody, did he talk about your involvement with what happened to Fletcher, to that Sergeant Clifton guy?"

Dr. Carter suddenly asked Michael as if he had read his mind.

"If my memory serves me right, Jose didn't say a word," Michael lied.

"Then its okay, nothing to worry about," said the doctor in a voice that was beginning to thicken from the shots he was gulping down.

"I am still trying to jog my mind, but no, Jose didn't seem to have mentioned my name," added Michael Ashcroft.

"Wait a minute, when you guys had that meeting at the Italian pub off Victoria Road, what were you discussing?" pressed the doctor.

"Oh my God, I remember," said Michael clapping a sweaty palm on his forehead so as not to let on that he had been fearing Jose's confession might come to haunt him. What a crazy mistake! I believe the sergeant knows what part I had to play in that whole Fletcher mess," answered Michael in a low tone.

"What exactly does he know, because this is now turning into some kind of bloody joke!" Dr. Carter exclaimed shock creeping into his drunken eyes.

"I will sort that out, please don't let's spoil this celebratory night," said Michael trying to placate the obviously horrified doctor. "I will sort everything out with him. I will try and meet him as soon as possible. Don't worry about it…"

"Are you nuts? Of course there is everything to worry about," the doctor hissed unbelieving.

"Don't worry doctor, all he knows is that I was not happy with Fletcher's infidelity," Michael said.

"And what else?" shouted the doctor before he quickly lowered his voice. Jose is freezing in a morgue and you think it's a small matter. What makes you think that the Sergeant will not be suspicious?" the doctor continued unable to hide his anger.

"I will deal with the sergeant and I will let you know how everything works out. You know me don't you doc?" Michael was trying to feign a positive mental attitude even though he was just as fearful of being connected with Jose's grisly death.

"We are done for!" the doctor said in disgust, his open palm up in the air.

"No, no, no, doctor, everything will be fine, just trust me," said Mr. Ashcroft reassuringly.

"Okay, okay. But for goodness sake, don't do anything stupid when you speak to him. This is serious stuff," said the doctor without blinking.

"I will sort him out. You know money always talks," Michael said and signalled to the waiter to bring the bill. He wanted to leave before the doctor got really agitated.

It was getting late and both men had work the next day. Michael had to think seriously about how to deal with the sergeant so as to ensure he was not a suspect in Jose's death. They finally parted with a promise to meet again on Saturday afternoon at the East Brighton Golf Club.

———

Linda Ashcroft didn't realize that the back, left tyre of her Range Rover was low on pressure when she decided to drive home. It was the unusual wobbling of the steering wheel that distracted her and made her decide to stop by the roadside. She was careful to avoid being knocked into by the flow of traffic behind her. Stepping out she walked around and found the flat tyre. Luckily for her she had not driven more than a few hundred metres away from her daughter's house. Fletcher Angleton was still there and she knew he could fix it for her. It didn't take Fletcher long to drive over and fix the tyre. He then wished her a safe journey as she started the engine. After she had driven off, he found his way back to Camila's.

After her mother had left the house, Camila Ashcroft felt worried as she continued to watch the repeated news broadcast of Jose Cameron's death.

The shock on Fletcher's face as he watched the footage on TV made her wonder if he was involved in some way. She remembered that they had almost fought physically in the street not too long before Jose's death, and this meant that he would be a prime suspect. This would dent his reputation markedly, but she also wondered what this would do to their relationship, which was already struggling to get back on track.

The night ended on a very low note for the two lovers. Although he tried his level best to comfort her after he came back from helping her mother change the flat tyre, Fletcher knew that Camila was struggling with whether she could still trust him. She turned towards him and pulled him up slowly from her sofa.

"I am sorry but you have to go now," she said unblinking.

"What's going on, I thought we agreed earlier that I will spend the night here with you," he said sounding incredulous.

"I need to be alone for now," she said matter-of-factly.

"But, please, why this change of mind?" Fletcher continued with both of his hands crossed over his chest.

"We will talk tomorrow Fletcher. I honestly need some time alone right now, there is a lot to think about," she told him.

"But I hope this has nothing to do with what we've just heard from the news?" he retorted.

"How can you think that?" Camila said feigning indignation.

"Okay if you insist. I guess I am left with no choice," Fletcher said gruffly while picking his jacket from the chair.

"Have a good night," Camila said standing behind him as he trudged reluctantly out of the door of her apartment.

"Good night," he replied without turning back.

Camila cried unashamedly after Fletcher left. All that had been happening between them was too much for her. She felt the love she'd been nurturing for so long was waning too fast. She loved him but still she felt honesty was crucial in any relationship. She had to choose to let go if that was the only way to protect her self esteem but the rift was too painful to deal with.

Fletcher Angleton had himself to blame for all that had taken place between him and Camila over the past weeks. His deceitful acts had led to increasing mistrust between them. He had neglected her and played around with other women even though he was her fiancé. After he had left Camila's house to help Linda outside with the tyre, his cell phone that was lying on the sofa had started to ring and innocently Camila had picked it up because she thought Fletcher had not yet reached her mother on the roadside, and that she was calling him again to ask him to hurry. But it wasn't her mother, it was Samantha. This had reopened the wounds that were not completely healed in her heart concerning Fletcher's recent infidelity. It was too much for Camila. It was too late to salvage the relationship. In addition to all that pain, there was this sudden news about Jose, and she had noticed that Fletcher was very disturbed about what had happened. She couldn't piece everything together, but one thing was clear, Fletcher could not spend the night in her house when she was feeling so hurt and confused about him. She cried till the early hours of the morning wondering what was to become of their love.

Chapter Twenty

Nothing could change Lesley Angleton's mind. She believed her son was innocent and was ready to pursue the case in his defense up to the bitter end. She escorted her son to the police station where he had been summoned for questioning. There was no way she could leave her son to face this difficult moment alone. He was now the hunted. She had also heard that Superintendent Victor Griffins was leading with the investigations and that he was a no-nonsense and shrewd detective. It was rare for his stone-face to break into a smile. They found him pacing up and down his small room, deep in thought. He waited for them to settle down then Lesley Angleton asked.

"So, why have you called my son for questioning?"

"I think he is mature enough to talk for himself," replied the detective rudely as he sat on the edge of his table.

"I expected more respect from a detective of such high standing!" she countered heatedly.

"This is a murder enquiry and it has nothing to do with you madam," he answered flipping open the only file on the table.

"Okay let's get on with it; we have plenty of other things to do," she said obviously not impressed.

"Why do you want to involve yourself madam? I know Fletcher is your son but for everybody's sake, please leave me to do my job, Okay!" he commanded with a pinched face.

All this time Fletcher Angleton appeared relaxed. He felt strongly that there was nothing to fear because he knew he was innocent of any crime.

He was only slightly worried about how he had met Jose in the town centre when they had almost fought in public. That was a while ago now so he knew there was no way, any right-thinking person, could link him with Jose's death, but it still niggled at his conscience now that the poor bloke was dead. Detective Griffins placed the opened file in front of him pointing to the signature as proof that the written statement in front of him was voluntarily written.

"Is that your name?" asked the detective pushing the file closer to Fletcher.

"Yes sir," Fletcher answered peering at the statement in front of him.

"Can you tell me why you were so aggressive when you met that day on the street, before his death," the detective asked again.

"The same reasons I gave to Sergeant Morgan Clifton," Fletcher replied trying to maintain his cool.

"And did you ever get in touch with him again after that incident?" continued the Detective.

"No," Fletcher answered.

"The reason why we called you here is because it's clear on our records that, at one time you threatened the deceased in public, and you were warned by Sergeant Clifton not to have anything to do with the man, as you can very well recall, is that not true?" asked the detective standing up.

"The truth is, since that day I've never seen him again," Fletcher answered matter-of-factly.

"What about your associates, did they meet with Jose," the detective asked.

"Not that I know of," Fletcher answered truthfully.

"Exactly what do you mean by that?" the detective asked banging the table with his clenched fist.

"I am telling you the truth; how am I supposed to know whether they met him, I don't live with all my associates you know," answered Fletcher Angleton startled and frustrated at the line of questioning.

The detective kept quiet studying Fletcher's every move then finally said, "I will let you go for now, but I don't want you to go thinking that it's over. I expect you to come here quickly as soon as you are summoned, do you understand?" Superintendent Victor Griffins was not smiling at all as he walked to open the door for the Angletons to leave.

The questions were a formality. Even the detective knew they couldn't pin anything on Fletcher unless the had sufficient, and hard evidence. Nobody had any idea what had happened to Jose, and this left the theory of suicide by poisoning as the only probable cause of his death. The detective snapped his file shut as the duo left. He had no choice but to seek answers elsewhere.

Henry Forbes shuddered when he got the news from Sergeant Morgan Clifton on Wednesday morning when he went for his usual reporting at the station. He knew of the incident but had no idea who the victim was and although he despised his association with Jose; he didn't expect that things would end this way. Being the only one known by the authorities for his involvement with the case of assault to Fletcher Angleton, he feared the repercussions to this turn of events. He only hoped that the case would be dropped owing to lack of sufficient evidence. When he learned he was being called for questioning about Jose's death, he was shocked.

"Henry, I know this has come as a surprise to you, but expect to be summoned any time by our homicide detectives," said the Sergeant.

"But I don't know anything about it, in fact I can't even remember the last time I saw this fellow," replied Henry Forbes.

"You don't have to worry about it then. If they ask you, just tell them the truth and don't dwell on irrelevant issues. Answer only what you are asked," the Sergeant advised. It seemed he could tell Henry was telling the truth; he had worked long enough with hard-core liars to sense when a suspect was telling the truth.

"I understand, but what happened to him?" Henry asked.

"Well the pathologists are still trying to connect the dots otherwise we still don't know what happened to the bloke," the detective answered.

"I hope they will get to know what killed him," Henry offered feebly, fear creeping up his spine as he contemplated the same thing happening to him.

"Sign here and let's hope so," the Sergeant said pushing the open file towards Henry. He continued, "I think that's all and you can go now, but remember what I have said to you,"

"Yes sir," Henry said and left bewildered.

Sergeant Clifton was sceptical about the whole episode. He recalled the admission of Michael Ashcroft when they met at the Italian pub on that Monday evening about his involvement in the assault and knowing the family's immense influence he wondered silently to himself 'could he have been the one who silenced Jose for his own protection?'

Left alone in his office, Sergeant Morgan Clifton took out his diary and scribbled down the date, time and the venue of their meeting on that Monday evening. Other than Michael Ashcroft there was Dr. Carter who followed later after he and Michael had finished talking. With a sigh, he picked up his phone and called Mr. Ashcroft who, luckily, was still in the office.

"Hello," Michael said when he answered the phone.

"It's Sergeant Clifton,"

"How are you Sergeant?" Michael asked.

"I am okay how about you?"

"I am doing fine, just the usual hassles of construction."

"Well, I don't know about your schedule but I wanted to see you some-time," said the Sergeant.

"Is it urgent?" Michael asked.

"Not really," the sergeant said.

"Let me check my diary," replied Mr. Ashcroft.

"Go ahead I am not in a hurry."

"The remaining days of this week I will be at the construction site moni-toring the activities there and if you can wait, I think we can meet on Saturday morning," Michael proposed.

"That will be fine with me and because it's not official, shall we meet at the Volks Bar and Club," the sergeant requested.

"Where is that?" Mr. Ashcroft asked.

"Driving from the A 259 junction, where Marine Parade and Kings Road meet, branch off to Madeira Drive and you can't miss it," explained the Sergeant.

"I know the place," Michael said.

"And the time?" he requested.

"Shall we say twelve o'clock," suggested Sergeant Clifton.

"That's fine with me."

"Okay then Saturday at twelve sharp please," the sergeant said and hanged up the phone.

From their first meeting, it had always been Michael Ashcroft who requested some time from the Sergeant, but this time it was the other way around. Michael remembered the old adage 'happiness was a word too elusive to those who didn't understand' and he realized that his world of happiness was on a collision path with unknown natural forces beyond his control. This could be a big deal. He sat down for a few minutes recalling his meeting with the Sergeant on that Monday evening at the Italian pub and asked himself, 'could it be something to do with the demise of Jose Cameron?'

His wife and daughter were both in his office that morning, each for different reasons. Linda had to go to the bank to negotiate an overdraft facility and Camila was to go to the Council Office to pay some bills. It started as a normal day for the family. From the small room they used for making snacks, Camila walked to her father's desk with a cup of coffee in one hand and a packet of biscuits in the other, but soon after placing them on the table she realized her father's mood had become quite glum and decided to confide in her mother who was still making some hot chocolate and placing some salty snacks on a white plate.

"Something is wrong mum," she started.

"What's wrong now?" Linda asked her daughter.

"I don't know, but I think there is something bothering dad; come and have a word with him," she said picking her own cup of coffee.

Michael Ashcroft's face was slowly turning pale like somebody with a fever; the cup of coffee on the table was untouched as he tried to focus on what he suspected was inevitably hurtling his way. He stood by the wide window with its amazing view of the city, but his mind was too disturbed to notice. He looked up to the ceiling and breathing hard, he tried to compose himself when he heard his wife coming from behind him. He could tell her footsteps anywhere. With immense control, masking the fact that there was anything wrong, he picked up his cup and took a sip before Linda sat in a chair in front of him. She looked searchingly into his face.

"You don't look okay my love what's wrong?" she asked.

"No, I am alright why?" he asked feigning surprise.

"Don't say no because I can tell that there is something wrong," she told him touching his forehead with her soft index finger gently.

"I am absolutely fine," he insisted.

"If your own daughter can notice there is something wrong, how about me, someone who has been married to you for God knows how long. I am your wife and you should tell me if there is anything wrong." Linda was not one to give up easily.

"Hey honey, I am being honest with you, I am fine, there is nothing to worry about," Michael said forcing a smile.

"Your daughter was concerned but if you are fine, then we are all a happy lot," she told him standing up.

Turning his head towards the small room, Michael called Camila. She walked dutifully towards him, a questioning look on her lovely oval face. She stood in front of her father.

"Sit down my girl," he said to her gently and continued. "Your mum told me that you are concerned about me. I don't want you to worry my love, I assure you that I am as fit as a fiddle and I don't have anything bothering me," It was a lie but he covered the tremor in his heart well. He was desperate not to get them worried.

"I thought I noticed something unusual," Camila probed.

"Relax, I am fine," he said taking a bite from a biscuits to keep from saying more.

"Dad, don't forget what I told you last week," Camila said smiling.

"Remind me ..." he said.

"You mean you've forgotten already?" she asked.

"I have so much going on in my head at the moment and sometimes I do forget things," her father said scratching his head.

"You promised to give me eighteen thousand pounds for my perfume project," she reminded him.

"Oh that? Sure, when did you say you'll need it?" he asked.

"Anytime next week," she replied.

"Remind me on Wednesday and I will see what I can do."

Camila picked up her jacket from the top of the side cabinet and followed her mother who was on her way out the door. She turned and waved goodbye to her father.

Alone in the office, Michael Ashcroft paced up and down trying to figure out what it was Sergeant Clifton wanted to see him for. He thought of all the possibilities and came to the conclusion that the meeting he was called for had everything to do with the death of Jose Cameron. He sensed that reason why the Sergeant had selected such an excluded location was because he wanted to know as much detail about Jose, and he needed a private space if he was to achieve this. The question in Michael's mind however was whether he had a good enough alibi to cover his ass over the Jose debacle?

Blackmail was inevitable either way he thought. This was all due to his dim-witted error of judgment, and there was no chance his best friend Dr. Carter could come to his rescue. Different scenarios raced through his distraught mind. The tension continued to build, even before his meeting with the sergeant, as his guilty conscience got the better of him. He had to prepare for the worst.

Unlike the previous days, Thursday started with a cold spell in the morning, warming up as the day progressed. A flock of birds swirled overhead as they migrated from one hemisphere to the other, for warmer climates as the weather in Brighton got chillier. On the footpaths, squirrels scavenged for remnants of fallen nuts from the tall trees beyond their reach. At a distance, a pair of bunnies hopped about playfully, sometimes disappearing into the thickets dotting the landscape at the slightest sound of cracking twigs or the startling sound of barking dogs

Janet Cooper had taken a day off to visit her dentist leaving Maria Kosgei to stand in for her at their Chartered Accountants Office. Business was flowing as usual with customers walking in and out randomly. Michael

Angleton was busy in his desk talking to a new client when the telephone on his desk rang.

"Yes," he answered.

"You have a caller on line three," said Maria Kosgei from the reception desk.

"Thanks Maria," he said pressing the button for line three.

Surprisingly the call was from Michael Ashcroft. He couldn't ignore him despite the fact that he had a new client to attend to. He decided to buy some time and persuaded Mr. Ashcroft to call back in a few minutes. He was puzzled however at the call. The last time they had talked was on Sunday outside the church compound and Mr. Ashcroft didn't seem to have anything urgent to tell him on that day. Michael Angelton hanged up the phone and scribbled a few notes in his diary.

Despite the slight distraction from that phone call, he concentrated on the work in front of him and even managed to clinch a new client, which was quite a Godsend taking into consideration the downturn he had experienced in his business due to the frustration high inflation rates, and the distraction of this police case and all that went with it.

It was during his lunch break that he finally decided to call Mr. Ashcroft. He feigned ignorance of what the subject of their phone conversation would be, hoping to draw it out this way from him. It worked because Mr. Ashcroft finally narrated how eager he was to end the case now that Jose Cameron was dead and stating that this would inevitably reduce the friction between Fletcher and Camila, something that this fracas had regrettably caused.

"I don't understand why you are suggesting that," said Mr. Angleton pretending disinterest.

"My friend, this matter is out of our hands. We can't change or control the way the system works; the investigations are still going on as far as I know and I think we should let nature take its cause," Mr. Ashcroft replied matter-of-factly. "I feel this issue has driven a wedge between our two families and my concern was only to defuse the tension between us."

"The fact that Jose Cameron is gone doesn't mean my son does not deserve justice! Don't forget that?" Mr. Angleton retorted angrily.

"No, you don't understand, it's for the sake of all of us," Ashcroft parried.

"You know what Mr. Ashcroft, I am a bit suspicious about how this young fellow died and I stand corrected if his death had nothing to do with the Fletcher case," said Mr. Angleton.

"What do mean, I don't understand," Ashcroft said.

"I mean just that, there's something fishy about all this I sense, but it's only a thought," replied Mr. Angleton.

"Is that what you think?" Ashcroft asked again.

"It's my thinking and I am entitled to it," Mr. Angleton retorted.

"Well, we will have to wait and see then what happens," Ashcroft said dejectedly.

There was no doubt in Ashcroft's mind after their conversation. He felt a fear clutch his heart; fear that would bring even the most powerful to their knees. He felt this surreal sensation building up in his mind, like an earthquake roaring from afar and menacingly threatening to demolish all in its path with a devastating finality. He knew after that brief, tense chat with Angleton that the man was resolutely pointing an accusing finger at him.

Reality was dawning; a standoff with the Angleton's was imminent and the dispute was threatening to tear down what held the two wealthy families together. It was as if each family was trying to maintain a footing on a slippery turf. The palpable tension was still based on speculation, but it was there. Like feuding tyrants, they had to face each other and square everything out before it exploded out of control, but who would initiate the truce? This all-important question still remained unanswered.

Pamela Wilcox walked through the park that morning for her routine exercises. She had regained her strength tremendously and felt able to do her normal chores. As she rounded a hilly section, she unexpectedly bumped into Janet Cooper who was walking her dog. They had been workmates in the past so Pamela stopped for a chat. They talked about life in general and gossiped about domestic matters as time passed. During the seven months Pamela worked at the Chartered Accountants Office Janet cooper was her mentor. Unfortunately, Pamela was guilty of gross misconduct during her time at the office and was summarily dismissed.

It had not really been her fault but she had failed to gather sufficient evidence to prove her innocence. Janet Cooper had tried to persuade the management of Pamela's innocence but somebody higher up was determined to make sure that Pamela was laid off. Apparently, she had something personal against Pamela and was determined to see her go. After chatting for a while, Pamela extended an invitation to Janet to visit her and James over the weekend. Pamela was eager to meet up again and they parted after confirming the time.

Sitting alone on a bench in the park, Janet Cooper was enjoying the scenery. She was also thinking of the regrettable events that led to Pamela leaving their office. She glanced at her wristwatch and noticed that she still had enough time before her appointment with her dentist. The sun was brightening up and the morning vapour floated away into the atmosphere above as the sun's rays filtered downward. Dotted along the rooftops above was a mix of pigeons and other bird species. They dipped their small beaks into their feathers from time to time as they preened themselves in the warmth of the brightening sun. A spectacular display of kites with their forked tails showed off in the skies higher up. It was a lovely day and how Janet wished she could stay there relaxing much longer but she had to leave for her appointment.

Driving along the busy highway, Fletcher Angleton was sure something was not right after talking to his father a few minutes ago. The tone of his voice gave him away even when his father tried hard to mask his true feelings. It was unusual for his father to call him for a meeting in a hotel instead of at the house, especially if his mother was not included in the meeting. Fletcher knew better than to disobey. He shrugged his shoulders as he wondered what the meeting, which was set for after work, would be about.

Heist Restaurant located on West Street was an ideal meeting place for them. It was hidden from most eyes in their neighbourhood. The eye-catching interior décor and the orange bright lights from the high ceiling, and the mahogany bar-top that extended to the stairway on the left were a refreshing change from the dullness of the outside world.

It was five o'clock and as usual the restaurant was teeming with revellers of all kinds. Michael Angleton walked in and stood by the bar looking around for his son. Fletcher who got there thirty minutes earlier was sitting on a stool chatting with two girls. He had his back facing the main bar. His father decided to call him on his cell phone after fifteen minutes. All he could hear was Fletcher's hearty laugh mingled with that of the girls he was with. The unbridled laughter came to an abrupt end when Michael Angleton tapped Fletcher's shoulder and pointed firmly towards an empty table on the other side of the restaurant.

It was one of the tensest discussions they'd had for a while. The light music that floated from the speakers placed on the side walls helped muffle their conversation. It pained Michael Angleton to discuss the details of the phone conversation he had earlier with Mr. Ashcroft, but it had to be done. They talked in length for almost two hours, analysing the conversation word for word.

Fletcher Angleton couldn't understand why Michael Ashcroft would want to harm him especially because, from his perspective, all his life he had respected the old man, especially when he and Camila became lovers. He couldn't really understand how anyone could be involved in this whole mess, however, after a lengthy discussion, he agreed that they needed to engage the help of private investigators to help decipher this whole mess, and what the connection with the Ashcroft's could be.

Chapter
Twenty One

Saturday came sooner than expected. With nothing planned for the day, Fletcher Angleton decided to pass time by going out for a drive through the sprawling landscape, away from the chaotic city life. He tried to overcome a constant throb in his head as he navigated his Mercedes Benz slowly through the terrain and listened to his favourite music. The memories of the past few days ricocheted back and forth in his already ragged mind.

Thinking of the last time he was with Camila at her residence, he felt even more restless. What had blown it was when she found out he was having other lovers like Samantha in the wings. That had been final straw and he had only himself to blame for the miserable turn to his relationship with Camila. He tried to justify it in his mind; he recalled how vehemently he had tried to ward off Samantha's approaches. But, Samantha's relentless charm got the better of him and he succumbed to her lascivious demands, but deep inside, what he felt for Camila was deeper, a love that meant the world to him; he was willing to do whatever it took to win her heart back.

It was not going to be easy because he had wounded her heart with his shenanigans. He had to evaluate his options carefully. Driving through the country roads on the outskirts of Brighton, he careened down the hills and let the wind blow through the open car windows, as if this might blow his troubles away. The meeting with his father at the Heist Restaurant kept flashing back into his mind, however much he tried to think about something else. He couldn't understand why his father was so worried about the Ashcrofts and this made him feel uncomfortable, and to wonder whether his father's fears were real or imagined.

He couldn't believe that Michael Ashcroft could be so protective of his daughter Camila, that he would succumb to such a heinous act and ultimately come between her relationship with Fletcher. This seemed too petty for a man of Mr. Ashcroft's stature and charisma Fletcher thought. It was also considered traditionally incorrect, and in fact, a taboo, for a father to interfere with the private life of a twenty-three year old daughter. Surely Mr. Ashcroft understood that such behaviour would lead to unpleasant repercussions. What could lead a man held in such high repute socially to do something like what Fletcher's father was alluding to? It was all becoming very difficult to understand.

Fletcher's naivety is what had led to the attack in the first place. He failed to understand that, though Camila was twenty-three years old, her father could not turn his head the other way regardless of what went on in her life. She was his only daughter and he cherished her. She was also not married to Fletcher and this meant that she was still under her father's jurisdiction and as her father, he would do all in his power to protect her. It was a deadly mistake for Fletcher to underestimate Mr. Ashcroft's devotion to his daughter.

Driving through Horsham Road towards the centre of Guildford, his cell phone rang. Fletcher couldn't pick it right away as it was in his jean pocket and he was driving. By the time he got it out of his pocket, it had gone silent. He didn't have to wait for long before it rang again. He slowed his car and stopped on the side of the road.

"Hello, who is it?" he answered without checking the caller's number.

"Hey, it's Samantha, what are you up to?" she asked.

"Nothing really but I am okay, how are you doing?" he asked.

"I was wondering if I could see you today."

"We can't talk now because I am driving. I will call you later" he replied agitated. He was strongly aware that it was especially because of Samantha that he and Camila had broken up.

"Okay I will wait. Make sure you call," she replied and hanged up the phone.

Fletcher Angleton felt frustrated. A call from Samantha was the last thing he needed right now. It had been three weeks since they last met and he wasn't sure whether to ignore her calls or not. Holding his cell phone in one hand he thought of Camila and shook his head.

It was approaching twelve o'clock. Seated alone outside the rear entrance of Volks Bar, under a canopy, was Sergeant Morgan Clifton. He held a glass of orange juice in his left hand, and was looking down at a tabloid newspaper. The club was surrounded by a scenic mass of water extending beyond the horizons. Looking around, Fletcher saw a happy group of people splashing and diving into the English Channel. It was mesmerizing to watch the women clad in skimpy bikinis compete with the men in different water games. In the far distance, small boats with their sails raised high pushed forward against the rising tide that carried them beyond the horizon.

Looking at his watch Sergeant Morgan Clifton felt dismayed; it was thirty-five minutes past twelve o'clock and Michael Ashcroft had not arrived yet. He had expected that he was a punctual person. 'Had he decided not to turn up after all?' Clifton wondered to himself. He waved at a waiter and looked at his watch again. He asked for another glass of orange juice and crossed his legs as he concentrated on the tabloid's lead story. It was then that the unmistakable figure of Michael Ashcroft emerged from the side patio. Michael walked majestically towards him with his hand extended.

As expected, Michael apologized for being forty minutes late. The earlier dismay that Clifton had felt dissipated into thin air as he thought secretly of what he could gain from this meeting. It suddenly mattered little to the sergeant whether the reasons he gave for his lateness were genuine or phony. He hoped Mr. Ashcroft didn't have any immediate commitments to warrant a hasty discussion.

For the first thirty minutes, they talked about life in general: the crumbling of the world economy and the rising cost of living everywhere that did not spare especially the up-market and middle-income professional elite. Big cooperates drew on the meagre savings of the lower cadres and interest rates soared to record levels. Michael Ashcroft was well-versed with such subjects and enthusiastically plunged into such discussions in order to ward off the nervousness he felt inside.

"I tell you what Sergeant; this world will only become a paradise if there is no divisive religion or racial segregation. Or what do you think?" Mr. Ashcroft continued. "Right now, though, the best we can do is to mop up the muck, don't you think so?"

"As a trained police officer, sometimes I feel it's my duty to lead the way," said the sergeant hypocritically.

"But don't you think it's hard?" Mr. Ashcroft asked.

"It's not hard, just self-discipline and respect will get us there," the sergeant continued pompously.

"I wish things would just work out right now," Michael replied.

That was the moment Sergeant Morgan Clifton had been waiting for and he jumped in with what he had in mind.

"Look for example what happened to Jose Cameron, I personally liked that lad and I can't understand why anybody of sane mind could carry out such a heinous act!" said the sergeant looking pointedly at Michael's face.

"It was a terrible loss," said Michael Ashcroft avoiding eye contact.

"Listen Michael, the Angleton family is intending to launch a private investigation into the matter because they don't believe the fellow died from a self-administered overdose of whatever killed him," the sergeant said in a deliberate tone.

Mr. Ashcroft's body language betrayed him. He slowly crossed his hands and stared at his empty cup of tea. He seemed stunned and hardly blinked. This is exactly what the Sergeant had wanted to happen so that he could launch into his incisive questioning.

"Mr. Ashcroft," started Sergeant Clifton.

"Yes Serge," Michael answered tentatively.

"As Jose's former employer, I think you will also encourage a thorough investigation into his demise or what do you think, especially since he was such a trusted and devoted employee of yours?" asked the sergeant.

"Sure," Michael answered clearing his throat.

"And there was this other thing; Mr. Angleton told me you had really wanted to end this case quickly, which raised many eyebrows. That is in fact why I wanted to see you in private," said Sergeant Clifton.

"You know Fletcher and my daughter are dating each other don't you?" Michael asked.

"Yes I know about that," answered the Sergeant.

"That was the reason why I suggested that the case would be discontinued so as to end the stress they have undergone because of it," Michael continued.

"Don't worry I am off duty and everything we discuss here today is off record, I just want to know the truth. Talk to me," the sergeant said meaningfully, leaning back in his seat and eying Michael quietly.

"Are you saying that Mr. Angleton is accusing me of something to do with Jose's death?" Michael asked.

"He didn't say that, but I am afraid that's how it might look if you insist that the case is dismissed," the sergeant replied.

"I am surprised", Michael said with a sigh.

"If you remember when we met at the Italian Club a few weeks ago, you told me of your involvement in getting Jose Cameron to hunt down Fletcher Angleton and discipline him for his infidelity to your daughter Camila. You also said that things seem to have gone out of control. Is that not true Mr. Ashcroft?" the sergeant asked.

"Do you want a drink, a strong one?" Mr. Ashcroft said trying to digress from the contentious discussion.

"I don't mind a Jack Daniels," the sergeant nodded sensing Michael's underlying desperation and taking his time about things.

Michael Ashcroft didn't expect such a grilling from the Sergeant. A thin sheen of sweat was forming on his forehead and he felt trapped. He drew his handkerchief from his trouser pocket and frequently wiped it off as he wondered how he would get out of this corner he was in. The sergeant was calling the shots and Michael Ashcroft felt extremely vulnerable. His mind whirled and he wondered why he blundered and shot himself in the foot in this bloody case by calling Michael Angleton to suggest they bury it. It was too late to change that; the milk has been spilt and his judgment had failed him.

Michael abruptly excused himself, pushed his chair back and stood up. He strode across the gravelled compound and away from the sergeant's vision. He walked aimlessly completely blind to the beautiful landscape before him. He agonized over what was going on and wondered how to shake the sergeant off his scent. He remembered suddenly the meeting he had arranged with Dr. Carter later in the afternoon, but realized that it would be impossible to make it if the sergeant was going to continue grilling him. He decided to call the doctor and cancel their meeting.

He then walked slowly back to the sergeant who was still seated at the table. He felt calmer and more able to face him. Everyone had a price. Michael's extensive experience in the business world had taught him that all-important lesson. He knew the only way to get away with it was to compromise the sergeant with a bribe. He had done it with enough people each time he found himself in a fix, and knowing Sergeant Clifton, he probably faced the financial constraints that most police officers had and this made it all the more likely that he would not hesitate to accept the bribe. That was why Michael had come armed and ready for such an eventuality.

Slowly, he pulled his chair close to the sergeant and ventured in a low tone. He explained what had taken place and expressed his regrets regarding the whole saga with Jose Cameron. He kept nothing back. He graphically gave a blow-by-blow account of what had happened to Jose, all this while, watching the sergeant closely. The sergeant was nodding his head at intervals as he listened to the shocking narration from Michael. His face looked increasingly incredulous. Michael was not sure he would manage to snare him into taking a bribe but he had to take the risk so he continued with his shocking tale nonetheless. He was not willing to lose the business empire he had built all his life for a nonentity like Jose Cameron so he decided to bare all to the sergeant.

Sergeant Morgan Clifton seemed to soften, as if he sensed that his financial status might transform remarkably after this meeting.

"The ball is in your court," the sergeant concluded looking at Michael meaningfully as he pushed his chair back so that they were looking at each other directly in the eyes with Michael who had also stood up slowly. Michael breathed a long sigh of relief. He could tell he had succeeded in baiting the sergeant. But, he needed to make a few things clear.

"You need to be sure of one thing though," he said.

"What is it now Mr. Ashcroft?" asked the sergeant.

"First of all, I want to remind you that I have had absolutely nothing to do with this case and that no one will ever be able point an accusing finger at me. I am certain that this can help you make sure of that," he said as he removed a thick, sealed envelope from his jacket pocket.

"Tell me what you want me to do?" the sergeant asked staring at the envelope like a deer trapped in a car's headlights.

"Destroy any evidence that's in your possession on this case," Michael said sliding the envelope over the table between them towards the sergeant.

"Okay. That would not be a problem. I know exactly what to do," said the sergeant dazzled by the sight of the thick envelope.

"Take it," Michael said to the mesmerized sergeant who had still not taken his eyes off the brown envelope, "It's yours".

Without a word, Sergeant Clifton took the envelope and stashed it swiftly into his inside coat pocket.

"See you some other time," the sergeant said and left without looking back.

———————

Linda Ashcroft left the house late in the afternoon after receiving a phone call from Lesley Angleton reminding her to join their family and her friends for a party. Lesley and her husband were celebrating their wedding anniversary.

Under a green striped canvas erected behind Lesley's back garden were tables neatly arranged and matching in colour with the decorative flowers hanging on the canvas. The mouth-watering aroma of a variety of barbequing meats filled the air. Fletcher Angleton was manning the fire and struggling to keep the delicacies from burning.

Before leaving the house, Linda Ashcroft called her husband and reminded him of the party. Michael had completely forgotten about it but he feigned remembrance and promised that he was on his way.

It took him forty minutes to get to the Angleton's residence. He pressed the door bell and though he could clearly hear it ringing, he could tell that the sound of the revellers rose above it. A stereo playing in the background made it harder for anyone to hear the bell buzzing. Exasperated, he removed his cell phone from his pocket and called his wife.

Michael Angleton was talking to the Rt. Reverend Crisple Wilson behind the tent when Mr. Ashcroft walked in and joined them after polite pleasantries with the guests seated inside. People of different trades and skills converged together to grace the occasion and with free alcoholic drinks doing the rounds, the atmosphere was carnival-like.

Pretending all was well Michael Ashcroft joined the conversation and even cracked a few jokes, which elicited gales of laughter from the Rt. Reverend.

The party progressed very well with women converging in small groups a distance away from their men folk. They gossiped and laughed heartily as they sipped on multicoloured cocktails. The men maintained a macho demeanour by chatting about politics and sports, even though the tension between the two Michaels was palpable.

Michael Angleton stood up to clear the table of empty beer bottles. He stuffed the tip of each finger into a beer bottle so that he could carry ten at a time and headed for the rubbish bin outside. Mr. Ashcroft quickly followed from behind. It was the moment he'd been waiting for and he didn't waste time when the opportunity presented itself.

"I wanted to have a word with you but you've been very busy throughout the afternoon," started Mr. Ashcroft holding the rubbish bag.

"We've been busy trying to make everybody happy," Angleton replied matter-of-factly.

"Very soon I will call you guys for a get together at our place as well," Ashcroft continued.

"That will be a nice thing to do, remember what the Reverend said when we were chatting with him?" Mr. Angleton asked.

"No I don't, remind me again," Ashcroft answered forcing a smile.

"He suggested that people should be meeting regularly to forge stronger friendships and encourage unity. We should teach this to the younger generation I'd say," Angleton continued

"That's true," Ashcroft said fidgeting.

"Let's get to the point. You said you wanted to have a word with me, what about?" Michael Angleton asked.

"It's about what happened to your son on that Sunday night when he was attacked outside the Ogaden Night Club," replied Michael Ashcroft.

"Okay, shoot," Angeton answered quickly.

"We only want to strengthen the relationship between your son Fletcher and my daughter Camila, nothing else," Michael said taking in a sharp breath to steady his nerves.

"Look," Angleton cut in suddenly not having understood what Michael Ashcroft was driving at "I don't really know what you are leading to, but I am determined to have justice for our son. I will do anything; surmount any boundary to make sure the blokes who did this to Fletcher pay for what they did!" Angleton was prodding the air in front of him as if at some imaginary figure's chest to make his point clear.

"I am also very concerned about what happened to Fletcher I can assure you," Ashcroft butted in quietly before he added, "I just think that because we have lost the main suspect in the case that the only way forward is to let bygones be bygones and move on with life, instead of wasting time trying to catch the culprits. It is only adding the friction between our children. I am sure you have noticed that this has not been good for their relation-ship so far; they are hanging by a thread and we are the only ones who can help them recapture the deep love they had for each other," Ashcroft said.

"Did you say wasting time?" Michael Angleton asked physically gutted by that comment.

"I didn't come here to offend you, it was just a suggestion," Ashcroft replied defensively.

"Tell me Mr. Ashcroft, how much do you really know about what hap-pened to my son Fletcher?" Mr. Angleton asked peering at him suspiciously.

"I don't know anything about it; that's why I am concerned. Don't forget the dead guy worked for me," Ashcroft answered.

They were going round in circles and Angleton could tell that something was not coming out clearly. Frustrated, he turned and slowly led the way back to the tent that was now teaming with additional revellers from his wide circle of influence. They both mingled with the affluent crowd, and no one was any wiser about the tense conversation that had just taken place. Nobody seemed to be in a hurry to leave, and definitely not when there were free drinks around. Michael Ashcroft had not intended to stay for too long but he couldn't leave his wife behind and she was engrossed in an animated discussion with her friends so he couldn't bring himself to interrupt them.

Conspicuously absent from the party was Camila Ashcroft who had never missed such family events before. On arrival at her house after his solitary drive through the country, Fletcher Angleton had called her to beg her to attend the afternoon celebrations. She was still nursing her emotional wounds and adamantly refused. He had said he could change her mind about them, but she still refused to meet with him. She was determined to ponder a future without Fletcher after his infidelity and lies and she was not willing to keep up the pretences at lively events like these when she was feeling so down in the dumps. She needed time to heal.

It was ten minutes to midnight when Michael Ashcroft got home with his wife Linda. The warmth inside the house was welcoming and despite what went on at the Angleton's residence, they found themselves in high spirits. Linda, as per her habit over many years together, put the kettle on and prepared a cup of tea for both of them. They hardly ever slept without taking a cup of tea together.

Fletcher Angleton sat next to his father in the sitting room, with his mother facing them. All the visitors had left. They decided to clean everything up the next day; it was more important to talk about what had transpired between his father and Mr. Ashcroft. Mr. Angleton narrated what he had been discussing with Michael Ashcroft earlier in the afternoon at the bin. He shared that he still had his doubts about how Jose had died. He told them he found it increasingly odd that Mr. Ashcroft wanted him to drop the case. He vowed to continue working with the private investigators until he got the truth about the matter.

Chapter Twenty Two

The weather had changed drastically and several weeks had passed since Jose's burial. Blustery winds were blowing from all corners, spreading the dry autumn leaves about the place. Memories of the grisly death were fast fading.

Sergeant Morgan Clifton, after being corrupted by Mr. Ashcroft, shrewdly manipulated the private investigations by destroying vital records on Fletcher Angleton's assault. Detective Victor Griffins tried fruitlessly to piece the evidence together after that, but found it impossible.

Suffering in silence was Fletcher Angleton. Even his work mattered little to him now. He felt betrayed by Sergeant Morgan Clifton who had not succeeded in capturing those who had attacked him at the Ogaden Night Club. It seemed the sergeant was too eager to forget about everything, choosing instead to put aside Michael Ashcroft's involvement in the whole episode. Fletcher's emotional involvement in trying to get to the bottom of the case had caused him to be so distracted that it alienated him more from Camila. He felt a stab of pain at what his aloofness with her as a result of the ambush had done to their relationship. 'A day will come and the truth will manifest itself', he thought to himself as he stood by the wide windows of his spacious flat.

A deep sense of guilt had been eating away at Dr. Carter, like a parasite that was sucking his life blood. Over the weeks following Jose's death, the doctor had become more of a recluse, confining himself to his house most of the time. He became increasingly fearful of the unknown. He had killed two people, both of whom had nothing directly to do with his life. He had used his expertise as a neurosurgeon to snuff their lives out. He had given in to the pressure of people who had the power to manipulate him, and corner him into doing things he really didn't agree with.

As there was no one to console him and fend off the ghosts he was wrestling with, Dr. Carter decided to take a walk to nowhere. He had taken a week off work to try and relax, on the advice of his superiors who had noted with concern his deteriorating performance at work. He had decided on finding solace in a small retreat centre within a church compound. He hoped he would find solace in its spiritual surrounding. It was a Friday afternoon in the last week of September. He quickly stood up, picked his jacket and walked out of the centre.

Outside the church yard he found himself facing a row of freshly dug graves – the last thing he wanted to see. A shiver ran down his spine as a lone grey fox dashed across the well-maintained lawn scavenging for the small dead birds or rodents around the old tombstones.

Sitting on a wooden bench under a well-spread canopy of evergreen eucalyptus trees, Dr. Carter suddenly thought of Michael and fumbled for his cell phone. He dialed his number.

Michael Ashcroft was alone in his office consolidating his end-of-the month records from his subcontractors. Files were cluttered across the desk, occupying every available space. He was in the process of trying to sort them out according to the most important to work on. His daughter Camila, who was meant to help, was confined at her house due to influenza and couldn't be there. He was grappling with the numbers in the various excel sheets when suddenly his cell phone rang, it was Dr. Carter.

"Hello doctor," answered Mr. Ashcroft.

"Hello Michael," Carter replied hesitantly. His voice sounded heavy and dull.

"How are you getting on?" Michael asked.

"I know it's been a while since we last met," Carter answered in a croaky voice.

"It's been a busy month but thank God it's almost over now," Michael said.

"There is something I needed to tell you," said Dr. Carter.

"Go on doc, you know you are free to tell me anything," replied Michael.

"Something terrible is going on in my mind and I don't know how to resolve it, I feel very weak and I need you to help me," he said without specifying.

"Anything you need from me, I am ready to help, whatever it is," Michael said listening keenly.

"At the moment, I am feeling like an outcast, nobody is interested with what I am doing even my work mates don't appreciate my efforts anymore. Am I being a fanatic or what?" the doctor asked his voice hoarse.

"I am your friend. I am here for you. Nobody can hear what you are telling me. I don't want you to struggle with macabre imaginations alone, so please don't let yourself go in that direction," answered Mr. Ashcroft concerned.

"Can I come and see you later today?" asked the doctor again.

"Where are you?" Michael Ashcroft asked.

"I took some time out of town to clear my head," the doctor replied chewing a blade of grass.

"Okay then, come to my office soon?" Michael suggested.

"Okay," was Dr. Carter's reply. A protracted and poignant silence ensued.

Michael had known Dr. Carter to be a strong personality, and he could sense his friend was struggling with something serious. He determined that when the doctor came to see him, he would encourage him to go for counselling. It seemed that the Jose incident had affected him more than he had imagined.

Dr. Carter glanced around him at the sprawling terrain. It was dotted with trees and electricity pylons with cables stretched out into the distance. Sparrows lined up along the long cables that disappeared into the distance.

He stood up and walked slowly back into the retreat centre and suddenly came face-to-face with the Rt. Reverend Crisple Wilson. He mumbled a quick greeting as guilt overwhelmed him, and dashed out of sight like a scared mongrel. Everything that happened in the past few weeks culminating in Jose's death had allowed a deep fear to descend on the doctor's soul. The reverend stared after him, bewildered by the doctor's uncharacteristic behaviour.

Dr. Carter wandered aimlessly out of the vicarage and towards the City Centre. He walked towards the busy main highway without focusing on what was around him. It was getting dark and he didn't even realize when he stepped onto the busy road without heeding the oncoming traffic. Out of nowhere, a speeding police Range Rover careened around the corner and knocked him off the ground. The impact lifted him two metres up in the air before he landed with a sickening thud on the dark tarmac below. His breadth was snuffed out in a frightening moment and the doctor lay contorted in a pool of his own blood. He was pronounced dead by paramedics who arrived at the scene shortly thereafter.

———————

Michael Ashcroft stood in shock, his mouth slightly agape as Dr. Rajesh Patel relayed the sad news. For the first time in years, Michael Ashcroft broke down and wept unashamedly. It was five fifteen in the evening the day after Carter died. Everything seemed to come to a standstill in his office. He slumped back onto his chair and seemed to lose focus momentarily. Everything around him developed a ghostly red, as if the room's contents were bathed in blood. The smell of blood filled the air and everything seemed to melt into nothingness. 'What is happening to me?' Mr Ashcroft wondered bewildered. Leaning his head back against the back of the big swivel leather chair, he closed his eyes and thought of the horrific incident. The neon lights from outside his office window blinked relentlessly, the light bouncing off his tired, closed eyes.

———————

Michael Angleton received the news from Dr. Rudolf from Radcliffe Referral Hospital. He knew Dr. Carter very well, especially as a close associate of Michael Ashcroft. Although he had heard of his failing health, the sudden news of the doctor's gruesome death came as a surprise.

Appraising the whole saga, he wondered to himself what the connection had been between Mr. Ashcroft and the doctor. Though he shared this with no one, he couldn't help wondering what all this was about. He had to admit that the whole situation was tragic and unnerving.

—————————

To the medical fraternity at the Radcliffe Referral Hospital and beyond, the doctor's ghastly demise was a shocking phenomenon and condolences streamed in after the news broke. Known to many as a person full of life and with unparalleled expertise as a neurosurgeon, Dr. Carter's death left a gaping crack in the profession. A palpable gloom descended on the hospital staff as the doctor had been held in high esteem.

The death of Dr. Carter was devastating to Michael Ashcroft especially when he recalled how much trust the doctor had placed in him and the many secrets they had shared together.

The loss was unbearable but unfortunately what had taken place was irreversible. He got home at eight o'clock that night relieved to find his wife Linda at home. At such moments, she knew best how to comfort him. She had heard the news and was equally shocked.

Chapter
Twenty Three

It was nine o'clock on Saturday morning when the delivery van stood outside Michael Angleton's residence. Armed with a thick, brown envelope, the driver knocked on the door to their house and received a warm welcome from Lesley Angleton who was alone in the house. She took the registered package and signed for it. She could not imagine the contents and since it was addressed to her husband, she put it on a drawer in the sitting room so that she would see it as soon as he entered the house. He was out of town on a business assignment. It was the classified dossier from the private investigators he had hired but Lesley did not know that.

Obsessed by a desire to make amends with Fletcher, Camila Ashcroft left her house heading south to the coast where she had agreed to meet with him when they had spoken on phone earlier. She drove slowly through the streets and stopped to park her car outside a florist's small stand. She walked up and purchased a small bunch of flowers – a token she hoped to give to Fletcher in the hope of initiating a truce.

Fletcher Angleton drove his car fast towards the coastal region of Brighton where he was to meet with Camila as they had agreed. He was eager to get there before her.

The Brighton Pier stretched out into the sea. Rising waves formed a frothy white line that reflected the receding sun rays. In the distance, boats with their masts raised high sailed in all directions. They dipped and bobbed in the waves of the English Channel as colonies of migrating Gannets soared overhead. Mountains were profiled in the far distance and a layer of clouds attempted to gather.

Throwing petals of assorted fresh flowers to the waters beneath, Camila Ashcroft leaned against the banister rail listening to Fletcher Angleton's sweet-nothings as he tried desperately to appease her. She had found him waiting eagerly for her. Droplets from the salty waters blew up at their faces but that did not impede Fletcher's desperate pleadings for Camila to give their love another chance. He was determined to woo her back. She hid her feelings well and he could not tell what was going on in her mind.

He was a desperate man at this point and poured on his charm without hindrance, pleading and cajoling relentlessly, touching her arm gently at intervals.

Overtaken by her own desire to feel close to him again, Camila finally surrendered to his imploring. With tears slowly dropping down her tender face, she held him close and kissed him. Fletcher clutched at her desperately and almost in a whisper, he begged to be forgiven.

"I want my life to be one act of goodness," he told her.

"It's never too late to work this out," she replied finally, closing her eyes and leaning against his broad chest.

"I will never let you down again Camila," Fletcher said earnestly. "I promise," he said.

"You promise?" she queried peering into his eyes.

"I promise," he answered.

"I love you Fletcher and you know that," she said a tremor in her voice.

"I know that my love and I love you too," he replied.

With her blue eyes staring into the distance, and her long, blonde hair swirling and weaving around her face, she moved closer and held his hands. She looked into his face lovingly and he smiled back. They vowed not to let any differences separate them again. They pledged to move on regardless of challenges around them.

A dark cloud swept across the horizon fading into the distance. A rainbow formed in the sunny sky above. Even as Fletcher held her close, he couldn't help wondering if the tension between the two families would really come to an end. Why did he have a niggling feeling that something tumultuous was headed their way? He wrapped his arms around Camilla as if protecting her from something that was inevitable.

Little did he know that the answers to these troubling questions were about to become very clear to them all.

Chapter
Twenty Four

Michael Angleton did not sleep easy that night; he tossed, turned, and wrestled with the linen sheets in his ornate, four-poster bed, as macabre scenes snuck in and out of his tired mind against his will. Lesley his wife tried fruitlessly to shake him awake once or twice in the deepening hours of the night out of concern and to ask what was wrong. She would then gently take the crumpled sheets off the floor and cover him up again when he would quiet down, and then she would sit up and watch over him with an increasing sense of foreboding.

The sun stole stealthily upward, as if reluctant to face the day, and dampness lingered in the air over Brighton. Even the usual dawn chorus to herald the morning from the birds chirping overhead, was muted and unnerving, and the clouds overhead had a depressing gray tint.

It was nine o'clock on a Saturday morning; a day when most people would venture to shop for the week's groceries in the large malls that littered the city, but this Saturday, the weather caused many to snuggle deeper into their duvets, in the hope of a warmer mid-day.

Michael Angleton had come home late the night before, after a gruelling day of finalizing on some large local government audit deals with wearisome sub-auditors who always tried to wheedle tiny-print clauses that would increase their profit margins into his bidding tenders. He had learned how to beat them at this game from his many years in the financial industry, but the experience still wrung all vestiges of energy out of his mind and body.

After his meeting with them, all he could muster was the strength to drive home to his wife, aiming to turn-in early for the night.

This was not to be however, for the first thing that caught his eye when he opened the front door and walked into the living room, was the unopened envelope that had been delivered by the private investigators he had hired to try an unearth the truth that he sensed lay behind his son's ambush outside the Ogaden Night Club a while back. In vain, Michael Angleton had struggled for weeks to push the picture out of his mind; that of his only son struggling with hours of haemorrhaging and excruciating pain in some gutter by the roadside, before being picked up by an ambulance and rushed comatose to the Radcliffe Referral Hospital. That was an image that would forever be seared in his brain. That notion alone is what drove him to seek the help of the private investigators in the case.

Also, the past weeks, Michael had observed with mounting suspicion and unease how the case with Jose Cameron had taken one discouraging turn after another. First, it was the fact that the Metro Police seemed to drag their feet over the investigation; then there was the obvious and unprofessional camaraderie between the sergeant and Michael Ashcroft; then there was the increasing nervousness with which Michael Ashcroft approached him nowadays and his shocker of a request to have the case dropped; all these experiences made Michael Angleton smell a rat in the Jose case. Most disturbing however, was Jose's sudden and mysterious death, followed by the demise of Dr. Carter, a close friend of Mr. Ashcroft. Michael stood looking down at the large envelope in his hands as all these thoughts raced through his throbbing skull. His fingers shook slightly and he wondered what Pandora's Box he would be opening once he saw its contents. Instinctively, he turned his head quickly when he heard the 'flip-flop' of Lesley's bathroom slippers approaching from behind him.

"What are you looking at sweetheart?" she asked as Michael quickly slipped the large envelope under a pile of memos on the small computer table in the living room. He turned to face her, donning a forced smile, and hugged her tight so that she would not sense his disturbing train of thought.

"Hallo darling," he said as he gave her a long hug before slowly but deliberately leading her into their fitted kitchen.

"I have just come in and was thinking of making myself some of that nice honey and lemon herbal tea I like, would you want some?"

"Yes, that would be nice as it's been quite nippy today," Lesley said pulling her warm housecoat tighter round her slim shoulders. "It seems you had a busy day today, you look dead beat."

"Yeah...same old haranguing with greedy sub-auditors at the office, but I was up to their game; I fixed them good," Michael said smiling at her broadly. He was glad that his wife had not noticed the large envelope from the private investigators. He glanced back at it on the computer table, and decided he would have to ignore it until morning so that she would not ask about its contents. He decided he was too tired anyway to get his head properly around the information in it. He decided to have a look at it when he was fresher the next day.

However, his gallant efforts to sleep early failed miserably when he got to bed, and it was then that he struggled with all those nightmares that got Lesley so worried.

At three o'clock in the morning, Lesley finally dozed off wondering what was bothering her husband.

An hour and a half later, Michael startled and woke up. He looked at his sleeping wife and rubbed his temples slowly. It had been a miserable night. Ghostly images of Jose Cameron and Dr. Carter pointing at him with thin, long fingers, and calling out to him in hoarse, haunting voices, kept filling his dreams. Michael would try to run away from them, but the ground seemed to shift and throw him towards the two men instead. They had blood dripping from their ears and eyes, and their grotesque faces were ashen. A repugnant smell reeked from Jose's mouth each time he opened it, and the horrific smell would hit Michael's face in waves and make him feel he was weak and fainting. It was as if they were desperately trying to tell him something of great importance; to warn him, but Michael could not make out what their raspy voices were saying to him, and to make things worse, the sounds seemed to fade in and out.

Michael Angleton with his face soaked in sweat slowly sat up on the edge of his large bed and shifted his weight away from Lesley. He wiped his drenched face with the back of his hand before stretching to reach for his dressing gown that was draped over the chair next to the bed. He put it on quietly as he shuffled his feet into his bedroom slippers, and then found his way quietly downstairs to read the contents of the envelope he had been careful not to open the night before.

———————

Linda and Michael Ashcroft had decided to brave the morning cold and find their way to East Gate Mall as Linda needed to buy a few groceries.

"We must pass by Prèt a Boire for a taste of their latté seeing as this is such a miserably cold morning," Linda said to her husband as they walked quickly through the large mall entrance into its warmer interior.

"Yes, let's do that," said Michael distractedly.

"Oh, and by the way," she continued, "Did Camila mention that next week she will be flying out to Los Angeles?"

"Of course she told me, Camila never conceals anything to me," he replied absentmindedly. He couldn't really remember his daughter telling him anything like that, but he had suddenly become tense because he had just spotted Sergeant Morgan Clifton in a small vegetable stall to their right. Linda walked on ahead of him into the coffee house to their left and straight to a small table in the corner. She sat down relieved to get out of the cold and waved at a petite waitress who was dressed in a small black frock, with tiny apron, like she was serving coffee in the warm climate of Hawaii. Lesley wondered to herself if marketing a product required such punitive dressing in biting cold weather. 'Never mind' she said to herself.

"Let me have the Café Machiatto, single, with some Vanilla syrup, and a chocolate-chip cookie," she said to the waitress as Michael feigned interest in the framed photos of jockey's on one large wall on the right of the coffee house. He wanted to keep an eye on Sergeant Morgan Clifton who was now standing just outside the green grocers opposite the café they were in and pretending to look at the large framed photos gave Michael a clear view of the sergeant. Michael watched quietly through the large, tinted glass windows that faced the mall entrance, as the sergeant spoke animatedly on his phone. It was getting to ten o'clock in the morning and life was picking up at the mall as Brighton roused itself.

The large envelope lay to the side of the computer and Michael Angleton was holding the last leaf of its contents in his left hand as he flung his head back to swallow his sixth shot of Vodka that morning. His left hand shook uncontrollably as he stared at the photos before him. He had spread them on the small table next to the computer and had just finished reading the last page of the private investigators' damning report of what had really happened to his son Fletcher. The minute he had gone through the report once, he had grabbed the Vodka bottle in a bid to steady his nerves, then he went through the contents of the envelope once more very slowly, as well as the scanned photos that came inside it.

'What the heck is this?' Michael had gasped to himself the first time he saw the photos as they fell out of the opened envelop. He had to constantly wipe beads of sweat that were forming on his forehead.

There were three photos in all: one was of Michael Ashcroft sitting at a table in some pub, talking with his head close to that of Sergeant Morgan Clifton and the expression on their faces was obviously conspiratorial; the other was of Michael Ashcroft with his arm around Jose's shoulders as if leading him somewhere, and standing to their right was Dr. Carter looking very satisfied with himself; the final one was of Michael Ashcroft handing the sergeant a small package in the same pub as in the first picture, and it was clear the package contained pound notes as some were sticking out of the top of the envelope; the sergeant was smiling and extending one hand out to Mr. Ashcroft as if to shake on an agreement. With his other hand, the sergeant stuffed the package greedily into his coat pocket.

'I can't believe this!' Mr. Angleton said as he smacked his forehead with one hand in consternation before grabbing another shot of Vodka. He felt that if he didn't take more, he would collapse from shock, even though he could tell he was already heady from the strong drink and the fury that he felt rising up in his guts. He grabbed his phone.

"Hallo," he barked into the handset.

"Hallo. Mr. Ashcroft's residence, may I help you?" said the butler slightly offended by Mr. Angleton's harsh tone.

"Where's Ashcroft? I need to speak to him immediately. This is Mr. Angleton," Michael said forcefully, the drink getting the better of him and the images in front of him fuelling the consternation he felt.

"I am sorry but Mr. and Mrs. Ashcroft have gone out," said the butler and continued "to the East Gate Mall. May I take a message?"

Mr. Angleton did not wait another second; he flung the phone down and turned suddenly towards the large wall unit on the right side of his expansive living room. He walked resolutely towards it and pulled open the large drawer at the bottom left hand corner. Only he knew of its fake bottom and the secret button to the left of the drawer. Sweat was starting to pour down his forehead and he was gritting his teeth as he scrounged around inside the secret space. Other than their pet cat purring and playing about, there was no one else around. Everyone else was still asleep upstairs. The cold had caused most of Brighton to sleep in and Michael was relieved by this fact as he wanted to deal with what was whirling in his head and heart all by himself.

"Got it!" he said in a whisper as his large fingers closed around the cold handle of what he was looking for. He got up and headed out the door to his car without a second thought.

———

"You seem disturbed Michael, is there something wrong?" Linda said quietly peering into her husband's eyes when he finally turned from the wall of the small cafe. She had not noticed that he had actually been staring out the window the whole time. She unwound her heavy scarf from around her neck as she waited for him to settle down and speak to her. She was feeling warmer now that she had taken a few sips of the Café Macchiato.

"No, I was just looking at those lovely photos my dear," Michael lied "have you ordered something for me? You know what I like."

Linda looked up at his face pleasantly after placing his order, and was about to speak. But it was the shell-shocked look that suddenly gripped Linda's eyes as they shifted from looking at him to staring at the entrance of the cafe behind him, which made Michael jump off his seat and turn around. The formerly quiet café exploded into screams and shouts as patrons rushed and converged at its small entrance.

Michael pushed his large body past the small crowd of onlookers; women screaming and clutching at their cheeks, and what he saw outside made his hair stand on edge. Sergeant Morgan Clifton was on his back on the floor, with blood splattered on his right temple, and Michael Angleton was atop him snarling and yelling out like a mad man. In Michael's hand was a .38 calibre handgun and as he wrestled with the sergeant, he repeatedly smashed the butt of the gun against the sergeant's temple. Blood splattered around as the sergeant tried to roll away from Mr. Angleton mad grip.

Michael Ashcroft rushed forward to see how he could help, but the words that were coming out of Mr. Angleton's mouth were what rooted him to the floor a few seconds later. He stood still in shock.

"You think I don't know what you and that hypocrite Ashcroft have done, huh, huh? I know what you have done and you are not going to get away with trying to kill my son," Mr. Angleton screamed with foamy spit flying out of his mouth as he and the sergeant rolled on the floor.

Suddenly, Michael Angleton jumped off the sergeant and with one hand waving the gun around so that people scurried under tables as others pushed back to avoid being shot, he stuck his other hand into his back jean pocket and pulled out a large envelope as the sergeant stood unsteadily on his feet to face him. The sergeant looked frazzled and confused. Blood was still trickling down his forehead. He stared at his attacker with one palm raised up as if to stop bullets if the gun was fired. Angleton continued shouting as he ripped the envelope open, strewing its contents onto the mall walkway as the photographic evidence fell out of the package.

"You think I don't know what you had planned? You think I don't know what happened to my son? Ashcroft tried to kill him with those ruffians, and he paid you to keep quiet...you think I don't know that? Here, here. I have pictures you crazy beast! You are a garbage-type of a police officer; I will kill you for this. I have all the proof," Angleton said waving the photos for all to see.

Sergeant Morgan Clifton stood unsteadily on his feet. He looked stunned and was still warily eying the small .38 that was swinging menacingly in

Angleton's hand even as the three, coloured photos were thrown at him. They fluttered towards his face and fell to the floor. Angleton then stuck his hand into the envelope again and pulled the shaft of papers that made up the damning report from the private investigators with details on what really happened to Jose, and the part that Ashcroft, the sergeant and Carter had to play in keeping it all under wraps. He threw these as well into the sergeant's bloodied face.

"There, there, it's all there, evidence of your crazy corruption! Eat it if you can you freak and cover up your heinous acts! You tried to cover up hooligans who wanted to kill my son!"

Angleton swung around and waved his .38 around to ward off any person from the crowd he had now realized had formed around him. He wanted no one to stop him from doing what he had planned to do. Revenge!!!.

"Stay back or I will shoot!" he shouted like a crazed maniac.

As he panned his eyes around the forming crowd, Angleton's eyes suddenly focused on Ashcroft who had been standing shell-shocked, listening to the ravings on what part he, the doctor and the sergeant played in hiding the hideous attack on Fletcher. Ashcroft had been listening to Angleton's delirious shouting and he had seen the photos, and the paper flying all over the place, as the private investigator's damning report was flung into the sergeant's face.

The fury on Angleton's face, when he realized he was facing Ashcroft was palpable. At first Angleton stood mesmerized, as if he had just seen a mirage. Then the full realization of who was standing in front of him hit him like a thunderbolt, and the sergeant was instantly forgotten. Angleton charged towards Mr. Ashcroft like a raging bull.

"You corrupt evil man, you murderer, you..."

Angleton raised the gun and pointing it at Ashcroft as he lunged towards him, snarling and shouting like a maniac.

"I will kill you for what you did....I will kill you for what you did!"

It was then that, sergeant Morgan Clifton grabbed the gun in the holster he had been unable to reach when Angleton was wrestling him to the floor.

Behind Ashcroft, an armed security officer in charge of the East Gate Mall had rushed to the scene when he heard all the commotion. He came speedily around the corner towards the café just as the raging Mr. Angleton was raising his .38 calibre handgun and pointing it towards Ashcroft. The officer was well trained and an expert in small arms. He raised his gun and pulled the trigger.

Sergeant Morgan Clifton had just drawn his gun from his holster and was pointing it to Angleton's back. He shouted at Angleton to drop his weapon. He hoped that Angleton would listen and not shoot at Ashcroft.

Such a horrific and gory scene had not been seen in Brighton's quiet and affluent neighbourhood in a million years. Two shots rang out: one from the security guard's gun as he came round the corner and met Angleton pointing his gun at Ashcroft, and one from Sergeant Morgan Clifton's gun as he fired to stop Angleton from shooting at Ashcroft.

Angleton fell to the floor, the bullet from the security guard piercing through his heart, just as the sergeant's bullet zipped past Angleton's falling frame and lodged itself in Ashcroft's large chest.

And just like dominoes, the two most powerful men in Brighton fell dead to the mall floor.

Checkmate!

A deadly game had reached its climax at a ghastly pace, and all the pawns were helpless to hold back its grand finale!

THE END